Death on the Dragon's Tongue

Other Penny Spring and Sir Toby Glendower Mysteries

MARGOT ARNOLD

Death on the Dragon's Tongue

A Penny Spring and Sir Toby Glendower Mystery

A Foul Play Press Book

The Countryman Press
Woodstock, Vermont

First Printing

This edition first published in 1990 by Foul Play Press,
an imprint of the Countryman Press, Inc.,
Woodstock, Vermont 05091.

Copyright © 1982 by Margot Arnold

ISBN 0-88150-183-2

Printed in the United States of America

To Joan Pring
Dear Friend and 'Dea Ex Machina,'
Who Is Really Responsible for All This

WHO'S WHO

GLENDOWER, TOBIAS MERLIN, archaeologist, F.B.A., F.S.A., K.B.E.; b. Swansea, Wales, Dec. 27, 1926; s. Thomas Owen and Myfanwy (Williams) G.; ed. Winchester Coll.; Magdalen Coll., Oxford, B.A., M.A., Ph.D.; fellow Magdalen Coll., 1949-; prof. Near Eastern and European Prehistoric Archaeology Oxford U., 1964-; created Knight, 1977. Participated in more than 30 major archaeological expeditions. Author publications, including: What Not to Do in Archaeology, 1960; What to Do in Archaeology, 1970; also numerous excavation and field reports. Clubs: Old Wykehamists, Athenaeum, Wine-tasters, University.

SPRING, PENELOPE ATHENE, anthropologist; b. Cambridge, Mass., May 16, 1928; d. Marcus and Muriel (Snow) Thayer; B.A., M.A., Radcliffe Coll.; Ph.D., Columbia U.; m. Arthur Upton Spring, June 24, 1953 (dec.); 1 son, Alexander Marcus. Lectr. anthropology Oxford U., 1958-68; Mathieson Reader in anthropology Oxford U., 1969-; fellow St. Anne's Coll., Oxford, 1969-. Field work in the Marquesas, East and South Africa, Uzbekistan, India, and among the Pueblo, Apache, Crow and Fox Indians. Author: Sex in the South Pacific, 1957; The Position of Women in Pastoral Societies, 1962; And Must They Die? — A Study of the American Indian, 1965; Caste and Change, 1968; Moslem Women, 1970; Crafts and Culture, 1972; The American Indian in the Twentieth Century, 1974; Hunter vs. Farmer, 1976.

CHAPTER I

Toby Glendower was in a state of complete happiness akin to ecstasy; he snuggled down in the dry, withered grass and looked lovingly at the large granite boulders above and on three sides of him. He blessed the labors of a long-dead people who had erected such a sturdy tribute to their dead chieftain, which now protected him so snugly from the cold summer rain of Brittany and a keen northeast wind off the English Channel that mourned and sighed around the ancient stones. Beside him on the grass in his rock-bound shelter lay two knapsacks. One contained his lunch, which consisted of a crusty baguette of French bread, a Pont l'Eveque cheese, a choice Breton onion, a bottle of St. Emilion claret, and a rare bottle of old Calvados, which his host at the local inn had so obligingly disinterred from his cellar. The other knapsack held his notebooks, his camera, drawing materials, and his spare tin of tobacco. He clasped his long thin arms around his long and equally thin shanks and puffed great plumes of blue smoke from his favorite briar pipe; the smoke rose like incense to a beneficent deity as he continued his silent litany of thanks.

He was so happy that he blessed everyone and everything he could think of. He blessed his absent French colleague, Charles Latour, and in particular Charles's ailing gall bladder, which had put Toby in sole charge of this site that now stretched in rain-swept desolation before his rocky shelter.

Charles—ridiculous man!—had been so apologetic about it. "I wouldn't have dreamed of asking, knowing how busy you are, but my doctor says I should not wait any longer for the operation, and the site *has* to be finished. It is a matter of great importance and some urgency. It is a stone circle, a henge monument, you see—common in your country, but, so far as I know, unique in France," Charles had told him.

"But, my dear fellow, I'd be delighted to help out!" Toby

9

replied. And he had been. He was still on his sabbatical, faced with writing a long-overdue excavation report with which he was thoroughly bored, and with no good excuse not to get on with it. To add to his woes, Penny Spring had taken off for America, ill-tempered and hell-bent on breaking up a budding romance between her one and only son, Dr. Alexander Spring, and a thoroughly unsuitable (in her opinion) nurse. Bereft of her stimulating, if often hair-raising, companionship, Toby had seen Charles Latour as an angel of mercy, albeit an extremely diffident one.

"There are—er—certain problems connected with the site," Charles had gone on.

"Such as?" Toby prompted, the gleam of archaeological battle in his eye.

"Well, for one thing, I'm afraid you'll not find anyone to help you." Charles's tone was abjectly apologetic. "You see, the position is this: they are having to move the henge, because the location is right in the middle of an area which is slated by the French government for a nuclear power plant. You know how provincially conservative and superstitious the Bretons are," he continued with all the chauvinism of the native-born Parisian. "Well, in addition to all the usual 'No-Nukes' and nationalist feelings a scheme such as this arouses, the locals are convinced that something terrible will happen on the Dragon's Tongue if the plan to move the henge is carried out. Hence none of them will have anything to do with it. I've been working with a couple of laborers imported from Paris myself, but they refuse to stay on. The locals have been after them, too. One of the many reasons I thought of you is that as a Welshman and fellow-Celt, and as a distinguished foreigner, you would be less likely to have trouble than would any of my French colleagues. I should add, on the plus side, that very little of the excavating remains to be done. There is the central portion of the site, which I think has a cist burial in it, and apart from that it is just a question of mapping accurately the position of the stones, prior to removal, and trying to find something that might give us a positive Carbon-14 dating for the site. So there really isn't that much heavy labor involved."

"Oh, that doesn't worry me," Toby had said absently.

"But I'm just trying to place where the Dragon's Tongue is—I don't seem to recall."

"That's just the local name," Charles interposed. "You remember how Brittany looks—particularly in the old maps— just like a reptile's head sticking out into the Atlantic? Well, this little isthmus looks like a forked tongue sticking out of its open mouth—hence the imaginative nickname. Its real name is the isthmus of Crozon, and the site is a little to the northwest of Morgat on the coast, near the little village of Cormel. It's a very isolated backwater, which is one of the reasons the French government decided to build the plant there. So you'll do it?" He had sounded eager, and it had only just then struck Toby as odd that a sick man—for Charles Latour had indeed looked very drawn and white—had taken the trouble to come over to Oxford from Paris, when he could just as well have phoned. They had discussed details of the excavation, and Charles had given him his own notebooks and had taken his leave in a very evident state of relief.

That had been over a month ago, and Toby, forewarned, had arrived here three weeks past, braced for some local trouble and hostility; but nothing had happened. True, he could not find anyone to come out to the site with him, but he didn't mind that. He rather liked puttering around it by himself; the sandy soil was easy to work, and, if worse came to worst and he could not manage all the surveying single-handed, he could always whistle up some student from Oxford. Money was no object and he was not about to cut short his own delighted dallying on behalf of the French government.

He had elected to stay at a little inn on the coast just outside of Morgat and away from Cormel where the center of the opposition lay, but so far there had been no sign of hostile action. Indeed his only worries had come from an unexpected source.

A rustling in the thick bushes on the opposite side of the site brought him out of his euphoric reverie and his round blue eyes behind their equally round glasses peered intently through the sheets of rain. A black shape flashed across his vision for an instant and was gone. That damn dog again! Where could it come from? What attracted it so? His brow under the splendid silver thatch of hair on his small round head knitted into a frown. He had never caught a closeup glimpse of the black hound, but it had to be huge, judging from the paw marks that he found in the light sandy soil of the site when he returned each morning. Not that it was a hazard or danger, exactly, but it was a nuisance. The animal had a tendency to dig holes in the yielding surface and to lurk, as it was apparently doing at the moment, on the outskirts of the site. Why? he wondered.

He had asked about it in the inn parlor one evening, only to be met with uneasy stares and blank silence. No one knew of such a dog in the district, no one knew to whom it could belong. One villager had finally said in a nervous voice what they all evidently had been thinking. "You are sure it *is* a real dog, M'sieu?"

"Of course it is!" he had answered testily. "What else would leave ruddy great paw marks everywhere and dig messy little holes?"

"The Dragon's Teeth is a sacred site of the old ones," the man had muttered defensively. "The Black Hound may yet guard it, and you know what that means."

Toby had dismissed this with a derisive snort, and a saner suggestion had come from a red-faced farmer who had been listening with interest to the exchange.

"Perhaps it comes from the Chateau de la Muette. The people there are foreigners and keep to themselves; we would not know about them."

Still, it *was* odd how the dog kept hanging around and yet never appeared when Toby was actually there. He took a small stone from the floor of the shelter and hurled it in the direction where he had last seen the black shape, but there was no startled rustle in response. The dog had disappeared again as quietly and as mysteriously as it always did. He sighed and began to unpack his lunch from the knapsack. He'd give the rain another hour to slacken before he packed it in for the day and returned to the warmth of the inn and the companionship of his fellow drinkers. They weren't a bad lot, he reflected, particularly when they had discovered he spoke Breton, which was close to his native Welsh, so fluently. No longer did they fall into a dead silence when he entered the bar, but continued with their gossip as if he were already part of the community. He had learned a lot of what was going on in the district while leaning quietly up against the bar, sipping the local hard cider, which was extremely good, and listening to their lilting Breton accents.

That reminded him. Apples—the cider was brewed locally from the sea-wind-bent orchards of the Dragon's Tongue. His eyes strayed back to the site. At one time this too had been an orchard, for he had found apple tree roots snaking through it everywhere. Was that what made it so revered by the locals? Apple orchards had been as sacred to the Bretons as they had been to the English Celts, for from the apples had been brewed the sacred drink of the Druids—the Lammasghal— used in all their ancient rites and ceremonies. He had even heard that very word muttered reverently in the inn, and wondered if, on this isolated peninsula, they continued to brew it in the ancient way. It was said that an animal body of some kind added to the brew increased its clarity and potency; in his youth he had heard that Somerset cider-makers still added a rat to their bubbling vat.

The henge itself, of course, had nothing to do with the Celts—despite the claims and manic goings-on of the modern so-called Druids. These ancient stone circles predated the entrance of his ancestors on the scene by a thousand years or more; they were relics of another people, another way of thought and life. His eyes roved lovingly over the silent circle of shaped granite monoliths, gleaming wetly gray-blue in the subdued light like giant teeth. The familiarity of their arrangement teased his mind—he had seen almost the duplicate of this henge across the Channel, whose murmur he could hear in the distance. If only he could recall where!

As he had so frequently found, when he wasn't forcing it, the right answer popped out of the computer of his mind on the instant: Stannon—that was it. Stannon on Bodmin Moor in Cornwall; how neatly that fitted, he reflected, because there had always been a lively intercourse between the Cornish and Breton peninsulas, long, long before the Celts had made their entrance on the screen of history. With a growing excitement, he thought about Stannon. It had astronomical alignments—solar ones. He'd have to check this site out for the same thing. Both henges were open rings forty meters across. The main difference was that here the stones were higher; some of them as tall as he was, a little over six feet. But Stannon had never been satisfactorily dated, he recalled. Perhaps if he could get a date for Dragon's Tongue, he could resolve the question of Stannon as well. Wouldn't that be something! he exulted.

His thoughts were interrupted by fresh rustlings from the bushes across the site, and he armed himself with another stone to hurl at the dog, but the bushes parted and the figure of a small man emerged, causing Toby's rounded jaw to sag with astonishment. He was carrying a black silk umbrella over his head and was dressed in an immaculate black suit, a snowy white shirt, subdued tie, and somber black trilby hat. He looked for all the world as if he had just stepped out of the French Foreign Office on the Quai d'Orsay. As Toby watched him pick his way gingerly across the site towards the shelter of the dolmen-tomb, he saw that his face did not match the rest of this immaculate image. It was raw-looking and weatherbeaten, with strong, bushy brows that were currently lowered over his small eyes in a formidable frown. The vision halted and raised the umbrella slightly in a parody of hat-raising. "Sir Tobias Glendower?"

Toby scrambled hastily to his feet. "Er—yes. What can I do for you?"

"Armand Dubois, Engineer for the Ministry of the Interior, charged with expediting the construction of Nuclear Power Plant 6 at Cormel." His voice was hoarse and raspy and somehow suited his raw-boned face. "I have had considerable difficulty in locating you. And I trust you can do a very great deal."

"I left my local address with the Department of Antiquities," Toby said defensively. "And the people at the inn at Morgat could have directed you to the site. I am usually here all day working."

The Frenchman's small dark eyes took in the half-empty bottle of claret and the bottle of Calvados on the grass. "So I observe," he said drily.

Toby began to bristle but then saw that, despite the umbrella, Dubois was soaking wet, his mud-spattered trousers clinging to his thin legs, so that they looked like black matchsticks. "Won't you come in out of the rain?" he asked, hastily shoveling the remains of his lunch and the bottles back into his knapsack and making room beside him. "And perhaps a tot of Calvados to warm you up?"

Dubois seemed taken aback by this pacific answer. "No, thank you," he said shortly. "I do not intend to stay long. I came to inform you that there will be a meeting tonight at eight o'clock at the inn, with the Mayor of Cormel and various other local notables, which I must ask you to attend. I would also like a status report on the site. It should have been finished by now, and I must inform you that I intend to start moving the stones in exactly one week."

This time Toby did bristle. "Impossible!" he boomed. "Absolutely out of the question! I was given to understand by Dr. Latour *and* your Department of Antiquities that I could have as much time as I wanted. I am working alone, so I shall need at least two weeks more, and if this rain keeps up, probably longer. You have to realize, Monsieur Dubois, this site is a national treasure; it is unique. And, in addition, I was told that, in view of the local opposition to your project, Paris would be sending a public relations man down here in advance to soften up local feeling before any construction or engineering personnel were sent in."

Dubois made an impatient gesture with his free hand. "All that is changed. The French government cannot wait upon or cater to the absurd pretensions and superstitions of these backward Bretons any longer. I have my orders. I intend to carry them out! These people must realize what a great favor we are doing them by erecting the plant here. When finished it will free the whole of Brittany from dependence on that damned Arab oil!"

"Oh? I thought the main reason they were putting it here was so that if there were a disaster akin to the Three Mile Island affair in America, only a few communities would be decimated," Toby said acidly. They glared at each other in mutual animosity.

Toby was usually a completely nonpolitical man. Only Athenian politics of the fifth century B.C. had ever aroused a spark of interest in him, and modern politics he shunned like the plague. Nevertheless, the cool bureaucratic indifference of this man placed him suddenly and fervently on the side of those who did not wish this site to be tampered with.

"Well, I do not intend to stay here, getting soaked and arguing about it," Armand Dubois growled. "We will have further discussion this evening at the inn, but I can assure you

I have the authority to do what I have stated, so suggest you adopt a more cooperative attitude. This affair is complicated enough without having the further interference of foreigners. I suppose you know this Gareth Winton—who also, as a land-owner, must be consulted?'' His tone was bitter. "Perhaps you could direct me to the chateau; he too must be warned to attend the meeting tonight.''

"I presume you mean the man who owns the Chateau de la Muette?'' Toby replied. "No, I don't know him, have never laid eyes on him, and don't particularly want to. An Ameri-can, isn't he?''

"So I believe.'' Dubois shifted restlessly from one soggy foot to the other. "Some crazy man who bought the old chateau for his cult center—the Order of Cosmic Conscious-ness. What rubbish!'' He snorted.

"I think the chateau lies directly north of here, about a mile and a half away, but you are going to get extremely uncomfortable if you try for it through the woods. They are very thick,'' Toby said gruffly, feeling a twinge of sympathy for this little robot of a man bent so sternly on fulfilling his duty.

"I have a car,'' Dubois snapped. "But I had to park it behind your Jeep back there on the cart-track. It was too narrow for me to pass—very inconvenient!''

Toby's sympathy evaporated. "Then you have no problem. Just go back to the road, head north for a mile or so, and you'll see the iron gates of the chateau on your right. I have never seen them open,'' he added with a touch of malice.

"I'll get in, never fear. So I will bid you *au revoir* until tonight. We can talk then about getting some assistance for you on the site.'' And on this surprisingly amiable note, he turned on his heel and retraced his steps.

Toby sat down again, relit his pipe, and took a healthy swig of the Calvados, but his state of euphoria had vanished. Damn the man! he thought crossly. Just when everything was so pleasant, why did he have to show up? Even the fact that the rain was letting up and the overcast sky getting percepti-bly lighter did nothing to lift the cloud that had descended on his spirits. Instead of a nice month or so of leisurely pottering, he had been given a week's notice to quit. If Dubois meant what he said—and he was very much afraid he did—he would have to work like a demon to get everything done in that time.

Drawing on his oilskin cape, Toby wandered out into the circle and looked gloomily down at the flat slab of rock, under which he was pretty certain lurked a cist burial, and which he had been keeping until last, like the cherry on the top of a sundae. Now he would have to excavate it in the next day or two and then get on with mapping all those alignments. Hell, he hated to be pressured like this. "No, damn it all, I'll have a go at the Department of Antiquities," he muttered. "Maybe they can get a stay of execution." But, knowing the slow wheels of French bureaucracy, he didn't feel very confident. "Damn Armand Dubois!"

He collected his things and stomped moodily off towards the expedition Jeep bequeathed him by Charles Latour. He flung the knapsacks in the back and vaulted into the driver's seat, feeling thoroughly bad-tempered. Behind him, in the bushes towards the site, came a sudden rustling and he looked over his shoulder, thinking Dubois might have returned. A large black dog was standing in the middle of the muddy grass-grown track, looking at him with big amber eyes. It was not quite as big as he had imagined from its paw marks, but on glancing down he saw that the paws were huge in proportion to the body. It wasn't fully grown! What he was looking at was an enormous puppy. The dog sat back on its haunches, threw back its massive head, and let forth an uncanny ululating wail. Howl after mournful howl rose to the rain-laden skies. Then, as suddenly as it had begun, it stopped, looked searchingly at him again, and, as if satisfied its strange message had been delivered and understood, bounded into the bushes and was gone.

Toby felt a queer chill and shook himself. "Just as well none of the locals saw that little exhibition," he thought, as he started up the Jeep. "Then they would have been certain the Black Hound of Death was on the loose. How very odd."

CHAPTER 2

A definite "maybe" was all he had been able to extract from the Department of Antiquities. "We'll do what we can," the voice from Paris apologized, "but I do not hold out too much hope of getting such a concession. With the price of oil continuing to soar at this ridiculous rate, there is considerable pressure on the government to produce alternatives, and the Cormel Nuclear Plant is top priority."

"The plant—if the ones in England are anything to go by—will take years to build," Toby said irritably. "So what difference will a week or two make? This site should be of equal priority to you. Not only is it the only henge on French soil, but I am pretty certain it has astronomical alignments as well. It is a twin of one in England which has solar alignments—once those stones are moved, this aspect of it will be destroyed forever."

"I appreciate that, but your best hope is to explain all this to the engineer down there and get him on your side." There was a pause. "If you like, we could probably send you an assistant to finish up."

"No, no," Toby barked, "By the time he arrived and I'd explained everything to him, the time would be running out anyway. This Armand Dubois said something about getting me local help."

"There you are then." There was relief in the distant voice. "If he is that cooperative, you should have no problems."

"*If* he produces," Toby said. "Do you know anything about him?"

"Never heard of him. Why? Was there anything in particular you wanted to know?"

"No, but he struck me as a pretty funny type for an engineer," Toby growled and rang off, feeling thoroughly ill-tempered.

His temper was not improved by another phone call, this time from Armand Dubois. "There has been a change in plan," the raspy voice informed him. "The meeting will not be at the inn after all, but at the Mayor's house in Cormel. Please be there at eight. You cannot miss it; it is a large granite house on the outskirts of the village to the west. My car, a red Citröen, will be parked outside."

"I'll be there. Have you done anything about finding me an assistant?"

"Yes, I have," came the quick reply.

Toby was astonished. "Oh? Who?"

"I'll tell you about it when I see you." There was an uneasy edge on Dubois' voice. "Not ideal, but the best I could do in these trying circumstances."

Toby dined early and then went for a quick walk along the cliffs to cool himself off and collect his thoughts for the coming battle. The majestic savagery of the towering cliffs, against which the restless Atlantic pounded in constant, impotent fury, had a soothing effect on him. He realized that he had to swallow his disappointment and stop acting like a spoiled child whose favorite toy had been taken away; he must be sensible and conciliatory. Maybe Dubois wasn't such a bad chap after all. If he had found someone for him already, he had to be damned efficient, and if he was that efficient maybe he was reasonable also.

He returned to his Jeep, drove through Morgat and started north towards Crozon, then turned west on the little road that ran through Cormel heading for the Pointe de Dinan. The village of Cormel, unlike Morgat, appeared to be crouched in a hollow, as if to hide itself from the gales that scoured the Dragon's Tongue. It was still daylight, but already there were scattered lights in the gray and white-washed cottages strung along the winding village street and in the little cluster of shops in the center of the village. A small gray stone church, set a little back from the road, flashed by his vision and then he spotted the red Citröen parked in front of the only house of any size he had seen. In contrast to the rest of the village, it had a prosperous air. Its shutters were freshly painted; a wrought iron gate gave onto the cement walk leading up to the front door, which gleamed with highly polished brass accoutrements. The Mayor of Cormel obviously did not lack for money, and Toby, as he parked behind the Citröen, wondered idly what its source was.

He was admitted by a small, dumpy maidservant with mouse-colored hair, which reminded him—with a pang—of the absent Penny. Wish she were here, he thought, as the maid opened the door to the left of the entrance and ushered him into a dining room. A group of men were seated around a polished mahogany table. Armand Dubois was seated at the bottom end, an open briefcase before him, while the opposite end of the table was dominated by a large, broad-shouldered man with curly fair hair and a broad, square face and head. It was a typically Anglo-Saxon face, which stood out markedly from the rest of the company who, to a man, were dark-haired, round-headed and smallish.

As Toby entered, Dubois rose to his feet. "Ah, good! There you are!" He indicated a chair to his right, and Toby sensed somehow that the balance had shifted and Dubois was relieved to see him. He was still wearing the formal black suit, which had the faintly crumpled look of wool that has been hastily dried before a too-hot fire. There was still a faint smell of dampness about him, accentuated by the shiny blackness of his thinning hair. He cleared his throat nervously. "Messieurs, may I present my colleague, Sir Tobias Glendower, a distinguished British archaeologist who has been excavating at the Dragon's Teeth on behalf of the French government."

Toby's silvery eyebrows rose a fraction. Colleague indeed! Here was progress. Heads bobbed in acknowledgment as eyes, some wary, some hostile, some calculating, fixed on him. Armand continued doggedly with the introductions. "At the head of the table, the Mayor of Cormel and our host, Patrice Villefort. To his right, Judge Herve Rouillé, Juge d'Instruction for this area." A hatchetlike face favored him with a blank stare. "To his left, Monsieur le Curé, Père Laval, who represents the villagers." A small man in a black soutane, with mild hazel eyes but a determined slit of a mouth, gave a jerky acknowledgment. "To the left of Monsieur le Juge, our Commissaire of Police, Pierre Pommard." The man was as broad in the shoulder as Villefort, but dark and swarthy of complexion. His pale blue eyes clamped on Toby's, then flicked away and resumed their contemplation of his hamlike fists, resting on the table. "And on Père Laval's left,

Monsieur Jean Sommelier, representative of the farmers of the district," Dubois concluded. Toby had already recognized the man as one of his acquaintances from the inn, who now favored him with a conspiratorial wink. Dubois' eyes fixed on the empty seat opposite Toby as the grandfather clock in the hallway chimed the hour. "Monsieur Gareth Winton was informed of our change in plans," he said. "But apparently he has not seen fit to honor us with his presence. So we will go on without him."

Dubois proceeded to shuffle through his papers, clear his throat several times, and appeared loath to begin anything. The big man at the head of the table moved restlessly. "Monsieur Dubois," he said in a high voice that ill suited his large frame, "We are ready to cooperate with you, but we are all busy men. Are we *waiting* for this Gareth Winton?"

"No, not at all!" Dubois said hurriedly, and launched into a long speech about the farsightedness of the French government, the need for the nuclear plant, and the blessings it would bestow on the area. The faces around the table took on a fixed, inward look, and Toby found his own attention wandering. Dubois' voice had an edge of desperation in it, as if he was being tried and was determined not to be found wanting. Toby tried to gauge the reactions of the other men, wishing again that Penny were here with her quick intuitive feelings about people. He could not sense any hostility; it was more like a stolid blankness, as if they were listening to what Dubois had to say but would then go about their respective affairs as if nothing at all was happening. But something *was* happening. Even Toby, who was no political tyro, could see that the whole tenor of life on this little isthmus would be completely disrupted and set on new and unexpected paths by the advent of the power plant; yet these men seemed totally unmoved, almost disinterested. The judge and the commissaire were not even putting on a show of attention, but were sunk in their respective thoughts, oblivious to the rasping tones of this danger from without.

Dubois finally seemed to sense this, for he addressed the policeman directly. "Commissaire Pommard, as I have just said, only a token work force will be sent down at first, to move the henge . . ." he shot an apologetic look at Toby, ". . . and to do the initial clearing of the whole area. Since it is summer, they will be housed in a tent town until prefabricated buildings, later to be dismantled, will be erected on the plant site to house them, together with their own mess halls and bathing facilities. As little strain as possible will be put on the facilities of your area, though naturally your local businesses will benefit from the additional trade. However, it is then the trouble will be likely to start, and it is up to you and your men to ensure that it is put down with a firm hand at the outset. The 'No Nukes' groups can probably be controlled from Paris or Brest, but I have been informed that the peninsula here is a hotbed of Breton nationalism, and we can expect trouble from them also. I trust you are equipped and ready to deal with this?''

Pommard shot a quick glance at the judge and then fixed Dubois with a steady stare. ''We know who they are,'' he said shortly. ''We'll keep an eye on them.''

''That's not good enough. You are to *prevent* any kind of disturbance or sabotage that could inhibit progress at the site or intimidate the workers. Is that understood?''

Villefort suddenly leaned forward. ''Monsieur Dubois,'' he said in a quiet voice which was nonetheless charged with authority. ''It seems to me *your* attitude leaves something to be desired. You appear to have a chip on your shoulder and to regard us all as potential enemies. If we were that, we would not even be here tonight. It is true that we were not happy with the decision of the French government to put the plant here. We liked the Dragon's Tongue as it was, but we have lost that fight and so accept what must be. But do not try and teach us our business—Monsieur Pommard knows what he is about. Start pushing our local people too hard and you will only fan the flames of resentment, and before you know it we'll have half Brittany up in arms. I am sure that is the last thing the government would want—such bad publicity!''

For the first time Judge Rouillé spoke. ''Do the Dragon's Teeth have to be removed? Cannot the government build around it? It is but forty meters in circumference. Surely your plans could accommodate such a small area when the plant is to be so big? No good can come from moving the stones, no good at all. It is that you should worry about.''

Dubois looked as surprised as Toby felt. ''But that would be absurd. A prehistoric monument sitting in the middle of a twentieth-century nuclear plant! I could never suggest such a thing to my superiors!"

"Why not?" Toby asked. "The same thought had occurred to me; such a small area is involved, as the judge has pointed out. And if this would allay local fears and animosities, it strikes me as a very small price to pay. I could enlist the aid of the Department of Antiquities, if need be." The judge gave him an approving nod, and Sommelier, his red face going even redder, muttered, "It would be well done. Then you would have only the hotheads to deal with—not the people."

"There is altogether too much catering to this heathen superstition," the priest interposed in a deep voice. "I would be against any such acknowledgment of the Dragon's Teeth. This is the twentieth century, as Monsieur Dubois says. It is time the people around here realized this. While the Teeth stand, they will always be the center of this witchcraft nonsense. If I had my way they would be bulldozed into the earth."

This unexpected support had allowed Dubois to recover his equilibrium. "Quite so," he snapped. "It is out of the question. If we made an exception in this case, then the next thing you know everyone in the district would be petitioning to save this or that. Their precious orchards . . ." he shot a glance of intense dislike at Jean Sommelier, which puzzled Toby ". . . .or their wishing wells, or the chateau people complaining their view had been spoiled. No. It would simply open up a Pandora's box—I'll have no part in it."

"I can see your point, but what none of you seem to understand is that this site is unique," Toby said earnestly. "It is the only one like it in France—indeed on the whole Continent, so far as I know. To destroy it is like having to tear down the Arc de Triomphe. In fact, I am absolutely astounded that it has not been recognized as such and thoroughly investigated scientifically long before this!"

There was a short silence and then the priest said tightly, "I think I can explain that, M'sieu. You see, M'sieu Villefort's grandfather, who was then still at the chateau, had the entire site covered in . . . about the turn of the century it was. It was a period of bad depression in these parts and, as always in such times, witchcraft reared its ugly head. He was determined to put a stop to it, so he had the site buried. If you are interested, there is an account in the parish records written by the priest of that time, who helped him.'' Suddenly he seemed ill at ease, and shot an apologetic glance at Patrice Villefort, who was gazing impassively at him.

"Was an orchard planted over it?" Toby enquired. "I have found evidence that apple trees were there."

"No." Now the priest was avoiding all their eyes and mopped at his brow which was wet with perspiration. "It was not so much an orchard as a grove of apple trees. He destroyed them, too."

Something between a snort and a groan of rage escaped from Jean Sommelier.

"And it has remained buried until now?" Toby was flabbergasted.

"No." The priest looked helplessly at Villefort, who put in in his high smooth voice, "I sold the chateau and its appurtenances to the present owner some ten years ago. He had the site cleared when he found out what it was. A rather clever move on his part, since the local people were pleased by the gesture and have left him and his queer disciples in peace."

"So the site is on chateau land," Toby murmured, trying to sort out this jumble of new ideas and impressions that had been flung at him.

"Not any more," Dubois cut in firmly. "The land has been requisitioned by the government, with due compensation to the owner, naturally. Only then could it be investigated. But we have wandered far from the point. There is nothing more to be said on the matter, so let us proceed."

With a sudden movement Judge Rouillé rose to his feet. "Proceed if you must," he announced. "But I warn you, Monsieur Dubois, you are playing with fire. No good can come from this, only ill. I have heard enough. I represent the law and so must perforce uphold you, but I beg you to take care—for you know not what you do."

His dramatic exit, however, was marred. The door opened and the head of the little maid appeared, her round face convulsed with agitation. "M'sieu Villefort . . ." she stammered, and then was propelled into the room by a figure behind her who paused on the threshold in order to allow the full impact of his appearance to sink in.

Toby saw a man of medium height clad in a long white robe of coarse wool, with what looked like a mirror of polished obsidian slung around his neck on a heavy silver chain. His pepper-and-salt hair hung down loose and bushy to his shoulders and his face was almost completely obscured by a huge black beard, liberally sprinkled with white. He wore Indian-style sandals, but the Eastern guru effect was ruined by a very American pair of thick, horn-rimmed glasses that masked his eyes.

"Why was I summoned here?" he said in a high, fluting voice. "Why was my peace disturbed? Why was I called back from the Higher Realms to this sink of mortality?"

It appeared that Gareth Winton, owner of the Chateau de la Muette, had finally arrived.

CHAPTER 3

"A rum sort of do, wasn't it?" Jean Sommelier said in Breton, as he and Toby emerged from the Villefort house into the deepening dusk.

"Yes, that sums it up pretty well," Toby agreed.

After the dramatic entrance of Gareth Winton, the situation had deteriorated rapidly. Armand Dubois had attempted to give him a short version of his opening statement, but everyone had begun speaking at once, and it soon appeared that the only thing paramount in Gareth Winton's mind was that he and the grounds of the chateau should remain inviolate from the intruders. "I will not allow anyone to intrude on our peace; *no one* is to come into the chateau grounds," he had repeated. "I appeal to you, Monsieur le Juge. Under French law am I not within my rights?"

On being assured that he was, he promptly lost interest in everything else Dubois had to say and appeared to sink into deep meditation, occasionally coming forth with a surprisingly deep-throated "Om." The meeting had lost all semblance of order, and Judge Rouillé, though his exit lacked the dramatic impact of his first attempt, had led the exodus.

As Toby and the farmer reached the wrought iron gate, Dubois' voice rang out. "Sir Tobias, I will see you back at the inn. We have still to discuss the matter of the excavation and your assistant."

"All right. In about half an hour then?" Toby turned to see him silhouetted against the light from the open door. As he did so, there was the clatter of a stone, which thudded against the frame of the door and fell harmlessly to the ground. "Go back to Paris," a voice called out. "We don't want you around here, nor your damned plant. Go, if you know what's good for you!" And there was the sound of running feet as Dubois swore and stepped back inside, slamming the door.

"See! Already it begins!" Sommelier said heavily, as he

made for his battered-looking truck parked behind Toby's Jeep.

"Any idea who that might have been?" Toby was uncomfortable.

"Oh, I've plenty of ideas! Could be anyone of about three-quarters of the local population," Sommelier replied, climbing up into the cabin of the truck.

"Will I see you later at the inn? There are some things I'd very much like to talk to you about."

"Yes, I'll probably be along eventually." Sommelier did not sound overly enthusiastic. "But I am not anxious to be seen with your Parisian comrade—so if I appear to ignore you, don't be offended."

"He's no comrade of mine," Toby said quickly, but with a strange twinge of guilt. "I never set eyes on him before this afternoon and am totally against what he is proposing. But is he also staying at the inn?"

"So I heard. Apart from the Auberge du Dragon at Failleul, it is the only good one around here, and I doubt whether Dubois could get in at the Auberge—the owner is a fervent Nationalist. You may have heard of him—Francois Canard?"

"I'm afraid I don't know the first thing about Breton Nationalists," Toby said.

"Oh, not as a Nationalist—as a chef! He used to be one of our leading chefs in Paris. Has been all over the world; a celebrity. He has retired down here and runs the auberge *pour s'amuser*—to amuse himself. A very gifted and a very strange man. If ever you want a good meal, I suggest you try the auberge. Mind you," the farmer chuckled, "it will cost you an arm and a leg. Canard knows his own worth."

"Well, perhaps you would join me for dinner there some evening?" Toby said, hoping to cement a link of friendship with at least one local ally.

"Perhaps. We shall see. But I warn you—it would probably be wasted on me and we would not be likely to get much. I am a plain man with plain tastes and to Canard that would be like casting pearls before swine. Cider I know and pigs and bees I know—otherwise I know nothing! Life is much happier that way." And with another chuckle he set the truck in motion.

Toby returned to the inn and took up his usual stance in the bar parlor. Though more than half an hour had elapsed, there was no sign of Dubois, but he had scarcely more than settled in a corner with his tankard of cider when Sommelier reappeared and raised a hand in salute. "Won't you join me," Toby said hopefully. "What'll you have?"

"If you're buying, I'd like a Scotch," came the frank answer. "Always the way, isn't it? You like our cider, we like your Scotch—except that it's too damned expensive to drink."

"If that's your choice, it's fine with me," Toby agreed—it was the one form of alcohol he personally couldn't abide.

The drink arrived and Jean cocked a bright blue eye at him. "So what did you want to know?"

"Oh, just some general things. I'd like to rally some support to put at least a little bit of pressure on Dubois so I can properly finish my work at the henge. I wonder if you could give me some background on the people at the meeting tonight so that I'd know whom best to approach. I took it from what you said that you'd like the henge preserved if possible."

Jean shot him a curious look. "Yes, you could say that. Who first then?"

"Villefort intrigued me. I assume he used to be the local lord of the manor, and yet he does not look as if he belongs to the region."

The farmer gave a little laugh. "Looks can be deceiving. Villefort belongs here all right. There have been de Villeforts here at least since the Middle Ages. His mother was from Alsace; a big blonde. He takes after her."

"He appears prosperous," Toby observed.

"Oh, yes. Patrice has never been one to let a good chance go by. Been on the make ever since he was a boy. Not that I blame him. He's a lawyer, you know. Got his training in Paris and lived there for a while. Came back when his father died, of course. People were shocked when he up and sold the chateau, but he was right; no money in the place, no money to keep it up. Winton paid through the nose for it and Patrice has made good use of the money."

"He lives in very nice style now," Toby observed. "Was that an estate house?"

Sommelier shook his head. "No. He married the local

doctor's daughter. It used to be hers—he fixed it all up though. Poor soul, she didn't last long to enjoy it.''

"So he is a widower?''

Again Sommelier gave one of his short laughs. "No. Patrice is not one to hang long on the vine. Married a real young one about five years back—they've got two small children. She leads him a merry dance—very expensive tastes has the second Madame Villefort. He'll have to keep piling it in to hang on to her. He's fifty-five, you know. Doesn't look it, does he?''

" No, he certainly doesn't.''

"But if you are looking to him for support, I wouldn't bank on it,'' the farmer went on. "There's no profit in the henge, you see, and maybe a lot for him in the plant being here. He did try and stop it—went to Paris and everything but . . .'' he shrugged. "He's a very practical man.''

"How about Pommard?''

"Our Commissaire of Police does exactly what Villefort tells him to do. No more, no less. Pierre has always been a lazy son of a bitch.'' He said it without a trace of animosity. "Rouillé has tried to get rid of him several times, but he'll never succeed—Pierre has his own local following—and, after all, what is there for him to do in a small place like this? A few drunks, a few family disputes, the occasional accident.''

"There may be a whole lot more than that soon,'' Toby put in grimly. "How strong is the Nationalist feeling around here?''

"Strong enough,'' came the evasive answer, and the farmer drained his glass.

"How about another?'' Toby was anxious to keep him talking.

"As long as you're buying—thanks!'' the red-faced man grinned at him. "Foreigners think our crowning sin in France is lust. They're dead wrong. Our chief vice is avarice, and in that we Bretons have the rest of France beaten at the post. We can make every *centime* scream like a stuck pig. I say this because if you are looking to me to support you, you'll get it so long as it doesn't cost me anything. If it is likely to hit my pocket, *adieu*, my friend! *Compris*?''

"I understand.'' Toby was somewhere between amusement

and irritation. "And do you think Judge Rouillé is of the same opinion?"

"The Judge is a man of high principles. Unfortunately he is also a man with many problems. . . ." Sommelier broke off, exclaiming, "Zut! here comes the enemy in our midst." He hastily drained his glass, and scrambled to his feet. "*Au revoir, mon ami*, I will see you again soon—*bonne chance*!"

A hush had fallen over the crowded bar parlor as Armand Dubois made his way to Toby's table and sat down with a weary thump. He appeared worried and perplexed, and for a moment he sat in silence, his brows knitted above his small dark eyes. "*Eh bien*," he said at length. "If they think they can get anywhere by this treatment they are bigger fools than I imagined. Yes, they will soon feel the weight of the power that is behind me." There was a bleak sort of satisfaction in his voice. "You saw what happened back at Villefort's?"

"Yes, but there is bound to be a certain amount of that. I think the important thing is not to overreact," Toby said cautiously. "It's a hard lesson I've learned over the years on excavations. Vandalism and harassment are often a problem, but if you react violently it seems to egg people on."

"Oh, I shall do nothing at the moment," Dubois said. "But when I do take action, when I do show my hand, a lot of people will be in for very nasty surprises. What did you think of Winton?"

The sudden question took Toby off guard. "He appeared a bit of a mountebank to me," he answered.

"I wonder. I think I shall send for his dossier from the Sûreté. I feel there may be more to Monsieur Winton than meets the eye."

"Goodness! Do you still go in for that sort of thing here?" Toby murmured faintly, wondering how his dossier would read.

"Yes. Occasionally it comes in very useful." Dubois gave him a grim smile. "I shall be interested to see if Winton's finances have improved markedly of late."

Toby suddenly was thoroughly fed up with all these mysterious undercurrents and anxious to get down to the only thing that was of importance to him. "How about the excavation?" he demanded.

"At best I can give you two extra days—nine in total.

Believe me, I would give you longer if I could, but it is impossible," Dubois said firmly. "The man I have found for you can start helping you first thing tomorrow morning."

"I am surprised you managed to come up with someone so fast. Charles Latour found it impossible and I had no luck either. Who is he?"

"His name is Paul Grandhomme. Unfortunately he doesn't quite live up to his name." There was apology in Dubois' voice. "To be frank, he's not ideal, but from what you have said it is only a question of someone to hold your surveying poles and chains and tapes and to help shift earth to the dump. He should be capable of that."

"What is he—the village idiot?" Toby asked suspiciously.

"No, he's not from around here at all. So he isn't tainted by this ridiculous superstition. To be honest, I found him in the local jail."

"A criminal!" Toby was dumbfounded.

Dubois waved a placating hand. "No, not really. Pommard had him locked up for drunk and disorderly. He's a vagabond. Sad case, really. I had a long talk with him. He's a '*pied-noir*' colonial—you know, from Algeria? So many of them didn't settle into life over here after they got kicked out of Algeria. He's been on the road for twenty years—doing odd jobs here and there as he wanders, just enough to keep food in his belly, but a chronic case of a footloose drunk. That's his problem. But I put it to him straight. If he does what you want him to do, Pommard'll drop the charge against him, and he'll be free to move on with a bit of money in his pocket. His kind don't like to be locked up in summer—it's their best time. So long as you keep him away from the bottle, he should be all right. Can you handle it?"

"I think so." Toby was thoughtful. Drinking problems he knew about. At one time he had almost drowned himself in the bottle—until Penny had come into his life. It was not that she had preached at him or tried to save him, it was just her being there that had made all the difference. He still drank a lot, sometimes too much, but he knew how to control it. His sympathies, however, were with those who could not. He had been in that particular corner of Hell.

"I told him to be at the site at 8:30 A.M.—and also that you'd meet him there, rain or shine," Dubois went on.

"How's he going to get there?"

"Pommard will drive him in the police van and drop him off. He and I are going over the plant site to discuss ongoing security arrangements."

"You'll be at the site then?"

"No, I hadn't planned on it," Dubois looked at him. "After Pommard I'm supposed to see Sommelier. More trouble about his damn orchards. He's trying to replant some of the threatened ones and wants the government to cough up the money for it. Some nerve! He's already been paid ample compensation. God, it's just one thing after another with these bloody Bretons. When this is over I shall need a prolonged rest cure in Alsace, where people know the meaning of the words common sense."

"Is that where you are from?"

"Originally." For some reason the question had disconcerted Dubois. "Well, if that's all, I think I'll turn in and leave you to your drinking. I have an important day tomorrow."

"It's not exactly all," Toby said mildly. "I feel it's only fair to warn you I intend to try to extend my stay at the site by any means in my power. And, getting back to Grandhomme, where will he stay?"

Dubois shrugged. "Technically he's supposed to go back to the lockup each night, but Pommard doesn't care. He strikes me as a lazy bastard, that one. I thought maybe Grandhomme could sleep at the site—a sort of watchman for you; he's used to sleeping rough and he could use that shelter you were in." He got up. "As to the other—well, you don't have a hope in Hell. I am not easily turned from my purpose, as you all will find out." And with a defiant glare at the ring of sullen faces at the bar, he stamped out.

There was no sign of Dubois at breakfast so, after collecting enough food to make a lunch for two, Toby set out in the Jeep. It was a mild, sunny morning, the rain clouds of yesterday banished by a stiff southwesterly breeze that sent high white cumulus clouds sailing like galleons across the pale blue sky. Toby's spirits began to revive as he drove down the cart track, pushing the Jeep as far as he dared because of the muddy ground, and then walking in to the sandy open tract on which the henge sat.

His first sight of Paul Grandhomme was a dramatic one: the man stood straddled against one of the sun-struck stones. He was tall and painfully thin, his sticklike arms braced backwards around the stones, his lined, weatherbeaten face, uplifted with closed eyes to the sun, so that he looked like a victim tied to a stake and awaiting the first crackling of the pyre. At the sound of Toby's footsteps, he struggled erect and peered at him with eyes that were dim and heavily bloodshot. "Ah, I see my lord and master approaches," he said in a surprisingly educated voice.

Toby came to a halt before him and looked at him critically. "Paul Grandhomme? Toby Glendower. How bad a shape are you in?"

Grandhomme ran his tongue over dry, chapped lips. "Pretty bad," he muttered, and Toby could see his thin frame quivering. "Another day in that lockup and I'd have had the horrors."

Toby reached with deliberation into the hip pocket of his work corduroys and produced a silver flask. "We both know the score, I think, so this is what I propose. I'll give you a drink now and then another shot at eleven. When we break for lunch you can split a bottle of wine with me as long as you eat. And I'll give you another shot before quitting time. Now, this can be the ongoing pattern *if* you do your part. Fair enough?"

"Fair enough." It was only with a visible effort that Grandhomme stopped himself from snatching the flask. He tipped his head back and with eyes closed, took a long swallow, then reluctantly handed it back and wiped his mouth on his sleeve. "What do you want me to do?"

"First, help me get the surveying equipment from the Jeep. Then you'll have to hold the surveying staff where I tell you, while I sight. Ever done anything like this before?"

Grandhomme nodded. "Done some road survey work."

"Good, then you know the ropes." They set to work and Toby found him quick to take directions. By the midmorning break, half the stones had been accurately plotted on the site plan, but the man was shaking violently again by the time his second shot was due. "Good medicine this!" he said with a wink, after he had taken a satisfying swig.

"It should be—it's five-star cognac," Toby said mildly.

"You're all right, you know that? I won't give you any trouble." He looked wistfully at the flask in his hand. "I don't suppose . . . ?"

"No. We'll have our lunch in an hour."

"*D'accord*. Where do you want me now?" He shouldered the graduated surveying pole.

"Over there . . ." Toby began, but was interrupted.

"Hello there!" Jean Sommelier stepped out of the bushes, looking with curiosity at the tall man. "Got an assistant, I see—what luck!" There was an odd intonation to his voice. "I dropped by to see if Dubois was around."

"No, I haven't seen him this morning."

"*Merde*! He was supposed to meet me at the orchard and he hasn't shown up. If you see him, tell him I went back to the farm. Can't dance to his tune—I'm a busy man, I've got things to do," Sommelier grumbled. Having said that, he showed no signs of leaving. He looked around the site. "I see the dog has been visiting you here again." The large paw marks were evident on the exposed sandy subsoil.

"Yes. A damn nuisance," Toby said impatiently. "He's been burrowing at the center again by the looks of it; nothing but a big overgrown puppy."

"You've seen it?"

"Yes. Yesterday. Looks rather like a big Labrador, but with some other breed mixed in. Should have asked Winton about it last night. Was there anything else?" Toby asked pointedly.

"No. Oh, do you have the time? My watch seems to have stopped."

"Eleven o'clock." Toby said impatiently.

"Thanks. Well, *au revoir*." Sommelier faded back into the bushes as noiselessly as he had come.

They broke for lunch, which they ate in the dolmen-shelter, and, heartened by the wine, Grandhomme soon had Toby chuckling over his anecdotes about his life on the road. The bottle empty, Toby scrambled to his feet. "Well, back to work. Oh, by the way, you have a choice; you can sleep in the lockup or you can camp out here and keep an eye on the site for me."

"Here," Grandhomme said promptly, and then slyly added,

"But I'll need some money for my dinner—say ten francs? I can walk into Morgat for it."

Toby shook his head at him. "No. I'll take you back to the inn and make sure you eat dinner and not drink it. I'll bring you back."

"Oh well, it was worth a try! What now? More of the same?"

"No, I'm going to excavate the burial at the center. I'll need your help to move that flat capstone over there. Then you can take that basket and sieve, and sieve the earth through it into the basket as I dig it out."

After considerable effort, they lifted the large flat stone to reveal a dark hole about three feet square and lined with flat slabs of stone of the same material. Toby knelt down and peered in. "Good God!" he exploded.

The remains of a crouched, crumbling skeleton and a broken pot, covered by a fine silting of earth, lay revealed, but resting on top was a collection of objects that had nothing to do with the long-interred dead. There was a white-handled dagger; a chaplet of withered flowers; a hank of white rope; and a long, glossy plait of dark red hair that looked as if it had been but newly shorn from the head of a Celtic princess.

CHAPTER 4

Toby was more than a little shaken by the bizarre cache. Although he was no expert on the subject, he knew enough to recognize that at least two of the foreign objects in the grave—the dagger and the ropes or *strigils*—were utilized in the Wicca branch of witchcraft, the modern cult that claimed descent from the fertility religions of ancient Europe. That there was little basis to such claims, he also knew, but this had not prevented the modern participants from utilizing the relics of their putative ancestors for their rites; he had heard of several similar cases in England.

But the problem here was—who? Whoever had been holding witchcraft rituals at the henge had done it in the recent past—judging by the state of the flowers and the hair, not more than a month ago—perhaps even in those few days before he had arrived and when the site was deserted. Winton and his merry band seemed the obvious choice, but maybe too obvious: according to the priest, the henge had been used by the locals for witchcraft in times of crisis long, long before Winton had appeared on the scene—and this for them was indeed a time of crisis.

He was now in a fine old quandary as to what to do. Remove the objects and carry on with the excavation as if nothing were amiss? That would be no solution, even if he swore Grandhomme to silence and the man respected his vow. Whoever was involved in this knew that sooner or later he would investigate the burial; the objects could so easily have been removed during his absences from the site that it was obvious he was meant to find them. Why? Was it a message, a warning, a signal of defiance? And, if so, at whom was it directed? Himself? Or the local power junta headed by Villefort? Or the French government in the person of Dubois? A witch had been dedicated at this site—to do what? Gazing thoughtfully at the glossy hair of that amazing shade of deep maroon red only found among the Celts, he reflected that the witch in question should not be too difficult to pinpoint; there could only be a handful of such redheads, and fewer still who had suddenly gone from long to short hair in the past month.

"So what are you going to do about this?" Grandhomme's ironic voice broke in on his reverie.

Toby roused himself. "Well, for the moment, I'm going to put that capstone back on and leave it as is. I suppose I'd better show it to Dubois. At least, it may cause him to take these local feelings about the henge more seriously. Then I'll try and get a line on who is involved, through the hair. That should be easy enough to trace, it's so unusual."

Grandhomme chuckled suddenly, "Perhaps not all that easy, *mon vieux*! Have you seen many of the Cormel women?"

"Why no, none. I've been buying what odds and ends I need at the Morgat stores. Other than that, the only women I've seen have been the servants at the inn. Why? What do you mean?"

"My one diversion in the lockup was looking through the window. You could see out from the top bunk in the cell. I particularly liked watching the women at their marketing— you know why? Because I'd say half of them had that very pretty shade of hair. It must be a peculiarity of the region, at least of the women—I've only seen one man with it."

"Damnation!" Toby said fretfully. "Well, to hell with it for the moment. We'll go on with the surveying for another hour and then pack it in for the day. I'll find Dubois when I bring you back for the night. After that he can bloody well take what action he chooses."

They put the capstone back on and Toby took some care to make the area look undisturbed. "I wonder if that is what the dog has been after," he murmured, as they returned to their surveying labors. "If so, it might lead us to the source of all this." But, to add to his irritation, that day brought no glimpse of the black hound.

Another anomaly occurred to him as they drove away from the site. "Why does Cormel have a jail? It's such a small place."

"It's the ancient market town for this area," his assistant replied. "It may be small, but all administrative power for the

Isthmus of Crozon is centered there; something to do with the Villefort estate, I believe. Not that that is saying much. The entire police force consists of Pommard and two constables. If anyone wanted to go on a crime spree, this wouldn't be a bad place to do it. I don't think any of 'em would be up to catching their own grandmothers.''

"They caught you," Toby pointed out.

"Only because I was blind drunk," Grandhomme said cheerfully. "As it was, it took all three of them to do it."

After dinner, Toby decided to relax his own rules and treat Grandhomme to a pint of cider before taking him back to the site. It was a move he regretted the moment they had settled at a table, because the occupants of the bar were in an obviously hostile mood and kept shooting black looks in their direction and muttering sullenly to one another. Even the normally affable landlord had caught the contagion, and when Toby had asked for the whereabouts of Dubois had snarled, "I haven't seen him all day and I don't give a shit where he is."

Toby was relieved when Sommelier came in and greeted them amiably. "Did Dubois ever show up?" he asked, seating himself beside them with his tankard.

"No, not a sign of him. You haven't seen Pommard or any of the others around?" Sommelier shook his head. "Damn. I hope Dubois cleared it with someone that Grandhomme can stay at the site," Toby said irritably, "I wanted to take him back there as soon as we've finished."

"Could you give me a lift?" Sommelier asked. "Had to take my truck in for repairs, and it's a long walk from here. You could drop me at the end of the lane before you turn off; my farm is quite near there."

"I could take you right home." Toby was anxious to remain on the good side of what appeared to be his sole ally.

"No, no. Drop me where I said. It's a fine night and the bit of a walk before turning in will clear my head. Still, if I haven't got to walk all that way, I think I'll have another." They all had another round, Toby hoping against hope that Dubois would put in an appearance so that he could shift this new burden of knowledge over to him. He was out of luck.

A full moon bathed the rugged landscape as they drove back, turning it into a starkly dramatic chiaroscuro of black

and silver. A short way before the turnoff to the site, Sommelier suddenly said, "Stop right here. I can cut through the
woods to my place." As Toby cut the motor and the roar of
the engine died, a strange sound came out of the woods to
their left—a long drawn-out ululating wail that rose to a
crescendo, then stopped dead for a pulse-beat and started again
on the same eerie note.

"What the hell's that?" Grandhomme gasped.

"Holy Jesus, it sounds like the Gwarch y Crozon—the
banshee!" Sommelier muttered, and crossed himself. He made
no move to get out of the car. They listened in silence for a
moment to the uncanny wailing. "Must be the dog baying at
the full moon, or could be he is caught in something," Toby
said. "Sounds as if he might be in pain."

"Shouldn't think so," Sommelier said in a hushed voice.
"Poachers don't use these woods—too near the Dragon's
Teeth for local stomachs."

"Perhaps we should walk you a little way into the woods
and take a look." Toby was groping under his seat for a
flashlight. "If nothing else, we'd scare it off to do its howling
elsewhere. Grandhomme won't get much sleep if this goes
on."

They got out of the Jeep and plunged into the darkness of
the trees, which were a mixture of huge oaks, beeches, and
ash so thick that the light of the moon could not penetrate.
Only the thin beam of the flashlight picked out the faint
pathway that wavered in front of them through the dense
underbrush.

"The sound seems to be coming from the right—more
towards the cart-track," Toby observed as they plodded on.
"God, these woods are dense!"

"Yes, nothing has been done to them for years," Jean
Sommelier said gloomily, as he led the way. "Should have
been thinned out long since, but Winton doesn't care and I
don't have the money or the right to do anything about
them."

The wailing stopped for a moment and then began again
with renewed urgency.

"Sounds very close," Toby muttered. "How about bearing
off here?" His scanning light picked up an even fainter path
leading in the right direction.

"If we get turned around in there, we could be wandering all night." There was a faint protest in Sommelier's voice. "These woods are damned easy to get lost in."

"Then you stay here and if I get adrift I'll shout and you keep shouting back until I find you."

"No, we must all keep together." Jean said firmly. "Come on then." And he shouldered into the new pathway, Toby close on his heels and Grandhomme more reluctantly bringing up the rear.

Toby was so intent on picking out the tenuous path with the light that when Sommelier stopped abruptly he cannoned into him. "Mother of mercy! What is it?" the farmer whispered in a strangled voice, and Toby, peering over his shoulder, went cold with shock.

A dark form lay on the ground in a little clearing upon which the moon gleamed fitfully. Straddled across the figure was the hound, whose wails cut off abruptly and were replaced by a deep-throated growl, as it advanced stiff-legged and bristling towards them. Its large fangs were bared in a snarl.

"Down, boy, down," Toby shouted, with a lot more authority than he felt. "Good dog, stay now, stay!"

The dog stopped uncertainly, the growling reduced to a rumble. "Sit, boy, sit!" Toby continued hopefully. The dog did not obey, but the rumbling stopped and he began to wag his tail feebly. Toby stepped forward cautiously into the clearing, and the dog backed up a step. Then, with a sudden huge bound, it crashed into the underbrush and was gone.

Sommelier ran over to the figure on the ground and recoiled. "Mother of God, it's Dubois!" he gasped. "I thought the dog had got him, but . . . look!"

Toby was right behind him and the flashlight illumined the little engineer, who lay as if peacefully asleep. His face was an ashy white, his hands were folded across his breast, his legs stretched out, the small feet in their polished black shoes neatly together. But across his breast, its freshly sharpened blade glittering wickedly up at them, was an old-fashioned, long-handled scythe.

Toby knelt down and touched the folded hands. They were ice-cold and completely rigid. Frantically he felt at the neck above the white shirt. "He's dead," he announced grimly. "And for some time, by the looks of it."

"But how?" the farmer gasped. "Look, there isn't a mark on him!"

"Maybe his heart?" Grandhomme asked in a hushed voice. "The dog attacked him and he tried to drive him off with that . . . that thing, and his heart gave out?"

"And then he tidily stretched out, folded his hands, arranged the scythe on top of them and gave up the ghost?" Toby growled. "Not in a million years! This looks like murder."

"But how? Without a mark on him?" the farmer repeated in a shaky voice.

"That's what we'll have to find out. Where's the nearest doctor?" Toby demanded. He was still numb with the shock of it.

"There's a doctor in Morgat," Jean said.

"Right. Well this is what you must do. You take Grandhomme in the Jeep to get the doctor. Grandhomme can guide him back here in the doctor's car. Then you go on in the Jeep, get hold of Pommard, and bring him out here as quickly as you can. I'll stay here and guard the body. Stop!" The imperative was to Sommelier whose hand had gone out to close the eyelids, which were slitted open and gave the uncanny impression that the dead man was peering slyly at them. "Don't touch the body! Grandhomme, did you hear what I just said?" He turned around to see the tall man slumped down on the ground, his face in his hands. "What's the matter? Are you all right?"

"No, I'm not," came the muffled voice. "It is not that I haven't seen death—I have, too much of it. It's just that I never get used to it."

"Well, pull yourself together. You have to go with Sommelier, it's for your own protection."

"What about you," the farmer asked. "Will you be all right?"

"I sincerely hope so," Toby answered. "You'd better get going—and here, take the flashlight."

"And leave you without light?" There was a quaver of fear in the Breton's voice.

"The moon will be out for a while longer, and I have a small pen-light." Grandhomme had scrambled to his feet and was stumbling back along the way they had come; after a moment's hesitation, the stocky farmer followed him. As the sound of their footsteps died away, an utter silence descended on the glade. In the dense encompassing woods, there was not so much as a call from a nightbird or the hoot of an owl. Toby shivered suddenly and reached for the comfort of his pipe. The sequence of familiar acts; the filling, the lighting, the drawing, soothed him and allowed him to collect his thoughts.

So it had happened again! Like it or not—and he didn't— he was involved with another murder. The vow he had made to himself in an ancient cistern in Israel dominated his mind; not only was he involved in murder, he was pledged to solve it. He looked down grimly at the peaceful figure on the ground. He had not really known this little bureaucrat, he had not even particularly liked what little he had known about him, but the one thing he did know was that Dubois had been deprived unjustly of his most precious right, the right to life; and for that someone would have to pay.

The scythe, sending its glittering message from the breast of the dead man, stirred memories within him. Witchcraft again! There had been a case, he recalled, in a remote area of southern England; an old man found dead in a ditch, his throat cut, and a scythe ceremonially placed across him; an old man suspected of black witchcraft. An English parallel, just as there had been English parallels to his witchcraft find of this very morning—a morning which now seemed a lifetime ago. It was odd this recurrence of English themes when, so far as he knew, he was the only Englishman on the whole peninsula. It did nothing to cheer him up.

How and when had Dubois come by his death? Toby had done a lot of reading on forensic medicine since he had been plunged into the unlikely world of detection during the Pergama affair, so he knew what to look for. He tested the folded hands again. They were still rigid, but there was a slight give to the arms as a whole, as if the rigor mortis was beginning to wear off. He checked his watch by the light of the pen-light and saw it lacked fifteen minutes to midnight. So, taking the warmth of the day into consideration, the death would have taken place roughly twelve hours ago, say somewhere around eleven that morning. The lividity of the body might tell him more. Disregarding his own admonition, he knelt and carefully inched down one of the black nylon socks to reveal the

pallid flesh beneath—there was no sign of lividity at all!
Puzzled, he slid the sock down almost to the ankle, then
froze. Here was something: a bluish-gray band about an inch
wide ran around it. Dubois had been tied, his feet had been
tied together; it was the first sign of violence. But why was
there no lividity? Systematically he shone the tiny pen-light
inch by inch up the body, seeking some sign of a wound, but
there was nothing. On the back then?

He sat and debated with himself whether he dared disturb
the body to that extent. Finally, his nerves getting the better
of him and unwilling to sit there doing nothing, he rational-
ized that he probably knew as much about violent death as the
combined forces of a country doctor and a rural policeman.
After removing the scythe with his handkerchief-wrapped
hand, he tipped the body over on its face with a grimace of
distaste. This time the only thing the search revealed was a
slight bump on the back of the head. It did not yield to his
testing fingers so there was no fracture; it might be enough to
cause a mild concussion, but death? Shock possibly, if Dubois
had had a weak heart, but, damn it, there still should be signs
of lividity!

Rearranging the body in its original position, he tried desperately to remember any obscure case where such telltale
signs of time and position at death had been totally absent.
Something teased at his mind, some sentence from a textbook, but try as he might he could not bring it to the surface.

He started pacing carefully around the glade, looking for
signs of a struggle or of the body having been dragged, but
there was nothing. Then came a faint rustling in the bushes to
his right and he froze, his scalp prickling. "Sommelier?
Grandhomme? Are you there?" he called. The rustling stopped
and he waited tensely, conscious of his total isolation. It
started again. "Who's there?" he called, trying to keep a
tremor out of his voice. Something between a whine and a
whimper answered him—the dog again!

"Here, boy, here!" he shouted, advancing cautiously in
the direction of the sound. He caught a glimpse of the animal
before it bounded away from him and instinctively went after
it, plunging through the underbrush, not caring about the
commotion he was making. Suddenly he was free of the
clinging entanglement and found himself standing on the

cart-track, with the hound loping down its muddy length to where the Dragon's Teeth quietly gleamed in the moonlight. As he pursued the dog, he thought he caught a flicker of movement among the stones. He raced into the silent circle and looked around. The dog had disappeared and there was no sign, no sound even, of anything else. He cautiously approached the dolmen-shelter and shone the tiny light into it; it lit up nothing but Grandhomme's bedroll and the shabby knapsack that housed his entire worldly goods. He stood there for a moment getting his breath back, his ears straining for the faintest sound, but there was nothing except for the faint barking of a dog in the far distance. He turned on his heel and marched back up the cart-track, aware of a new, grim fact. However Dubois had come by his death, it had happened within easy shouting distance of the site, and it must have happened some time on that serene summer morning while he and Grandhomme were quietly about their survey work—and yet there had been no sound, no sound at all.

He located his point of egress on to the track and followed the trail of broken and bent saplings back into the clearing, where all was as before and the ashen, peaceful face of the dead man silently mocked him. Suddenly the textbook phrase he had been seeking popped out of his photographic memory. "Absence of lividity: in certain rare cases the usual telltale signs of lividity are not present, but this only occurs when a cadaver has been entirely drained of blood."

Drained of blood! How could that be? Heedless now of disturbing the body, he knelt down and pulled up the white shirtcuffs. The arms yielded flaccidly, although the hands were still rigid, showing the rigor to be wearing off fast; but there were no cuts on the wrists, any more than there was any sign of violence on the throat. His examination of that area had moved the head and caused the jaw to sag slightly. It was then he noticed a darker rim on the pale lips. He shone the light into the partly open mouth and recoiled. "Oh, dear God, no!" he exclaimed.

When Grandhomme and the elderly doctor forced their way through into the clearing, it was to find him sitting on the ground beside the body, his head bent upon his crossed arms. He looked up, his face almost as ashen as the dead man's, his round glasses gleaming like pale moons. "I have established the cause of death,'' he informed them woodenly. ''But I would be glad, doctor, if you would verify it. Arnold Dubois was murdered by having his tongue cut out, and then being hung upside down by the ankles until all his life's blood drained out of him.''

CHAPTER 5

"It may seem a hideous barbarism to you, but one could almost say that it is the execution method of the region," Jean Sommelier said quietly to the brooding Toby. "And I do mean execution. It started with a particularly nasty affair perpetrated by the Germans here in World War II. There was a lot of Underground activity going on in Brittany—as you can well imagine—and the Boche around here got thoroughly fed up with it. They caught a 16-year-old boy who'd been injured in one of the partisan raids and had been hidden out by two old-maid sisters who had a little farm just outside of Cormel. Well, the Germans took them all outside the village to another part of these very same woods, cut out their tongues, and hoisted them up on the trees to bleed to death, with notices pinned on them that anyone found acting against the Germans would suffer a similar fate. They should not have done that. When the Germans were losing the war and started pulling out of Brittany, there was a regular bloodbath here. The partisans picked up as many as they could and did to them as had been done. I was a kid at the time, but I remember it well—they seemed to be hanging from every tree."

"World War II was a very long time ago," Toby said in a monotone. "Are you asking me to believe a relic from that time perpetrated this . . . . this beastliness?"

"No, I'm not saying that at all. You see, it didn't stop with World War II. There have been a few cases since—mainly tied up with the extreme wing of the Nationalists. Like the IRA in Ireland, they are not exactly gentle souls and, well, the few who have been treated so were informers or traitors of one sort or another. But the point I am making is that anyone in the region knows these stories and you would not even need to be a native to copy the method."

47

"I see." Toby was still remote, cemented in an icy rampart he had built around himself.

It was several hours later and much had happened. The moon had set and the glade, which now seethed with activity, was harshly lit by Coleman pressure-lamps, hastily culled from Jean Sommelier's barns. They hissed and spat around the perimeters of the clearing, making grotesque giant shadows of those who crossed their line of light.

By the time Sommelier had returned with Pommard and Villefort—he had found them together—the doctor had confirmed Toby's gruesome findings and had tentatively agreed upon the time of death. "I'll be able to tell more accurately when I've done the autopsy, but yes, I'd say somewhere between ten and eleven this morning—or, rather, yesterday morning. But there are some unusual features I do not understand. The man wasn't a hemophiliac by any chance?" Toby had thought it highly unlikely.

Pommard had not so much arrived as erupted onto the scene and appeared to be in a mood to arrest anyone and everyone in sight. He had been all for clapping Grandhomme in jail as the guilty party, but had backed away from that when Toby, supported by the doctor, had pointed out that if the time of death was 11:00, Grandhomme had an airtight alibi, since he and Toby had been working at the site together from 8:30 onward. Pommard had started to bluster then that they both were involved and were as guilty as hell; that Toby had been heard quarreling with Dubois in the inn parlor; that he would arrest them both, when the wind was completely taken out of him by Grandhomme, who had turned quietly belligerent. "I think it would be most unwise to try and make us the scapegoats," he had hissed. "You'd have so much explaining to do to the man from the Sûreté, who will be here in a few hours. I may be nobody, but Sir Tobias Glendower is an important man, and we were together."

"What the hell are you saying? What kind of crap are you feeding me?" Pommard had blustered, and Villefort, who had remained silent up to that point had said sharply, "Yes, you'd better explain, if you know what's good for you!"

Grandhomme had not replied immediately, but just stared at them with a cynical smile, evidently savoring their sudden unease. "I suspected you might try some nonsense like this," he said at length, "so the doctor was kind enough to let me use his telephone. I thought the authorities in Paris might be interested to know that one of their government officials had been murdered. They were—*very*. They are sending a senior inspector down from the Quai des Orfevres. He'll be here to take charge as fast as a car can drive him from Paris. So take care, Monsieur le Commissaire, or your own neck may be on the line!"

Pommard had backed off, but had then turned on Sommelier. "You!" he had accused, with a shaking finger. "You were the last one to see him!"

"Not I," the farmer said quickly. "He never did turn up for our appointment and, if he was killed at eleven o'clock, well, I was with these two. Isn't that right?" he appealed to Toby.

"Yes, that's right," Toby agreed with a twinge of unease, recalling what a point the farmer had made about the time of his unexpected visit.

"In fact," Sommelier went on with distinct malice, "When the man from the Sûreté turns up, you'll have a lot of explaining to do, Pierre. By the looks of it you were the last person to see him alive."

"The last I saw of him was when he left in that red car of his to keep his appointment with you," Pommard stuttered. "That was at ten o'clock. We'd been all over the plant site, had a run-in with Winton. . . ." He stopped suddenly, as if aware he was talking too much. "Anyway, there is much still to be done. It's plain he was not actually killed in this spot. We have still to find where the murder took place, we've got to find his car. . . ." He trailed off and looked wearily at Villefort. "I don't have the men or the resources for this. I don't know where to start."

"With dawn, we can organize the villagers to look for the car." Villefort, after a quick look at his bemused police chief, took charge. "In the meantime, I think the doctor needs the body to be taken to his surgery for the autopsy. The constables can take care of that. Presumably the man from the Sûreté will bring some help with him. The best thing you can do is to get statements from these three about the finding of the body, so that the Paris inspector will have nothing to complain about. You've tested the scythe for fingerprints and there are none. I suppose you could try tracking it down, but there may be many such.''

"I can save you the trouble," Jean Sommelier broke in uneasily. "When I went back to pick up the lamps, I checked in my barn, where I had several. They haven't been used for years and were all rusted up. One of them is missing. This may be it. You can see it has been recently sharpened and polished." There was a moment of heavy silence, only broken by the sleepy chirp of an awakening bird.

Toby cleared his throat. "I'd like to suggest also a search of Dubois' room at the inn. The doctor and I have noticed an unusual circumstance about the body. It is rare that a cadaver can be so completely drained of blood as this one was. Normally blood will clot long before that point. So, in particular, we are looking for any kind of medicine for a blood condition or a decoagulant of some sort. Otherwise we will be left with a mystery within a mystery. There is also his briefcase, he mentioned to me. . . ."

"You shut up," Pommard said savagely. "You've nothing to do with this investigation. You've no business here at all. I ought to run you out of the district—you and this bloody vagabond.''

Toby ignored him, but looked steadily at Villefort. "I think I should inform you that I have had considerable experience in cases of violent death and, I may add, considerable success in solving them. I do not intend to stand idly by on this one. I did not know the murdered man at all well, but he struck me as an honest man trying to do an honest, if difficult, job, and was certainly undeserving of this hideous death. I am involved and, whether it suits you or not, I intend to see justice done. You have the reputation of a practical man; as such you should welcome all the help you can get. I should like to think I could work together with the people of this area and not in opposition to them, but work is what I intend to do. Apart from the wild and baseless accusations Pommard has chosen to hurl at the three of us here, it is evident that he has no idea where to start or even in which direction to look. There are all sorts of possibilities, all sorts of directions. I should think the more people you have looking, the better it will be.''

Villefort was once more his smooth self. "We have all had

a great shock, Sir Tobias, and doubtless things have been said that should not have been. Naturally we should welcome any kind of assistance or information you can give us, but I have the feeling that it may all be taken out of our hands with the arrival of the Sûreté, who are not noted for their tolerance of amateurs.'' There was a faint stress on the last word. ''I suggest we all go home and get a few hours of much-needed sleep before his arrival. I feel we are going to need all our wits about us.''

How true a prophet he turned out to be was borne upon Toby when he was awakened out of a troubled sleep several hours later by what appeared to be a minor riot taking place in the inn parlor beneath him. There was much shouting and trampling of feet and, as he dressed hastily and grabbed a quick shave, he could see from his window small groups of men stomping out of the inn. Their outraged mutterings sounded like a distant rumble of thunder. The cause soon became apparent with a hammering on his door. ''Sir Glendower, Sergeant Auvergne from the Sûreté. Inspector Favet wishes to see you at once in the parlor downstairs.''

Favet looked exactly like a ferret—a greasy ferret. His small glittering eyes were so closely set that they seemed to be gazing into each other, his face was long and pointed, but square at the temples, with a lot of furry-looking, close-cut dark hair growing low on his forehead. He was seated at a table but still wearing a shabby dark-blue, tightly belted raincoat, which had ashes strewn down the front from the cigarette that dangled from his thin, tight-lipped mouth. The beady eyes scanned Toby briefly before reverting to the folder in his hand. He said nothing, and Toby, his eyebrows lifting slightly, drew out a chair and sat down. ''I didn't tell you to sit,'' Favet suddenly rapped out.

''So I noticed,'' Toby replied haughtily, favoring him with an icy blue stare. ''An error on your part, I presume.'' He wriggled into a comfortable slouch and lit up his pipe.

Favet shut the folder with a snap and flung himself back in his own chair, his mouth opening in a mirthless grin that revealed sharp little pointed teeth that added to his ferretlike appearance. ''So! Sir Tobias Glendower. Millionaire-archae-ologist, and who no doubt expects to be treated like one. Tell me, *Sir* Tobias, just three things. What are you doing here?

How many oil shares do you own? And what oil company do you represent?''

To say that this took Toby's breath away was an understatement. If he hadn't had his pipe in his mouth, he would have gaped in astonishment. As it was, he was beginning to appreciate the growls of outrage that could still be heard from outside the inn. Toby took his time in answering. "As to your first question, I am here on behalf of your Department of Antiquities, excavating a unique henge-site, having taken the place of a French colleague, Charles Latour, who fell ill. As to the third, I represent no oil company, and as to the second, I haven't the faintest idea—such matters are handled by my lawyers. But that, in any case, is none of your business. And may I ask what the devil such questions have to do with the murder of Armand Dubois?''

Favet leaned forward, grinning with delight as if Toby had fallen into some trap. "Oh come now, you can't pretend to be that naive! Surely you must realize that from the first the big oil companies have made efforts to stop all nuclear plant construction in France, since this will eventually rid us of dependency on their products, and also that foreign powers would do almost anything to stop the growing strength and development of France?''

"And you think the murder of Dubois—one lone government man—will effect that end and put a stop to the plant?'' Toby countered.

This seemed to put Favet off his stride. "Well, no, of course not. The murder of Dubois is a terror tactic, which is why I am here. I am an expert on terrorist groups and their methods.''

"And are you accusing me of being part of such a group and of employing such tactics?'' Toby said acidly.

"Well, no, but. . . .'' Favet began again.

"Then what the hell are we talking about?'' Toby roared. "I expect to be asked substantive questions on what has happened here, not some damn tarradiddle about being a foreign agent! Check with your Department of Antiquities, check with your Foreign Ministry. They'll tell you what and who I am; an archaeologist—*tout simple!*—and with no political interests or bias. An archaeologist, moreover, with considerable expertise in questions of violent death, who would be only too willing to cooperate with you in an intelligent investigation, which has so many possible avenues to explore—the witchcraft angle for one.''

''The what?'' Favet looked blank.

Toby rapidly outlined his findings of the previous day, the local feelings about the henge, and the implications of the scythe. But as he went on, a disbelieving smirk played about Favet's mouth and he began to fiddle impatiently with the papers on the table.

When Toby paused for breath, he cut in, ''Oh, really now! Whoever is behind this must have seen you coming. Witchcraft indeed! And you talk of tarradiddle! Surely you can see this is nothing but window-dressing? No, no, this is just a simple terrorist murder, and now it is simply a question of rounding up the terrorists.''

The arrogance of the man simply took Toby's breath away. ''Well, if you have already solved the murder to your satisfaction and are not even prepared to listen, I may as well get on with my own business,'' Toby said with heavy sarcasm.

''And what is that?''

''Excavating a henge. I'll gather up Grandhomme and be on my way—unless of course you have him locked up as a foreign agent, too.''

''Oh, no. Grandhomme has been most useful to us. Mind you, I'm not sure how useful he's going to be to you this morning—a little under the weather I believe.''

''What have you done to him!'' roared Toby, flying into a fine Celtic rage.

''Why, nothing!'' Favet looked at him with mock surprise. ''Anyone who is as cooperative an informant as Grandhomme is always treated well by the Sûreté, but he seems to have a certain weakness for the bottle.''

''You made him drunk!''

''I? He did that to himself.''

Toby controlled himself with difficulty. ''Where is he?'' he said, getting up.

''Out back, sleeping it off, I believe. But one moment, Sir Tobias. Sergeant Auvergne will fingerprint you before you go.''

''Fingerprint!'' Toby was just about to give an outraged refusal when he saw the hopeful gleam in Favet's eye. ''We are fingerprinting everyone we know who had any contact with Dubois in this area,'' Favet continued, watching him closely.

"And what exactly is that supposed to prove?'' Toby asked, understanding now the outraged groups of men outside.

"Ah, we cannot disclose all our secrets,'' Favet said smugly. "But fingerprints are such useful things to have on file, I've found.''

Toby allowed himself to be fingerprinted by the stolid and impassive Auvergne. "I really can't believe your Inspector,'' he muttered, as he wiped off his fingers. "Does he really expect to get anywhere around here with these tactics?''

Auvergne carefully avoided his eyes. "He's a very good man with terrorists.''

"And if this murder doesn't happen to fall into that category?''

Auvergne's bulky shoulders rose in a slight shrug. "We shall see.''

Toby found Grandhomme sodden and insensible. He shook him awake, none too gently, ordered the scared-looking landlord to pump black coffee into him until he returned, and took off in search of Pommard. Predictably, he ran him to earth at Villefort's, where both of them were sitting at the dining room table drinking cognac and looking extremely harassed. They did not seem overly pleased to see him, but Toby was in no mood to be thwarted.

"I have just had a session with Favet,'' he stated. "And in my opinion the man is an arrogant ass with whom it will be impossible to cooperate, and who is likely, in my opinion, to precipitate a far worse crisis on this peninsula if he goes on in the way he has started. Now, I made my intentions clear last night, so it is up to you whether I go it alone or whether we can work together.''

"What do you want to know?'' Villefort asked cautiously.

"First, the doctor's report; then, anything about the car and Dubois' briefcase. Also I'd like to hear from Pommard about this meeting with Winton yesterday.''

A brief glance passed between the two men and Villefort gave a slight nod. "Well,'' Pommard growled. "The doctor says he can't be more exact about the time of death, but he thinks between 10:30 and 11:30 yesterday morning. Some medicine was found in Dubois' room—a decoagulant containing CXB. He must have suffered from phlebitis recently, according to the doctor. The car was located parked by a disused gate of the chateau about a mile from where the body was found; no sign of violence nearby and the briefcase was still in it.''

"Could I see it? Were his papers intact?''

Pommard looked up from under his heavy brows. "Favet has it,'' he growled. "And how do we know? We've no idea what he had in there to begin with. As to Winton. . . .'' He shrugged. "I think the man is insane. We were going along the iron railings behind the chateau—it used to separate the gardens from the old orchard, but is part of the land acquired for the site—when Winton suddenly appeared out of nowhere and started to scream at Dubois. Some nonsense about us having crossed the circle of protection he had erected around the chateau and setting in motion forces over which he had no control. He yelled at Dubois that unless he kept the workers away from that part, Winton could not be held responsible for their safety. Dubois got angry. He took him aside, out of my hearing, and talked to him steadily for about five minutes—I have no idea what about. Finally, Winton ran back towards the chateau, but just before he went inside he turned, shook his fist at Dubois, and screamed, "You have destroyed my peace and you shall pay!'' And that was it. Dubois seemed more amused than upset, and we finished up what we had to do and then went our separate ways—he in his car and I in the police car.''

"And that was when?'' Toby prompted.

"Just after ten. I thought he was on his way to meet Sommelier. I came back here and at eleven we were together.'' Pommard looked at Villefort who nodded agreement.

"I see. Thanks,'' Toby said absently. "Have you any idea how many people live up at the chateau?''

"Not many,'' Pommard said. "There were a lot more to start with, but they seem to have dwindled over the years. There are five foreigners besides Winton—they have to register with the police, of course, but there are a few French weirdos there, too.''

"Do you think I could get in to see Winton?''

Pommard shrugged. "You could try. There's a big bell

next to the main gate. You ring that and wait. Sometimes someone will come, sometimes they won't answer.''

"No phone?"

'No.''

"If you are thinking of trying, maybe you should let us know when," Villefort put in. "Just to be on the safe side.''

"Any idea how many women in the group?''

They looked at him in surprise. "No idea. There is one middle-aged female—kind of raddled looking—who takes care of what little marketing they do." Pommard volunteered. "Same weird get-up that Winton wears. Drives an old truck painted all over with kooky signs.''

"What color hair?''

"Black—why?''

"Just so that I'd recognize her," Toby evaded. "Well, I won't try it today. Grandhomme should be sobered up by now—I'll get over to the site.''

"You are going on with it!" Pommard was astounded.

"Naturally. Dubois' death may have delayed things, but I don't imagine it has altered anything. The site has to be finished before they send someone else down to move it. Don't bother to get up, I'll find my own way out.''

He let himself out into the hallway and was conscious of someone's eyes on him. He looked up into the shadows of the stairs and saw the slim, girlish figure of a young woman standing at the top, a baby in her arms. She had a pretty, slightly vacant face, but her most outstanding feature was a burnished helmet of short-cropped, dark red hair.

CHAPTER 6

Toby found Grandhomme contrite and in no shape to be of any immediate use. To add to his woes, the rain had started again; so, thoroughly disgruntled, he drove Grandhomme out to the site, instructed him to sleep it off in the rock shelter, and moodily began to take some sitings on the possible solar alignments. But he found he could not concentrate on what he was doing. His mind wandered over the convolutions of the case, worrying over the elusive details that seemed to be slipping through his fingers like quicksilver.

If the police didn't hurry at their task, this rain would blot out forever any clue as to where Dubois was murdered. Even if they found the site, what would it tell them? Practically nothing about the all-important who, only the where, and what did that really matter? This was a brutal murder without any leads that went anywhere; the scythe was a non-starter—except, perhaps, to point a shadowy finger at Sommelier—the car and the briefcase, likewise. If only he had talked more with Dubois, had known something of what was going on behind the hints thrown out by the dead man. So far as he could see, the only viable thread he had to follow, however tenuous, was the witchcraft angle—and that involved the tracking down of a woman. His gloom increased, for women and their ways were not his speciality. Shaking himself out of his fruitless meditation, he came to a sudden decision. He needed help; he needed Penny. Somehow or another he had to get hold of her and have her join him.

Heedless of the rain, he took out his wallet and extracted her last letter: Penny was one of the last great letter-writers. "Let's see," he murmured. "Today is the 26th of July. Her conference ended on the 12th and she was going to visit Alex to straighten him out right then and there. Knowing her, she's probably already done that, so she just may be back in Oxford. She was talking about starting her new book. I have to find a private phone. If I can get her on the scene with no one knowing the connection between us, she could pursue the female angle. Yes, that's what to do."

His mind made up, he came to another decision and set off in the Jeep in search of Sommelier's farm. It was a surprisingly prosperous and substantial looking group of buildings, its rustic beauty only slightly marred by the overwhelming aroma of pig. Sommelier himself opened the door and looked suitably surprised and not overly delighted at the sight of him. "*Eh bien*, what now?" he said.

"I've come to ask a favor—a favor for which I am willing to pay. I'd like to make several overseas long-distance calls on your phone. Not only will I pay for the calls, I'll pay anything you think fair on top of that for the privacy."

"Hmm. Like that is it? Well, all right. In here." Jean ushered him into a cluttered farm office, which was tacked on to the main house. "Put the phone in here so the wife wouldn't gossip her time away," he said complacently. "You want me to get the local operator? Overseas calls aren't exactly everyday affairs on the Dragon's Tongue."

"Anything that will save time." Toby tried to curb his impatience.

There was a prolonged exchange between Sommelier and the operator before the former signaled for the first number. Toby handed him the number of Penny's cottage at Littlemore. "I did say private," he repeated significantly.

"Right, right. Understood," the farmer snapped back. "But there isn't any answer."

"Try this one then." He handed him their office number at the Pitt Rivers Museum. The connection was made, and Sommelier reluctantly handed over the phone and left, banging the door closed behind him.

"Who is this?" Toby barked into the phone.

"Ada Phipps, and who is this?" snapped back the secretary he shared with Penny and with whom he had enjoyed a running feud for years.

"Toby Glendower. Is Dr. Spring back?"

"Oh, it's you." The sniff was palpable, even over the noise of the bad connection. "Yes, she's back."

Toby curbed his irritation. "She is not at home," he said

carefully. "Is she in her office? And, if so, would you connect me."

"All right," came the reluctant answer; Ada Phipps was evidently disappointed that they could not spar a few more rounds. The phone rang and rang, and Toby's spirits were plummeting towards zero when the receiver was lifted and Penny's breathless voice panted, "Yes? Dr. Spring here."

"It's Toby," he boomed in his relief. "I'm calling from Brittany."

"OK, OK, but lower your voice a little, I'm not deaf," she said. "And I've just had to run up all those damn stairs from your office, so give me a second to get my breath back."

"What were you doing down there?" he asked, completely sidetracked.

"Reference books. I've started my new book at last, Chapter 1." She did not sound markedly enthused by it.

"Well, listen, is there any possibility you can drop what you are doing and join me here? I need you," he pleaded.

"Are you in trouble again?"

He ignored the 'again' and rapidly launched into his carefully thought out resumé of what had happened thus far. "I don't know which of the locals I can trust. The inspector from the Sûreté has a one-track mind and seems to be a thoroughly nasty piece of work into the bargain, and I really need someone on the outside who can operate independently. There is an American involved and a woman. I thought you'd be better on both than I would," he concluded.

"Poor Toby," Penny sounded amused. "You have been having a time! Yes, that inspector doesn't sound too bright if he took you for a latter-day James Bond."

"Who's he?" Toby asked suspiciously.

There was a faint sigh at the other end of the phone. "Never mind. So who's the woman?"

"I don't know, other than that she has dark red hair and is involved in witchcraft."

"Good heavens! Then I'd better come quickly. If there is a Guinevere knocking about, God knows what trouble you'll get into with your Lancelot tendencies."

"She's more likely to be a Morgan Le Fay." If he didn't know who Bond was, at least he knew his Malory. "In fact, this whole place seems like a slice out of a medieval romance, what with dragons and witchcraft and crazy cults—all that is lacking so far is the dungeons.''

"Well, what's the deal you have in mind?"

"I thought if you would come over—you'll probably have to fly to Paris and hire a car, and it's all on me, by the way—you could put up at a place called the Auberge du Dragon. It's quite near here on the coast and is run by a man named Francois Canard. He used to be a famous chef, so it should be right up your alley; lots of good food. He's supposed to be an ardent Breton Nationalist, so that's yet another line you can follow up. Pose either as a tourist or, better yet, someone who is doing a book on modern cults. You are going to have to try and get in to see Gareth Winton's outfit, so that might be the best line to take.''

"Gareth Winton—is that the American?"

"Yes, do you know him?" he asked.

"The name definitely rings a bell, but I can't quite place it. Something to do with the Sixties—I'll check up on him before I come.''

"Good. Get established there at the inn and don't try to contact me. I'll contact you, and we'll set up a meeting somewhere outside Cormel. It's best and safest if you don't seem to be connected with me in any way.''

"But how will you know when I arrive?"

"I've got a man helping me on the site, a French Algerian called Grandhomme. He's a drunk, but not a bad chap and not involved in any of this. I'll send him to scout when I think you've had time to get here, but I won't tell him why. Then I'll phone you at the inn.''

"Good grief! You're even beginning to sound like James Bond," she chuckled, and added hastily, to cut off the inevitable question, "I'll tell you all about that when I see you. Is there anything else? If not, I'll rush home and throw a few things in a bag. With any luck I'll be there by tomorrow evening. Depends on how booked up the airlines are. It's high vacation season.''

"No, I can't think of anything else that can't wait until I see you," he said reluctantly. He was loath to let go of the comfort the sound of her voice was bringing him. "The only woman I've seen so far with hair the color of the plait I found in the henge is Madame Villefort, the wife of the mayor of

Cormel, but, according to Grandhomme, the region is just crawling with women with that color hair."

"How about in Gareth Winton's outfit?"

"I don't know. They don't come out and nobody can get into the chateau. The only cult member who does venture forth is a middle-aged woman who does their marketing and she doesn't fill the bill."

"This man who was murdered—you say he wasn't local?"

"No—from Alsace, I believe."

"A nasty way to go," her tone was grim.

"Yes indeed. Look, I'm sorry I've thrown a crimp into this new book of yours." Toby wanted to keep her talking.

"Oh, don't be an idiot! You know damn well this is a lot more important—and a lot more interesting," she said gently. "Well, I'll be seeing you. Take care!" And before he could say another word, she hung up.

He found Sommelier lurking just outside the door and wondered how private his private conversation had been. After further conference with the operator, he paid the farmer double the price of the call, which brought a smile back to the latter's rubicund face.

"You're welcome to use it any time," he said affably. "That is, if that madman from the Sûreté hasn't thrown me in jail!"

"He has been around, has he?"

"His lordship? Oh, no—summoned to the inn I was, along with most of the rest of the population by the seem of it. By the way the talk was going, *he'd* better watch out if he doesn't want to end up on a tree," Sommelier leered.

"Well, if you have any local clout, I should warn everyone to calm down. Favet will have the Army in, if you don't watch out."

The rain was teeming down now, putting any further work on the site out of the question. He went back to the Dragon's Teeth, unloaded a Primus stove and some cans of food for the hung-over Grandhomme and, after charging him not to let anyone mess around with the site until he returned, took off once again in the direction of Cormel. Until Penny arrived and they could work out a concerted plan of action, he intended to keep a very low profile. While waiting, he felt it could do no harm to have a word with Father Laval about the weird past of the Dragon's Teeth, and an even quieter word with the judge, whom he hoped might prove a more reliable ally than any of the locals he had encountered thus far.

Toby found the priest huddled before a small coal fire in the rectory beside the church; it was a small dark house that reeked of dampness. He had not expected an enthusiastic welcome, nor did he get one, but he was determined to be amiable, so he put his case in the most diplomatic way he could think of. "As you perhaps know, I am excavating the Dragon's Teeth on behalf of an ailing French colleague, Professor Latour. Questions will be undoubtedly asked after the henge is moved as to why it was not investigated before. It is evident from his notes that the professor did not know the previous history you related at Villefort's the other day. I would therefore be most grateful if you would show me the account you mentioned and indeed tell me anything further about the henge and the people at the chateau, so that I can give him a full report."

"All right, I can see no harm in that." But the little priest made no move to get up. With a shake of his head, he went on, "This is a bad business, a very bad business for the region. The devil stalks among us. I feel so helpless." He looked miserably at Toby. "The young do not listen any more. They do not come to Mass; they run after heathen ways. And all the old ones do is grumble. If only I could still say the Mass in Latin! The old people do not like the new services, and the ones that do come grumble that they are not given in Breton. But what am I to do? The Church in France has decreed the Mass be said in French and I must obey, but they think it is my fault and will not heed me."

"Very difficult for you," Toby said, with as much sympathy as he could muster. "Have you had much trouble with the chateau people? Are those the heathen ways to which you were referring?"

"No, not really. Whatever they do up there, at least they keep it to themselves. I visited Winton when he first arrived. It hurt me to see the chateau stripped and bare as it was. I remember it as it used to be in Villefort's father's time— shabby, perhaps, but gracious and right. Now . . ." he shrugged, ". . . it is like a smelly old woman who has had most of her insides taken out."

"Have you talked with some of the other cult members?"
Toby asked.

"Only the woman who comes into Cormel. We have chatted several times. She talks much of love, but I do not think she and I have the same definition of the word. Her name is Jane Smith and she is an American." His pronunciation made the ordinary name seem odd. "Like Winton I would say she is a fanatic. And her eyes are always strange. I think she is on drugs." The priest's voice was heavy with disapproval.

"If I may see those papers?" Toby prompted.

"Very well." The priest rose reluctantly and went to an old black cupboard in the corner, returning after a moment with a heavy ledger. "I cannot allow you to take it out of the rectory," he said, "but you may read it over there." He indicated a small table set by the window, where the rain streaming down the glass cast a greenish gloom over everything. "You may make notes if you wish."

Toby settled himself at the table, conscious of the priest's eyes upon him as he opened the yellowing pages of the ledger, and started to study the cramped handwriting of the long-dead priest. It was heavy going and not too informative, the style verbose but vague. There was much talk of heathenish practises and rites, but nothing was specified, although two dates caught his eye. "June 21st. Midsummer solstice. It has happened again. M. Villefort very angry and much disturbed. He caught no one but found the fire." And then on August 1st. "Lammas. No doubt remains. It happened again. Villefort determined to stop it and asked for my help." There followed a lengthy description of the loads of earth brought in by wagon, the difficulties with the laborers brought in from Le Mans, their refusal to work and disappearance, and finally the long labors of Villefort and himself in the final covering of the site, "in spite of Rouillé's threats and the black dog." Toby looked up in excitement. "I see here someone called Rouillé is mentioned. Was he any relation to Judge Rouillé?"

The priest roused himself from his contemplation of the smokey fire. "His grandfather. A farmer here—and a hot-head, who was suspected of being behind it all, though nothing was ever proved."

"Behind the witchcraft?"

"In a way. He was a rabble-rouser by all accounts, an early

communist, you might say. Dead against the Church and the establishment, and always on about the rights of the working man and the real meaning of the Revolution. His son, the judge's father, had to move away from here after his death, the scandal was so great."

"So the judge was not brought up here?"

"No, but he came back. Hotheads run in the Rouillé family," the priest added obscurely.

"And this business about the black dog?"

Father Laval looked uneasy and cleared his throat. "More of the heathenish superstition. The peasants always believed the site to be guarded by a black hound. It was thought, after what happened to Villefort, that Rouillé had got hold of a savage dog somewhere to terrify the people."

"What did happen to Villefort?"

"It's all in there." The priest waved a hand at the book. "Shortly after they had finished covering the henge in, he was found dead in the woods. His throat had been torn out by an animal. The peasants said it was the Black Hound of Death."

Toby flipped quickly through until he found the passage which was written in a shaky hand, but he found the present Curé had given an admirable précis of it. He turned another page, but this one was blank. "That's the last entry," he exclaimed in surprise. "What became of the priest?"

Father Laval cleared his throat again and avoided Toby's enquiring stare. "The people boycotted him because they said he had brought the curse down. For several months he stood it. Then, on Christmas Eve no one came to midnight Mass. Poor soul, it was too much for him. He was found wandering about the mound where the henge lay buried, raving about the Devil Triumphant and the black dog. They took him away to a hospice in Brest, but he never did recover his wits."

"A very terrible story," Toby mused. "At least the present black dog seems to play a far less sinister role. In fact, you could say he was on the side of the angels."

It was the priest's turn to look surprised. "How so?"

"If it hadn't been for the dog, the body of Dubois might still be lying out in those woods undiscovered. He led us to the body."

"And you think that is good?" the priest asked. "When it all begins again?"

"But not as it was before. At the risk of seeming rude, I feel you may be allowing this very superstition to influence you unduly. This dog is a very real dog, there is nothing uncanny about him. And this murder is a very real murder, with a motive behind it. What that motive is remains to be seen, but it is most likely to be linked with the construction of the nuclear plant. I may point out that the henge has lain uncovered for the past ten years, during which time nothing untoward has happened. It strikes me that now that something highly unpopular has been foisted on this region, somebody is making a very conscious effort to get all these superstitious fears stirred up to camouflage what is actually happening. And I fully intend to find out who that somebody is."

"Well then, may God protect you," the priest muttered. "And I shall pray for you. Have you finished?"

"For the moment, yes. I may want to look it over more carefully later on." Toby rose and the priest restored the ledger to its place in the cupboard.

"I must say my Office now, so I will bid you good day," Père Laval said.

"Yes, well, thank you for the information and your help." Toby felt awkward. "If I might make a donation to the church?"

"That is not necessary." There was a trace of asperity in the little priest's voice. "Just take care, Sir Tobias, take great care. There are evil forces at work here."

"I do have one more question for you. Did Gareth Winton ever read that account?"

Laval shook his head. "Not to my knowledge. He has never been near this rectory."

"But is the story widely known?"

"The bare bones of it, but not the particulars. Unless. . . ."

"Unless what?"

"Unless Villefort's father left an account of it in the chateau library. That I do not know, but he was a young man at the time of his father's death. Perhaps Patrice Villefort would know."

"Well, thanks again." Toby drove off in a thoughtful mood. He tried to call on the judge, only to be informed that he was not at home, so he went back to the inn and made a neat précis of his interview with Laval. After he had finished, it was still too early for dinner, and he felt disinclined to face the bar parlor. Finally he decided to drive to the site, check on Grandhomme, and bring him a little pick-me-up. He filled his flask from the cognac bottle and set off in the Jeep in the gathering dusk. The rain had stopped and a watery moon was rising, but just as he turned off onto the cart-track, an obstruction in the road caused him to slam on his brakes; a small sapling tree was leaning drunkenly across the path, blocking the way.

He got out with a curse and tried to push it off the track. Suddenly there was a rush of feet and then his arms were seized from behind and wrenched behind his back. At the same time a bag was crammed down over his head. As he struggled, he fell heavily, cracking his head against the fender of the Jeep. His last conscious thought was one of surprise. Damn it, he was being kidnapped!

CHAPTER 7

Still semi-dazed and partially suffocated by the burlap bag, which from the smell had evidently once contained coarse flour, Toby was lifted bodily onto the floor of the Jeep. There was the grinding of gears and as the Jeep backed up he thought he heard a distant shout. Then there was the smoother surface of tarmac and the sensation of the Jeep shooting off at a high speed. The ride that followed was painful and seemed interminable. His face was pressing down hard on the jumble of digging tools in the back and a booted foot on his neck prevented him from moving. The Jeep finally slowed, the road became extremely bumpy again, and when the engine stopped he could hear the roar of the sea. Surely they aren't going to drown me? he thought, but was soon disabused of that gloomy idea as he was helped to his feet, taken by each arm, and half-carried into a building. They were descending, and by the echo of their footsteps, he concluded that they were in a stone building of some kind. A door creaked and his feet dragged across what felt like large flagstones. He was pushed down into a chair and he could feel ropes snaking around his chest and legs as he was pinioned to it.

A voice suddenly spoke in his ear. "You are now a hostage of the Underground Liberation Army of Brittany." It was a very young voice and, by the uncertain way it wavered up and down the scale, a very nervous one.

"If you don't get this damn flour sack off my head, I'll be a dead hostage," Toby managed to choke out. "I'm suffocating!"

Several voices held a whispered consultation behind him and someone fumbled with the hood. As it was pulled off, he took a grateful gulp of the damp air, which smelled faintly of the sea, and fell to coughing and wheezing. The flour had completely coated his glasses and he could not see a thing. His back was thumped gently until he stopped coughing and he gasped, "Clean off my glasses, I can't see a bloody thing." An unseen hand twitched them off his nose and then put them back on a mite crookedly, their lenses still smeary. Toby peered through them and found he was sitting at a rough wooden table, facing a decrepit dresser full of books and papers set against a gray stone wall, which was illumined by a paraffin lamp. As he read off the titles of the books from sheer force of habit, his round blue eyes widened slightly and he began to feel a little less alarmed. His captors stood in a whispering group behind him and he thought it wiser in the circumstances not to turn his head. "So what the hell is all this about?" he said with what he thought was admirable restraint. "What the devil do you expect to gain from kidnapping me?"

"You are a prisoner of the Liberation Army of Brittany," another young voice repeated in French. "If you cooperate with us, you will be treated well. If not, I warn you, you are going to be very uncomfortable. We mean business." There was some more muttering, this time in Breton, and Toby's interest quickened as his sharp ear caught the English intonation of one of the speakers. "We will be back shortly," the second young voice said, and there was the creak of the heavy door and then the sound of bolts being shot into place.

Toby wriggled into a more comfortable position on the chair—his bonds were not tight—and examined his surroundings. He was in a large, windowless, vaulted stone chamber with a crude stone fireplace at one end, from which came a penetrating draft. The script was now complete, he thought with grim amusement. Here was the dungeon. It had, however, the aspect of a very lived-in dungeon. There was a pile of bedrolls in one corner, knapsacks, and another dresser on which reposed a small Primus stove, some crockery, and a hodgepodge of groceries, including several bottles of wine. Toby ran his tongue over his dry, flour-caked lips—he could certainly use a drink, and he had a frantic desire to scratch his neck and back where the flour had sifted down the collar of his shirt and was tickling him. His brief amusement gave way to irritation, so that when the door creaked open again, he glared at the four youthful figures who appeared. They all wore ski masks and were dressed in black leather jackets, black trousers, and black boots. There was no doubt that one of the group was a girl, and this shocked his old-fashioned soul, particularly since she was armed with a revolver.

"Look here," he growled as they approached him. "If you want me to be cooperative, you damn well better start doing something about making me comfortable! I want to be freed of these bloody ropes so that I can get this flour out of my clothes, and I need a drink to get it out of my throat. When that is done I am prepared to talk to you, otherwise not. There are four of you and only one of me, and I see you are armed—so what have you got to lose?"

After a brief consultation, they advanced in a group and two of them slipped off his bonds as the girl stood back, covering him with the revolver held in a not-too-steady hand. He stood up, ignoring them, stretched the cramp out of his limbs, and, turning his back on them, stripped off his jacket and shirt and brushed himself free of the clinging flour. Then he walked over to the dresser and filled one of the glasses with wine from an open bottle. It washed down the flour, but he grimaced at the taste—cheap rotgut. "Got any cider?" he asked coolly when he had finished it. "This stuff is awful!" He could almost feel their amazement. "In the cupboard under the dresser," one of them stuttered. He looked, saw an earthenware flagon, poured himself another glass, tasted it, nodded approvingly, and said, "Yes, this is much better. Now then, what is all this nonsense about?"

He sat down with his drink at the table and regarded the group with almost fatherly concern. He was so used to students and their addlepated ways that he found it extremely difficult to take the young people in front of him at all seriously. In his opinion, all students were slightly mad, it was a phase they had to go through before they grew up, and, looking at the world around him, he was also of the opinion that many of them never did make it all the way.

"This is far from being nonsense." The girl spoke in a high clear voice; his calm had obviously irritated her. "We know who you are, Sir Tobias, and you will remain our prisoner until the French government has acceded to our demands. You will write a note which I shall dictate to go along with them."

"And may I ask what these demands are?"

"That the plan for the construction of the nuclear plant

here be stopped. Why should the people of the peninsula be put in danger of hideous death just to suit the pockets of the big business men of Brest and Nantes? Also that the program of victimization and persecution of Breton patriots be halted, and that serious consideration be given to allowing Brittany participation in the greater confederation of Celtic states."

"Young woman, I have no objection to writing a note. I'll write you a whole book, if you like, but do you honestly believe for one moment the French government will give a damn whether you have captured me or what happens to me?" Toby said mildly. "If you wanted a hostage they would have been concerned about, you ought to have picked an important Frenchman."

"Your English government will put pressure on them; they will insist on it. You are a very important Englishman. If they don't, they would have trouble with their own Celtic national-ists, who will take their lead from us!" Her voice was shrill.

"If you expect that, then you really have captured the wrong man." Toby began to chuckle quietly and then to roar with laughter. He laughed so hard that he had to take off his glasses and mop the tears from his streaming eyes.

"He has gone mad," one of the young men whispered nervously, while the others stood rigid, torn between amaze-ment and anger.

Still laughing, Toby stood up and extracted one of the shabby volumes from the dresser against the wall. "Are you familiar with this book?"

"Naturally we are! It is by Arthur Pendragon, one of the greatest Celtic nationalists of all time," one of the young men replied.

Toby switched into Breton. "And do you know who Arthur Pendragon really was? Among other things he was my father."

There was a moment of startled silence. Then the young man with the strange nasal accent said, "You're lying. Your name is Glendower. We know that."

Toby's infallible ear suddenly placed his accent. "My Liverpudlian friend, I have no idea what you are doing here, since you are very far from home, but you are wrong. Arthur Pendragon was the pen name of my father, Thomas Glendower. Having squeezed his millions out of the sweat of his fellow Welshmen, he spent his declining years writing a series of pipe dreams for them." There was a bitter edge on his voice. "So if you are planning to use me as a rallying point for your fellow Celts across the water against the English, I can only say you could hardly have made a worse choice. In fact you'll be the laughingstock of the Celtic world. Moreover, I really can't see the British government going to great lengths to secure the release of the son of a man who was always a right royal pain in the neck to them, particularly since I will appear to be in the hands of compatriots. They will think it is a put-up job and probably will not even make a move. After all, the French and British governments, as you must know, are not on the best of terms these days."

He had obviously disconcerted them, but the girl, who seemed to be the leader of the group, was not vanquished. "Even if what you say is true," she said, "you are still valuable to us. By holding you hostage we will show that this murder that has taken place has nothing to do with us. It is not our method—not this terrible barbarism. We believe in peaceful persuasion."

"Then, young lady," Toby boomed out, "I can only say that you have behaved in a singularly muddled-headed manner. Surely you must know by now that the man sent down from Paris, Favet, is an expert on terrorist groups? In fact he seems to be incapable of thinking about anything else. And what you have just done is a typical terrorist tactic. If this gets out, he won't look any further, but will be after your hides for the murder like a bloodhound. No, I really believe your best course would be to blindfold me, take me back to where you captured me, and let me go. I will forget this ever happened and I suggest you do, too. I don't know who you are and I don't know where I am. What is more, I do not care for Favet and his tactics either, and would not like to see you railroaded for a crime you say you did not commit. Whether you did or not I will most surely find out, but I am inclined to take your word for it."

"Why?" asked the young man with the very deep voice.

Toby began to chuckle again. "Because anyone who is woolly-minded enough to read the works of Arthur Pendragon and take them seriously would not have the stomach for that kind of murder. I am looking for a ruthless, cunning killer."

"You're the one who's making a big mistake if you think

we're a joke." The man from Liverpool's voice was flat and ugly. "We are going to check up on what you've said, and if you've been lying you're going to be very sorry. But even if you have been speaking the truth, if you think you're going to walk out of here, you've got another think coming. At least you'll pay through the nose before we'd let you go. I imagine you'd spend a pretty penny to keep that hide of yours intact, and the Cause can use the money."

There was a chorus of outraged whispered protests from the rest of the group. The girl made an imperative shushing gesture and, jerking her head in the direction of the door, she pushed her colleagues out. Before she left the room she turned back to Toby. "I should tell you it is no use trying to break out of here, and if you try shouting no one will hear you. This door is the only exit and it will be guarded at all times. If we find you making the slightest attempt to escape, you will be chained. If you cooperate you can have the freedom of this room. We will return." She closed the door with a bang and the bolts once more slid into place.

Toby crossed over to it swiftly and pressed his ear against the oak panels. He could hear voices raised in anger, but they were too muffled to make out any words. It seemed the man from Liverpool's money-mindedness was not getting a favorable reception from his co-conspirators. Of the group, he was the only one that Toby was at all uneasy about. Who was he and what was he doing here? Liverpool, he knew, was a hotbed of disaffected Irish; perhaps then a professional agitator sent over to stir up these obviously fervent young amateurs?

He turned away from the door and surveyed his prison, then looked at his watch. It was after nine in the evening and he had had no dinner. He strolled over to the dresser and made himself a sandwich of French bread and liver sausage, washed it down with another glass of cider, and then helped himself to some goat cheese and crackers and a handful of raisins. Munching on the snack, he peered up into the fireplace. The chimney, in which the salt-laden wind sighed mournfully, soared to an incredible height, the small opening at the top showing pale moonlight. Well, obviously that was out as an escape route. He explored around its angle and found a chemical toilet discreetly hidden behind a blanket.

"The dungeon comes with all modern conveniences," he observed to himself.

He wandered over to the bedrolls, undid them, stacked them one on top of another, and stretched out on top of their multiple softness. "May as well make myself comfortable while in durance vile." He lighted up his pipe and, with a sigh of comfort, clasped his hands behind his head and gazed up at the vaulted stone ceiling. Where was he? The stonework had an ecclesiastical look to him, and he brought to mind the map of the Dragon's Tongue. That was it! The gothic lettering for antiquities on the map leaped up at him: 'RUINS OF THE ABBAYE ST. JACQUES.' That was almost undoubtedly it—it was on the coast, a short way from the Pointe de Dinan, and only about eight kilometers from Cormel. What else was near here? He concentrated and smiled faintly. He had been told the Auberge du Dragon overlooked the Anse de Dinan, so that could only be about two kilometers away, which explained in all probability the excellent quality of the liver sausage he had just eaten. He wondered if the young people were on their way at this very moment to consult with Francois Canard— that ardent Nationalist—who, he felt, would be very unamused by the caper those young idiots had pulled off. The more he thought about the situation, the more certain ideas came to him. What he had in mind was a bit risky, but the advantages outweighed the risks.

His reflections were interrupted by the door opening again and the deep-voiced young man saying in alarm, "Where is he? He's disappeared!"

"No need for panic. I'm over here on your bedrolls," Toby announced from his shadowy corner. "I must say you run a very comfortable prison. Francois Canard's liver sausage is really excellent!"

There was another moment of startled silence and then the girl demanded, "What do you know of him?" Her voice was slightly hoarse, as if she had been arguing loud and long. "That he is a great chef, an ardent Nationalist, and lives approximately two kilometers from here at the Auberge du Dragon. I am in the Abbaye of St. Jacques, am I not?"

Once again he had startled them into silence. When the girl spoke, there was an edge of desperation to her voice. "Sir Tobias, we have come to a decision. You will be taken from here and released somewhere in Brittany. The conditions are that you do not return to this region, that you do not inform the authorities, and that you go back to England immediately. If you agree, we will let you go. But if you break them, it will be the worse for you. The Liberation Army has a long arm.''

Toby swung himself up into a sitting position, tucked his legs under him like an improbable swami, and looked up at them with a benign smile. ''No, I'm afraid that won't do at all,'' he said firmly. ''I've decided this suits me very well. You all can be very valuable to me in the days ahead. You see I have work to do—a murder to solve. And I have no intention of leaving the area until I've done just that. You have stated that your group had nothing to do with this murder, and I hope for your sakes that is true. So you should be equally interested in bringing the real culprits to justice. Ergo, you should, if you think about it, be eager and willing to help me get to the bottom of the matter. I have been handicapped so far by being too much in the public eye, and this you have rectified. I think I can find out from behind the scenes far more than I could otherwise—with your help, of course.'' His smile became positively sunny.

''He's crackers, just plain crackers!'' the man from Liverpool exploded. ''Why the hell should we help you? You're our prisoner.''

Toby's smile vanished. ''To get your group off the hook! You have put yourselves in a very dangerous position with this muddled scheme, which hasn't the faintest chance of success in present circumstances. I just won't go along with it and that leaves you with only one alternative; the only way to get rid of me is to murder me.'' He knew it was a rash gamble, and he held his breath, waiting for their reaction. ''You're really asking for it, really sticking your neck out,'' the Liverpudlian snarled. ''Well, the Dragon's Tongue might just be in for a nasty accident—a drowning. Too bad!''

The girl's voice cut in sharply. ''We are not murderers,'' she repeated. ''So you shut up! You have no authority around here, and much more of this and you can pack up and leave. If this is the sort of help your people had in mind, we can live without it. We've enough problems as it is.''

Toby let out his breath slowly; the crisis point was passed.

"So how about the help?" he ventured. "Time is of the essence, you know."

"We know," she said tersely. "I expect tomorrow they will start looking for you—unless we go ahead with our original plan. I do not see how you can stay out of sight or we can help you in those circumstances."

"I can buy you some time," Toby volunteered. "Listen, I don't know if you are local, but you must have local contacts to operate at all, so this is what I want you to do. Get into my room at the inn. Here's the key. And pack up one of my bags. I'll need some things if I'm going to stay here. I'll write a note directed to Grandhomme, my assistant, that you can leave in the room. It will say that I've gone to Paris for a few days to check on some things. That should keep the authorities quiet. After that—well, we'll just have to see how things develop and what happens."

"But what sort of things do you want us to find out?" she countered.

"Ah!" He got up. "Let's go over to the table and I'll make a list."

They sat in uneasy silence as he busily scribbled away, then he looked up, cleared his throat, and read off the list. "I'd like you to find out the following. *One*: the ownership of a very large black puppy, part Labrador. May be from the chateau. *Two*: what woman with dark red hair in this neighborhood has had it cut short in the past month. *Three*: whether the place of the murder has been discovered, and if so where. *Four*: how many people live in the chateau and who they all are. And *five*: what Inspector Favet is up to. I think that will do for a start."

He could almost feel their incredulity. "I told you he was crackers. Clean round the bend!" the Liverpudlian announced. "Only the last thing makes any sense."

"It all makes sense to me," Toby retorted. "I want to see how you do on these before I give you anything more substantive to work on. After all, you are new at this murder investigation business, and I'm an old hand." Again there was a shocked silence.

"How about that note to this Grandhomme character and a list of things you need?" the girl said. "As to the rest, we'll have to think about it."

"I know the answer to one of them," said the nervous young man. "The black dog sounds like Hercules—and it is from the chateau. It belongs to Patty Winton."

"What relation is she to Gareth Winton?" Toby asked excitedly.

"She's his niece."

"Is she a redhead?"

"No, a blonde." The young voice was muffled with embarrassment. "But what has the dog got to do with anything?"

"Shut up! Don't say any more," the girl commanded. "We haven't decided what to do yet." She got up and took the notes. "We're leaving now. We'll let you know tomorrow."

The door slammed behind them, leaving Toby staring at the lamp's flame. With a contented sigh, he lit up his pipe and watched the blue plumes of smoke eddying over the funnel of the lamp. Taking it all in all, this had been a most interesting day. The young people, he felt, would be extremely useful to him. And he still held an ace in the hole: tomorrow Penny would arrive. As he settled cosily into one of the bedrolls, he wondered how the Dragon's Tongue would survive the impact.

CHAPTER 8

By the time the door to his dungeon opened the following morning, Toby had already brewed some coffee on the Primus, breakfasted on the remains of the bread and a delectable raspberry confiture, and trimmed and filled the lamp. He had washed in a tin basin and was generally feeling at peace with the world. Only one small thing about his captors still worried him; the presence of the man from England. Not that he thought that the youth was English; it was far more likely he was a disenchanted Liverpool Irishman who had embraced the extremist IRA cause, but he had been looking for another person who had the same knowledge of English witchcraft as himself, and here was a likely candidate. However, common sense argued against it. Young people who embraced political causes, however off-beat, were not usually interested in witchcraft. It was, perhaps, just an odd coincidence. Still, he'd love to know the color of the girl leader's hair.

When the four trooped in, they once again wore their ski masks and leather jackets. Otherwise they were dressed in the universal garb of the world's youth: jeans, T-shirts, and sneakers. They were a very subdued lot as they trooped over to the table, where he was sitting skimming through one of his father's books and marveling at how such a tough-minded businessman could ever have conceived such romantic rubbish.

The girl dumped his bag on the ground. "I think everything you asked for is there. We left a few things in the wardrobe and just lying around in case someone thinks you skipped. By the looks of it your room had been searched, none too carefully either. Looks as if you may have riled up Favet."

"That is entirely possible," Toby said with distinct pleasure. "Thank you. So what have you decided?"

"I suppose there is nothing for it but to trust you," she

said, evidently not too pleased with the idea. "But you are going to have to stay here. We can't let you go."

"It suits me well enough to stay here for the moment, so long as you become my eyes and ears," he returned. "Have you got anything for me?"

"There hasn't been time. But we have heard plenty about Favet."

"That's a start," Toby said encouragingly, getting out his notebook. "But before we begin, why don't you take off those ski masks? Since we are all in this together now, anonymity is pretty silly, and they must be uncomfortable. After all, from the point of view of the authorities, having written that note I am now technically your accomplice in the Underground movement. They'd find no difficulty in believing that, since I have openly stated my objection to the proposed destruction of the Dragon's Teeth."

The girl hesitated a second and then with a resigned "Why not?" ripped the ski mask off, revealing a mop of short dark curly hair and a strong-jawed, interesting face with snapping dark eyes. The others followed suit; not one of them appeared to be out of their teens. The deep-voiced young man also had dark curly hair and bore a faint resemblance to the girl, though Toby, noting the adoring way he kept looking at her, surmised correctly that they were not brother and sister. The Irishman stood revealed as pale-skinned, sandy-haired, with a pair of cold gray eyes set in a craggy face, but it was the fourth member, the nervous young man, who riveted Toby's attention. His hair was the deep shade of red Toby had half-expected to see on the girl, but the face underneath it was unmistakable—long, aloof, hatchetlike, with deep-set dark eyes. Toby suppressed a smile; he had been brought face to face with at least one of Judge Rouillé's problems. He thought he would strike while the iron was hot. "Well, apart from young Rouillé here, do I get to know some names as well?" he asked amiably.

They looked thunderstruck, but the girl recovered quickly. "First names will be enough," she snapped. "I am Nicole, this is Alan, Shaun, and Yves you apparently know already."

"Only his father," Toby said, and saw the young man wince. "Are you and Alan local too?"

"No, but we have ties here. What does that matter?" she said with sudden suspicion.

"I just wanted to know how much information about what is going on you will be capable of getting," Toby said peaceably.

"Don't worry about that. We have plenty of contacts." She hesitated. "We have one problem though. Yves will probably have to come in here with you. Favet is having all the known Nationalists rounded up and questioned. Yves got arrested in a demonstration in Nantes not too long ago, and the way Favet is going, he may lock him up. He'll have to stay out of sight."

"A pity," Toby grumbled, "since he apparently is the only one with a contact in the chateau. Do you want to tell me more about that setup now?" He looked enquiringly at Yves, who blushed and avoided the eyes of the others.

"I don't know a great deal. Patty and I, well, we didn't talk much about them," he said. "She's so fed up with it all, we talked mostly about getting her out of it. She's only been there about a year. Her parents were killed in an auto crash and Winton's her guardian. He brought her over and now she's stuck. He handles all her cash."

"How old is she?"

"Seventeen." Yves went an even deeper red. "Next year he'll have to cough it up. We were—er—waiting for that."

"She must have said something about the others there. I mean, like how many, what they do, and so forth."

"Only that they're a bunch of weirdos. There's a couple of old people—besides Winton. In their forties at least." It was Toby's turn to wince. "And a few French recruits. She told her uncle she wasn't into their mumbo jumbo, so I guess they leave her pretty much alone. Before I came along, she was so penned up all she could do was talk to Hercules."

"How and when did you meet her?" Toby asked. "And have you been in the chateau?"

The boy shook his head. "No. It was about three months ago. My father had kicked me out and I was camping in the woods." His tone was bitter. "She slips out at night sometimes with the dog; there's a place in the iron railings she can get through. We met in the wood and—well—things have developed. . . .'' He trailed off.

An idea had been burgeoning in Toby's mind. "Do you think she could get you into the chateau? As a new recruit, I mean? It would keep you out of sight and you'd be in a position to keep your eyes and ears open about what's going on there. Not that I'm against sharing quarters here with you, but you'd be a lot more useful there.''

Yves pondered. "I'm not sure they'd let me in. I think you've got to put up some bread before you can be admitted. Patty says her uncle is a regular old moneygrubber.''

"If that could be managed, would you be willing to try it? I take it you are not averse to seeing more of the young lady?''

"No, of course not.'' Yves shuffled his feet with embarrassment. "It's possible she could smuggle me in and no one would be the wiser. They don't use much of the chateau. But what am I supposed to do once I'm there?''

"A lot of ground-clearing, I hope. The henge has been used recently for witchcraft rites. I'd like to know whether the people come from the chateau, because if not, we're going to have to do a whole lot more digging locally. In four days, August 1st, it will be Lammasghal, one of the great witch festivals. So, if they have been practicing, something should be going on then. Also I'd like to find out if Gareth Winton is just paranoid about his privacy or if he is actually up to something at the chateau that he doesn't want the local authorities to know about. I have no idea what, but Dubois, before his death, did throw out some hints to me along that line. He had sent for a dossier on Winton. Favet might have it. I don't know if any of you others would be in a position to find out what was in it.''

"We could try,'' Nicole replied briefly.

"And, finally, I'd like you to ask Patty about her dog. It has been haunting the site, and on the night of the murder I think there was someone at the henge with it. If it was Patty, ask her if she saw or heard anything besides me. If it wasn't, try and find out who else is friendly with or controls the dog. And,'' he added, "we are still looking for a woman with dark red hair who has had it cut recently.''

Yves looked at the others. "Do you think I should?"

Nicole shrugged. "We'll talk about it some more outside. I've another idea, that might help the Cause. But why don't you get your things?"

Yves obediently collected one of the bedrolls and a knapsack from the pile in the corner. What babes in the woods they are, Toby thought uneasily, as he watched Yves' thin young back. "One more thing," he said. "Be very careful. You don't know what you are going into, so if you sense any kind of trouble or danger, get out of there fast. Right?"

"He knows how to take care of himself," Nicole said with scorn. "We all do. So there's no need to play Big Daddy with us."

"God forbid!" he countered. "Just as long as you have enough sense not to do anything else rash. I may point out that we are probably not up against a murderer, but murderers. Though Dubois was a small man, I think it would have taken more than one person to do what was done to him—and Yves will be on his own."

She brushed his admonition aside. "Do you want to hear what we've got on Favet or not?"

"Certainly."

"Well, he's been putting pressure on Pommard to identify all the Nationalists in the area. He even had Canard hauled in for questioning. His mistake. Canard knows half the important people in the government and Favet ended up with very red ears. He's tromping around Cormel like a storm trooper and getting people thoroughly riled up. Not that it's helping him any—he's so desperate for leads he's been investigating the dead man, and throwing out dark hints about him."

"Dubois!"

"Yes. Seems he was heavily into oil engineering at one time—in Algeria. Then he took sick and they brought him back to a desk job in Paris. This was his first assignment on a nuclear project. Favet has also been raving on about papers missing from the briefcase, but he doesn't appear to know what papers."

"What has Pommard been doing?"

Alan answered that one. "Sitting on his duff and sulking mostly. Favet and he had a set-to over Sommelier. Favet was all for arresting him—he's that desperate for results—but the farmers came in a body to Pommard and pressured him into standing up for Sommelier. The man might be a mean old s.o.b., but he's the best cider-maker in the district and the harvest is almost ready.''

"Not to mention the time for the Lammasghal," Toby murmured.

"That old nonsense!" the boy snapped, but he did not look at Toby. "Shouldn't we be going?" he said pointedly to Nicole.

"Yes, I suppose so. You ready, Yves?" She got up. "We'll bring you more supplies later. Stay cool!"

Left to his own devices, Toby found his thoughts wandering down strange paths. In light of this new information, he wondered if Grandhomme's appearance in the area was as fortuitous as it appeared. There was no question that he was a drunk, but what if he and Dubois had been old acquaintances from Algerian days and he had been sent to smell out the situation here? For a vagabond he had been a surprise to Toby, both in his level of education and in his very prompt action in getting the Sûreté on the scene; a move which had so disconcerted Pommard. But where did that get him? Nowhere. If Grandhomme were connected with Dubois, he certainly was not physically involved in his murder. He toyed with the idea of trying to get a message to him, but decided his young captors would never agree. What else did he need to know? The chateau investigation was being taken care of by Yves. Rouillé—that was it!—the enigmatic judge who was so against the henge being moved. When Nicole and Alan returned, he would question them about the judge. Hotheads ran in the Rouillé family, the priest had said, presumably meaning Yves, who had been enough of a thorn in his father's flesh to get kicked out of the house. He struck Toby as a very mild sort of hothead, and he wondered if there were any more Rouillés around who would better fit the appellation. What was the source of Yves' red hair—certainly not the judge, so either from the mother or a throwback to a previous generation.

Extracting his shaving kit from the suitcase, Toby gave himself an absentminded shave as he continued his reflections. Nicole and Alan were not from the Dragon's Tongue, but presumably were related to someone locally. From the prompt way Alan had answered about Sommelier, he suspected that's where his kinship might lie. But what about Nicole—whom was she linked to? He realized he would have to tread very carefully with his captors if he was going to get anywhere and wondered perhaps if he hadn't been somewhat rash in choosing to continue his captivity and assume this passive, waiting role. Still, what else could he have done? "Young idiots!" he muttered crossly to himself. "I only hope they don't get into any worse mess." His toilet completed, he took out his site notebooks and plunged into the thorny question of working out the solar alignments. After a while he became so absorbed in what he was doing that the walls of his dungeon receded and he entered a realm in which he was totally at home and at peace.

Above his prison, the four young people lay sprawled at their ease on the short turf. The gray stone walls of the ruined abbey rose around them like jagged teeth, sheltering them from the brisk breeze off the Bay of Dinan and from sight of the world. Under the disapproving eye of Nicole, the three young men were smoking joints, and the sweet smell of marijuana competed with the tangy salt-laden air. The bucolic scene under the bright sun was only marred by the sharp, shrill tones of her voice as she attempted to keep the group in a businesslike mood. Nationalist rhetoric did not seem to be having much success, so she switched tactics. "Yves, you don't suppose your sister can be mixed up in this witchcraft business he was talking about?" she asked in a hectoring tone.

"Who, Marie? Nah, she's too much under the old man's thumb to try anything like that," he said uneasily.

"She *did* have her hair cut short recently."

"What does that matter? So have half the women around here who are at all 'with it'—like Jacqueline Villefort. It's the fashion."

"If you ask me, the old boy has a bee in his bonnet about witchcraft," Shaun put in lazily, taking a long luxurious drag on his joint. "Potty, that's what."

"I did some checking on him last night," Alan said, with

an apologetic glance at Nicole. "He's everything he says he is. He's solved a whole series of murders—usually with some woman in tow."

"Oh, a dirty old man is he?" Shaun said with interest.

"No, no, not like that at all. Always the same one—another Oxford professor."

"Will you two keep to the point!" Nicole snapped. "I mean it shouldn't be all that difficult to pinpoint a redheaded witch. Why shouldn't it be Marie? After all it wouldn't be the first time the Rouillés had been mixed up in that kind of thing—your great-grandfather. . . ."

Yves flushed. "That was all a damn lie!" he said angrily. "A damn lie put out by the Villeforts. He had nothing to do with old Villefort's death—more likely the son took the opportunity to do the old boy in and get the property. There was a lot of talk along that line at the time as well, but everyone chooses to forget it. Patrice Villefort is a real chip off the old block too. I wouldn't put anything past him, up to and including murder. And he has a redheaded wife."

"I bet our Jacqueline would be an eyeful capering around in the nude," Shaun said with a leer.

"She's too dim-witted to go in for anything like that." Nicole was acid. "All she thinks about is clothes and jewels and having a good time. Anyway, why not have a quiet word with Marie, Yves? She trusts you, doesn't she?"

"I thought I was supposed to stay out of sight," he said sullenly. "Hadn't I better cut along and contact Patty? That is if you still think we should play along with the old boy. Want me to get you some more pot?" he asked the others.

"That's another thing." Nicole shot a frigid glance at Alan, who was nodding enthusiastically. "Where the hell does Patty get her supplies from, if she's cooped up in there? Keep your wits about you, Yves, if you do go in on the up and up. I don't think Winton is up to any good. You know, I heard a rumor that there have been boats seen off the coast at night at La Haye beach. Some of our people thought it might be Irish gunrunners but HQ knows nothing of it. There's that old tale about a tunnel from the chateau to La Haye—see what you can find out. We might be able to put the screws on Winton to let us use it."

Shaun was scanning the area with a pair of binoculars. He watched as a bright green Triumph Spitfire climbed into view and turned into the windswept parking lot of the Auberge du Dragon. "I see the inn has some fresh trade, Nicole," he said with a yawn. "A limey by the looks of it. Nice nippy little car there. I wonder who goes with it?" He fiddled with the binoculars. "Ah, that's better! Mother of God, will you look at that! What a flaming shame! A nifty little car driven by some dumpy old broad with hair like a fright wig. I tell you there's no justice in this world—no justice at all!"

CHAPTER 9

As she climbed out of her Triumph Spitfire, her mouse-colored hair teased into spikes by the rollicking wind, Penny felt a profound sense of relief. There had been moments on the trip when she had doubted the wisdom of bringing her own car, but now these doubts had been firmly banished. When she had checked the airlines and found them gloomily promising nothing but stand-by flights, she had made an instantaneous decision. After a quick look at the map, she had hopped in the car and headed for Southampton and the Le Havre ferry. Just as she had arrived, the Triumph had shown signs of clutch trouble, and she had had to spend the best part of a day fuming and fretting around an MG garage while the clutch was repaired. But, that done, the ferry and the trip down from Le Havre through the Normandy countryside had been uneventful; and here she was. Now the only thing that could go wrong was if there was no room at the inn. Hitching her capacious shoulder bag more firmly onto her shoulder, she marched into the gray granite inn, determination writ large on every inch of her five-foot-one body.

There was no problem, and one glance at the prices on the hotel tariff told her why—they almost took her breath away. She was glad that Toby was footing the bill for this, otherwise she would have rushed screaming into the daylight. As it was, she simply hauled out her credit card.

"Would Madame perhaps care for luncheon, which was just now beginning?" the young man at the desk suggested.

Madame most certainly would. She was ravenous from the drive. She bustled into the low-raftered dining room to find it thinly populated with elderly, well-dressed couples. At these prices, no wonder! she reflected as she gazed happily at the enormous menu.

Much later she let out a sigh of replete bliss and sat back. She had started with a terrine de lapin, progressed through

Coquilles St. Jacques to Coq au Vin, then a delectable raspberry tartine, and had even managed to peck at some cheese
with her coffee. The magician who had produced these minor
works of art was now progressing through the room, receiving homage from his awed vassals. He was a very small man,
only topping Penny by about two inches, and almost eclipsed
by his tall chef's hat. The face under it was that of an
intelligent gnome, made remarkable only by a pair of glowing
amber eyes with very small pupils. The catlike eyes clamped
on her mild hazel ones. "Madame has enjoyed her meal?"

"I have eaten in many countries throughout the world, but
I can truthfully say that I have never had such a delicious
meal. Monsieur Canard, is it not? My most profound homage."

He preened slightly and inclined his head. "You are most
kind. You are English?"

"American," she smiled up at him. "But I have just come
from England."

"And you are passing your vacation here with us in
Brittany?"

In with both feet, she decided. "No, actually I'm here on
business, though staying at your inn will make it a pleasure."

The eyes narrowed slightly. "Business! On the Dragon's
Tongue?"

"Yes. I'm writing a book—on modern cults." She extracted
a card from her shoulder bag and handed it to him with a
flourish. "I am an anthropologist, and I understand there is
an American cult leader established near Cormel in the Chateau de la Muette. I was wondering if anyone here could
provide me with instructions as to how to get there?"

"From Oxford University," he murmured thoughtfully.
"A most prestigious place. The man at the desk will be able
to provide you with a map, no doubt. I know nothing of such
things myself. You will be dining here?"

"Oh, yes. I do not intend to miss a single meal under the
roof of the most famous chef in France."

"Ah, you are most kind, but one grows old, I fear," he
sighed. "Until this evening then, chère Madame!" and he
resumed his royal progress.

Having examined her room, which was unremarkable; tested
the comfortable bed; looked at the spectacular view over the
bay; washed up; and unpacked; she found herself pacing

around in a fever of impatience. When would Toby contact her? She had so much to tell him! The food had revived her and she was dying to get going. "Well, there's no sense in hanging around here waiting for this Grandhomme to show up," she murmured. "I may as well get cracking on my own."

She went down to the desk, where the young man obliged with a sketch map of how to get to Cormel and a larger map of the area. She almost asked him to watch out for Grand-homme, but then decided against it; it could be unwise to draw attention to herself at this point before she knew the local setup.

She wandered out into the parking lot and looked around. On the headland to her left lay some ruins perched precari-ously on the edge of the cliff; to the right was the great sweep of a beach on which the waves creamed and foamed in constant thunder. "Damn, I forgot to pack my bathing things," she thought, then climbed into the car and turned it down the narrow ribbon of tarmac that linked the auberge to the sec-ondary road.

She had no trouble finding Cormel, but the chateau was more difficult. She observed that the stone wall surrounding it was topped by a menacing array of spikes, and one gate was rusted shut and padlocked. By the rank vegetation rampant beyond, it had evidently not been in use for years. She drove on in increasing frustration and, seeing a well-traveled dirt road, turned down it in hopes of finding the main gate. It led her to what was obviously a pig farm, to judge by the smell. "Now that I'm here, I might as well ask directions," she murmured, as through an open door in one of the out build-ings she saw the outlines of a huge cider press and smelled the pungent aroma of apples, which mingled uneasily with the pig miasma. She knocked on the solid front door of the farm house, which eventually opened to reveal a plump, faded-looking woman.

"Who is it?" she said in a suspicious voice.

"I'm afraid I've lost my way. I'm looking for a way into the Chateau de la Muette."

"You won't get in there. Nobody does."

"Well, that remains to be seen, but there must be a main gate they use somewhere. Could you direct me to it?"

The woman gave her some reluctant directions and closed the door in her face.

"The natives appear far from friendly," Penny observed as she turned and headed in what she hoped was the right direction. "No wonder poor Toby needs help!"

Unfriendly or not, the directions turned out to be correct, and she soon found herself before two high wrought-iron gates, a metal bell set in a little wooden tower standing to one side of them. She rang the bell and its tolling sent flocks of startled crows into the air from the thick encircling woods. After a couple of minutes she desisted and waited hopefully; nothing happened. "Sooner or later someone has to take notice of this racket," she said with determination, and rang the bell again. Peer as she might through the gates, there was no sign of the chateau or any building, and she was just about to explore further when she caught a glimpse of a white robe fluttering among the trees. She kept tolling and was rewarded a minute later by a tall figure, who stepped out of the bushes and advanced on the gate with a set, angry face.

"Who is it that disturbs our peace? If you are a reporter— go away! We have nothing to say to you." It was a middle-aged woman, with long dark hair that lay loose on her shoulders and ill-suited her thin, sallow face. She peered through the bars. "Go away!" she repeated in French, but with a pronounced American twang.

"I am here to see Gareth Winton," Penny said in English. "And I intend to stay here until I do. My name is Penelope Spring. I am an anthropologist, and, like you, an American. I am not a reporter. But I would like you to take a message to Winton. Tell him that I was in Chicago during the riots of '68 and that I know all about him."

The woman hesitated a second, then said, "What is that to us? It is gone. All that matters is the Now and the Forever."

"I need to see Winton," Penny came back with mild menace. "When I say I know all about him, I mean it. I just wondered if the local authorities here did. If I don't get in to see him, I might have to enlist their help."

"Wait here. I'll check." The woman turned abruptly and was gone. Something about her was vaguely familiar, but Penny could not place the fugitive memory. She searched in her shoulder bag for something to while away the time and came up with a crumpled pack of cigarettes and an equally crushed candy bar. Still full from the excellent lunch, she decided on a cigarette and smoked it propped up against the wall in the sunshine, contemplating the woods and the deserted road. A dilapidated truck driven by a red-faced man rattled along, and he stared curiously at her as he sped by.

"What do you want?" The voice was high but masculine, and she turned to see two white-robed figures at the gate.

"Ah, Mr. Winton! I'm so glad you found it convenient to see me," Penny purred. "I am most interested in your Cult of Cosmic Consciousness. As an anthropologist and a writer, I am preparing a book on modern cults and their impact on modern culture. I have traveled a long way to see you, knowing what an important figure you were in America during the '60s." She could not tell what impression she was making, for the heavy beard effectively masked his face and the heavy glasses, which glittered directly at her in the bright sunlight, shielded his eyes.

"We have progressed beyond that; the past has no meaning, only the Now and Forever," he said, paraphrasing the woman's words.

"Exactly what I'm interested in!" Penny said enthusiastically. "Cultural evolution is my business. I am anxious to talk to you and to other cult members to see how far your thinking has progressed. After all I know what you used to believe and advocate: Resistance on all levels to the Establishment; the advocacy, along with Tim Leary, of mind-liberating drugs for all . . ." She paused, as Winton seemed to wince a little at that, ". . . the primitive communism of your 'One for all, and all for one' doctrine. I would like to see what you have retained and what you have discarded in this evolution. It would make a fascinating chapter for the book and, I may add, I naturally would submit the manuscript to you for approval before I actually sent it to my Boston publisher." She thought a timely lie might be appropriate. "I did the same with Tim Leary, who was most cooperative, and since you were an equally important figure, well, naturally I wanted your point of view too."

It seemed he hesitated, torn between vanity and suspicion. "It would take some time," he mumbled.

"I could suit my time to yours," she pressed. "Obviously

we can't make much progress talking to each other through this barrier. Why not let me in and we can talk at the chateau? Even if you do not care to pursue it, at least it will give me something to add—even if it is only a footnote to the Leary chapter,'' she added artfully.

He nodded to the woman. "Open the gate."

She produced from the folds of her robe a huge iron key and, with ill grace, undid the heavy padlock and chain. Penny, slipping through the opening with alacrity, felt a little thrill of triumph; she was in!

The walk up the weed-strewn driveway explained why the chateau was invisible from the road, for after about a hundred yards it swung sharply left and the rundown chateau, its long shutters gray and free of paint, sprang into full view. Some mental gymnastics informed her that its main face, which they were approaching, faced east towards the woods; its back was therefore towards the sea, and the encompassing woods also shielded it from the north winds.

They entered a large empty hall with a fine staircase. Penny's serviceable brogues echoed hollowly as she followed her host across the marble floor towards the rear of the house, where he opened some double doors and ushered her into a long, narrow wood-paneled room lit by three large French windows. The room was empty of furniture, save for piles of rather grubby-looking cushions strewn around its beautiful but unpolished parquet flooring. It had the sad look of a gracious lady who has come down in the world.

Winton seated himself on a high pile of cushions and indicated a lower pile at his right hand. "We live very simply," he said, explaining the evident.

The woman hovered above them like a displeased hawk and he looked at her with a flash of the thick glasses. "You'd better see to the others."

She lingered a moment longer. Then her sandals flip-flopped across the parquet and she was gone with a decisive click of the door.

Penny got out a notebook and tried to look businesslike, well aware that before she asked any questions she would have to lull him into a sense of security. "Now, Mr. Winton, if you would explain the principles behind Cosmic Consciousness for me?"

He launched into a long monologue, his voice settling into a high-pitched drone. There was nothing new in it for Penny—it seemed an inane and meaningless hodgepodge of Tibetan mysticism and Hindu philosophy mixed up with cloudy twentieth-century political thinking and slightly inaccurate scientific jargon. After a while her mind began to wander, distracted by the frantic barking of a dog somewhere in the chateau, and the pleasing prospect of the sunlit garden seen through the dirt-grimed windows. In contrast to the ill-kept grounds in front of the chateau, it appeared to be neat and well-kept. As she listened with half an ear to her host's lecture, she caught a glimpse of two youthful figures sneaking through the vegetation; a blond-haired girl with her arm around the waist of a redheaded young man. They reached the corner of the house and disappeared from view, but she could see they were giggling and laughing together like a pair of naughty children up to mischief. Her heart lifted. So all was not muddled mysticism at the Chateau de la Muette—the oldest game in the world was afoot!

Her host showed signs of slowing down, so she brought her attention back to business. "How very interesting," she murmured tactfully. "An amazing evolution over your original ideas! But why did you come to this particular place, the Chateau de la Muette? Why did you not remain in America? Was there something particular here that drew you?"

The question seemed to disconcert him and he hesitated for a minute before launching into a diatribe about the materialism of America blocking "the Way"; that he had long sought a spot where "the Route" was open to the greater Etheric; that Brittany had always been noted for its sacred spiritual tradition; that he had been "led" to this very spot.

"Because of the henge in the chateau grounds?" she said with a touch of mischief.

This also threw him off his stride. "Er—well—yes, among other things," he admitted. "But how did you hear about that? It is not well known."

To allay his sudden suspicion, she said easily, "Oh, the region sings your praises for having put it back as it was; a very gracious gesture." She decided to switch to a safer topic. "And how do you organize and run your community in this remote region?"

He greeted this with relief. "Well, we are mainly self-supporting. We are vegetarians and grow most of our own food right here," he waved an explanatory hand at the windows. "Though we are not fanatics, you understand, we also eat fish, poultry, and eggs—we keep chickens here too. Perhaps you would care to see the gardens?"

"Yes, indeed!" She almost sprang to her feet, anxious to be away from this stale, dust-filled room and into the fresh air. They walked through one of the French windows and started to pace through the large vegetable garden with its long lines of potatoes, cabbages, runner beans, carrots, and other vegetables, all in neat orderly rows. She saw a line of equally well-kept greenhouses, their windows whitewashed, to her right, and she noted with quickening interest that the doors were firmly padlocked. They reached the limit of the garden, bounded by a fence of open iron railings, which she peered through to see trees heavily laden with apples beyond. "And this is your orchard?" she asked.

"Not any longer," his voice was forbidding. "The government took this land for an access road to the proposed power plant."

"How maddening for you!" she sympathized, turning and looking back at the chateau. "So close to you, too."

"It will never come to pass," he said unexpectedly. "The Cosmic Force will prevail and our peace will remain."

To her dismay, the tall figure of the woman appeared from the direction of the chateau and came towards them with purposeful strides. "And how many followers are with you here?" she asked quickly.

He did not give her a direct answer. "The road to Cosmic Enlightenment is difficult and only open to a few. Many fall by the wayside," he droned. "Many are torn by materialism from the Path."

"So how many are with you here?" she persisted, watching the woman's progress with an anxious eye.

"Including Sister Smith and myself, a round dozen," he admitted reluctantly.

"I should very much like to meet with them and talk with them on another occasion. We have made such an excellent beginning. Would it be all right if I came back about the same time tomorrow to continue this?"

"Well. . . ." he hesitated.

The woman called out, "The study hour is here. You are needed."

"Oh, all right, I suppose so. I must go now," he said and turned back to the house.

"I am so happy to see you have young people among your following," Penny babbled on, anxious to keep him interested. "A tribute to your leadership in these changed times."

"How do you know who is here?" he asked with sudden wariness.

"While you were talking inside, I saw a couple of them walking in the garden. A blond girl . . ."

"That would be my niece, Patty."

"Oh, how nice to have family here!" The woman had joined them and was moving restlessly up and down, her eyes fixed on Gareth Winton. "And how about the redheaded young man?" Penny continued.

They both looked at her with blank expressions. "You must be mistaken," Winton said stiffly. "There is no red-headed young man among us."

CHAPTER 10

The woman had accompanied her to the gate in funereal silence, but before they turned the bend in the driveway, Penny caught sight of another white-robed cult member, who stepped out of the front door and appeared to be staring after them. He was a big man, his face shrouded in a beard like Winton's, and as he turned back into the mansion Penny noticed he walked with a heavy limp.

"Until tomorrow then," she said, with a bright grin at the forbidding female. "I'll be back here around the same time." Jane Smith did not reply, but slammed the gate shut with unnecessary force, again sending a few startled crows into the air.

Penny went back to the Triumph and sat behind the wheel thinking things over. How far had she got? She had managed to wheedle her way in on the basis of the veiled threat of going to the local authorities—meaning Winton felt he had something to hide. But was that something past or present? He had struck her as more of a vain mountebank than a man of power or of evil. He was a sort of sad aging relic of the Savage Sixties, who now played only to a small, dwindling audience in a remote backwater; a man whom the times had passed by. And yet at one time he had had quite a following—way up there with Leary and Jim Jones and the like. The hasty research she had done on him in England had indicated he had been arrested several times, but never convicted of anything. There had been rumors of ties with the violent Minutemen, but nothing ever proved. Although he had championed radical causes, he had been comfortably cushioned against personal want at that time by his wife's fortune. She had been a flaky heiress of a tobacco fortune who had been even more vocal than he. What had become of her? Was she one of the present inhabitants of the dilapidated chateau? If so, she certainly wasn't much in evidence. Jane Smith seemed to be Winton's right-hand woman. But Penny was willing to bet it was his wife's money that had purchased the chateau; Winton, prior to his brief notoriety, had been a lecturer at some mid-West college with no money of his own. He had not fled from the States under threat of arrest as others had done, he had simply dropped quietly out of sight in the early seventies. He had turned up here shortly thereafter—and since then?

She wondered if he really believed in any of the mishmash he recited so glibly. It was possible, she supposed, but there were one or two facts that didn't quite jibe—those locked greenhouses, for instance. What was in them? And why deny the presence of a boy she had seen with her own eyes? She gave a little sigh of frustration. "Tomorrow is another day. The main thing for me is to play this role convincingly enough to keep him on the hook. I wonder if I could con him into letting me stay there?" The thought of giving up the gourmet delights of the Auberge du Dragon for a diet of cabbage and carrots did not make the prospect too tempting.

Thinking of the inn reminded her of Grandhomme and she looked at her watch—almost five. She was so close to the henge and it would be near quitting time for the day. Dare she just drop by like a tourist to signal to Toby she had arrived? Maybe she could even catch him alone and they could cut out all this 'I spy' stuff. She decided yes and, after a quick consultation of the map, shot off at breakneck speed. She located the track leading through the woods easily enough and, bumping along, saw the gray outlines of the monoliths ahead. Her spirits sank slightly as there was no sign of his car and no sign of movement on the henge. "May as well take a look while I'm here," she told herself and walked out into the circle of stones.

"What are you doing here, lady?" a voice called out, as a tall, thin man stepped from behind one of the stones; Grandhomme, for sure!

"I was told there was an archaeological excavation going on here," she said, peering around like an eager tourist. "I'm staying over at the Auberge du Dragon and they told me the Dragon's Teeth was a must to see. Are you an archaeologist?"

"No, just an assistant." He eyed her warily and she saw he was shaking.

"Is the archaeologist around? I would so like to meet him. My name is Penelope Spring," she said with emphasis and looked at him hopefully. There was not the slightest gleam of recognition in his eyes at her name, and she felt a twinge of unease—that was strange.

"He hasn't been here today, and my instructions are to let nobody onto the site."

This was even stranger; it had been a perfect day for digging and Toby had told her on the phone he meant to continue with it until she arrived. What was he up to?

"The dig isn't finished, is it?" She was too puzzled to be cautious.

"No. I'm afraid I must ask you to leave." He advanced towards her, and as he did so she saw something that jolted her heart. Toby's silver flask was sticking out of the hip pocket of the man's shabby jeans. Toby never went anywhere without the flask; it was as much a part of him as his pipe and tobacco pouch. He had said Grandhomme could have in no way been involved in the murder, and yet this demanded an explanation and quickly.

"Wait!" she commanded, her sudden fear making her angry. "Where did you get that flask? That belongs to Sir Tobias Glendower."

He stopped dead in his tracks. "Who are you?" he asked uneasily.

She was so alarmed she threw caution to the winds. "I'm a friend of Sir Tobias'. I was sent for." She fumbled in her shoulder bag and snapped open a wallet to show him a picture. It was of her, grinning broadly, and Toby, looking like a monument of misery, resplendent in top hat and morning coat. It had been taken when the Queen had presented his Order of Merit for his role in the affair of Zadok's Treasure. "See! We are friends. And I ask you again—what are you doing with his flask?"

"I found it," he whispered, running his tongue over his dry lips. "I found it last night, but it's been worrying me all day, because he hasn't shown up. You see, yesterday it rained heavily, and I'd been sleeping a lot . . ." he jerked his head towards the dolmen-tomb, ". . . over there. Sir Tobias had been by earlier to drop some things off for me. Then later I thought I heard his Jeep again. I started to come out—it was darkish because of the rain—and I heard the Jeep backing up. I thought I saw several people in it with him. I gave a shout and went up the lane and found a tree down blocking it. By that time the Jeep was gone, but on the ground I found this:'' He took out the flask and handed it to her. ''It was full, so I figured he didn't want to risk the Jeep getting stuck and had just left it there for me. But when he didn't show up today. . . . I don't know what to do.''

Penny was really alarmed now. ''I must go to his inn. Tell me how to get there.''

''Take me with you!'' There was a desperate plea in his voice. ''I have to have a drink or I'll get the horrors—and I want to know where he is, too.''

By the time they reached the inn he was shaking uncontrollably—partly from his need and partly from Penny's hectic driving. Penny, however, had calmed down enough for her caution to reassert itself. ''Money for a drink?'' he pleaded.

''Not before you've checked on Sir Tobias' room. Then I'll give you enough for a flagon of cider,'' she said firmly. ''I'll wait here. If he is up there, tell him to tell you where I should meet him.''

''I don't see the Jeep,'' he said, but got out and did as he was bid.

She waited with mounting anxiety, until Grandhomme shortly reappeared, grinning broadly and waving a note. ''It's all right!'' he exclaimed. ''He left me this letter. He's gone off to Paris for a few days, and he's left me some money, too.''

She took the note and scanned it hastily. ''That's Toby's handwriting all right. Was there anything for me?''

He shook his head. ''Not that I saw.'' A worm of unease still gnawed at her. ''Is there anybody around? I'd like to go up to the room if I can manage it unseen. How did you get in, by the way?''

''The key was in the door. No, there's no one around. It's too early yet for the evening trade.''

''OK. Show me the way and go get your drink. Don't have too many. I'll drive you back to the site in about fifteen minutes.''

He directed her to the room and departed in frantic haste. She went over to the little writing table by the window and searched it thoroughly, but there was nothing there for her, although she did find a pile of notes Toby had apparently been collating on the case; these she promptly pocketed. Further search revealed that one of his suitcases and a good proportion of his belongings were gone. "He obviously has gone somewhere, but how very odd he didn't leave any kind of word for me. Perhaps he'll phone me from Paris," she fretted. "What could he have got onto?"

It was a question she repeated to Grandhomme when he appeared twenty minutes later, his shaking under control and much brighter of eye. He deposited a flagon of cider in the cubbyhole behind his seat and sat back in the car with a relieved sigh. "He might have got a line on the oil angle."

"What oil angle?"

"It seems Dubois—that's the man who was murdered—gave him some hints that somebody around here might have been paid off by the oil interests to throw obstacles in the way of the power plant. Dubois was doing some checking on anyone who had got a fatter bank account of late. He said something about the man at the chateau. Perhaps Sir Tobias got something more on that angle and has gone off to Paris to do some more checking. Seems reasonable to me."

"I suppose so." But she was not entirely convinced. "Did he leave anything else of his with you at the site?"

"There's one of his knapsacks at the rock shelter. Want to look at it?"

"I may as well." She parked the car and was starting to walk across the henge with him when he let out an exclamation. "*Merde*! Somebody has been here!" He hurried over to a flat slab of rock at the center, which to her eyes appeared exactly as it had been. "Quick!" he panted, tugging at one side of it. "Give me a hand with this." Between them they managed to shove it aside enough to open a six-inch crack. He rushed over to the shelter and, returning with a flashlight, shone it inside the black pit. "*Parbleu*—they're gone!" he swore.

"What's gone?" Peering in beside him, she could see a mouldering skull and a broken pot.

"The witchcraft things—the hair and the dagger and the cords." He stood up and swore fluently in French for a solid minute. "It's all my fault. I should not have left the site. He told me not to."

"How did you spot it so quickly?"

"Because, when we put the rock back the first time, Sir Toby put some twigs in certain places so we could tell if anyone had tried to tamper with it." He pointed a finger to where one showed, snapped in two.

"The police?" she guessed.

"The police weren't interested when we told them of it. Favet just laughed at us both. Besides, if he had been here there would have been bootmarks everywhere around it." He waved a hand around. "As you can see, there is nothing."

She felt a little chill. "Whoever did it must have been watching your every movement," she muttered.

"Which wouldn't be difficult." He looked around at the thick, encompassing woods. "Though why they should have waited until now—unless. . . ." He did not finish his thought.

"Do you think it is safe for you to stay on here? Would you like me to take you back to the village?" she asked.

"Why should they bother me now?" he said bitterly. "They've got what they wanted and at least here I have a place to sleep. No, I'll stay until he gets back."

"Well, take care. I'll drop in on you tomorrow and see if there is anything you need. I'll be going to the chateau in the afternoon. And if anyone does show up here, besides Sir Tobias, say nothing about me."

"*D'accord*, but . . ." he eyed her thoughtfully, "you take care also. You realize that whoever was watching saw you, too."

She hurried back to the Auberge du Dragon, only to find there had been no messages, telephone or otherwise. She was disappointed and a little annoyed. "I know he told me to get on with the chateau and the redheaded woman," she fretted. "But you'd think the least he could do was to tell me what he was up to. He really is an infuriating man!" Still smarting from a sense of injustice, she decided she had done her bit for the day. Tomorrow she would see the denizens of the chateau and, if that did not yield anything, start scouting Cormel for a likely redheaded woman. Tonight she was going to relax, have a good dinner, and maybe have another chat with the chef, to whom she had taken quite a fancy.

When she got down to the dining room, the guests were being entertained by a dark, curly-haired young man, singing

French folk songs in a deep bass voice and accompanying himself on a guitar. It somehow suited the atmosphere of the low-beamed, candlelit room and was very pleasant. She dawdled through a Moules Mariniere and had progressed to a Lobster Newburg, when a pair of new arrivals riveted her attention.

A large, fair-haired man came in with a young redheaded woman on his arm and was led obsequiously by the waiter to a table near the folksinger. The woman was dressed in a short evening sheath of some glittering, clinging material that contrived to make all the other women there look like dowdy frumps. She casually discarded a stole of natural mink on the back of her chair, revealing magnificent creamy-white shoulders. Every man in the room was eyeing her covertly and her escort was obviously very proud of her. It seemed to do nothing for the redhead's spirits, for she looked both petulant and bored. She watched the singer, and then, Penny saw with interest, stared at her with undisguised curiosity.

No sooner had Penny marked her down on her scorecard of possible redheads than she had another surprise. An aloof-looking man entered with a girl whose resemblance to him was so marked that she could only be his daughter—but she had the exact same shade of red hair as the first woman's. The new arrivals recoiled slightly at the sight of the first couple and then the man bowed stiffly in their direction before heading for a table at the opposite end of the room. Penny went on to her chocolate mousse with renewed zest, wondering how she could find out about the newcomers.

"I hope, madame, you do not find the music too intrusive. On the weekends it is necessary to cater to modern trends, however much I personally abhor these trimmings." She looked up to see Francois Canard. He was in a dark business suit and, bereft of his chef's hat, seemed somehow shrunken and insignificant.

"Oh, not at all, Monsieur Canard! Nothing could detract from the magnificence of your cuisine," she gushed. "And it is obvious your patrons enjoy the music. The young man's voice is very pleasant."

The amber eyes swept the room and then returned to hers. "Perhaps, madame, since you are alone, you would allow me, who am also alone, to join you? May I offer you a liqueur with your coffee?''

"Why, I would be most honored—not to say flattered. But wouldn't I be keeping you from more important guests? The couple over by the singer for instance?" she hinted.

He sat down with what sounded like a sniff of scorn. "They are not visitors, they come here often. Those are the Villeforts. He is the nearest thing the Dragon's Tongue has to a lord of the manor.''

"She is very lovely," Penny remarked wistfully. "Quite exquisite, in fact."

"A case of beauty being but skin deep," he snorted. "Jacqueline Villefort is an empty-headed mischief-maker."

"But such a remarkable shade of hair," she murmured. "I noticed it on another young lady over there. Are they related, by any chance?"

"Not so far as I know." He looked over at the other couple, a puzzled wrinkle on the high brow beneath his grizzled hair. "That is our local judge, Judge Rouillé, and his daughter, Marie. I have never known them to patronize my auberge before. The judge's finances must have improved lately.''

"You are of this region, then?" she asked.

"No. I am Breton, *bien sûr*," he said with pride, "but from Concarneau to the south—from Cornouille, just like Cornwall in England.''

"Oh, really? I have some Cornish ancestors," Penny said, making them up on the spur of the moment.

"Ah, I knew it!" He positively beamed at her. "The moment I saw you I felt this empathy, *chère madame*, for a fellow Celt. And you Americans, I have heard, are so clever about tracing your ancestors.''

"Oh, yes, it is a fascinating subject, genealogy," she said, feeling slightly ashamed of herself. "But difficult. I imagine around here it is a lot simpler, with people rooted for generations and everybody related to everyone else. You have relatives here?"

"My late wife was from this part." His brow drew down as if the thought was not a pleasant one, but he did not elaborate. "*Tiens*, how the young Rouillé girl is examining us!"·

"Well, you are a very famous man," Penny said tactfully, but wondered herself about the covert glances the girl kept shooting at them. "Again, may I say that I have never enjoyed a dinner more than the one I have just had?"

"It is a gift from God to have a good digestion, and an even greater one to appreciate good food." He sighed. "My late wife now—*a 'mal á la foie' terrible*!—she could not enjoy anything; always medicine, medicine and more medicine, and slops to eat in between. It was a nightmare!"

"I'm so sorry," she murmured absently, for she was watching the tableau being enacted at the Villefort table. A waiter had spoken urgently in Villefort's ear, and with a courtly bow to his wife, he had hurried out. She in turn had summoned the waiter with an imperious finger and was saying something in a low vehement voice. The waiter's eyes turned immediately to their table and it didn't take genius to deduce that Madame Villefort was asking about her. Interesting, Penny thought, very interesting; Grandhomme's final words ringing in her ears. Here are two redheads, both apparently curious about me. Is it one of them? Or both?

The young man had finished his set of songs and disappeared in the same direction as Villefort. Jacqueline Villefort gazed after him, an enigmatic expression on her face, that quickly faded as her husband returned and with another courtly bow sat down opposite her again.

"You are interested in the Villeforts?" Canard's voice brought her up with a start and she realized she had been staring. "She really is so very lovely," she said hastily. "I was also wondering about your singer—an interesting-looking boy and a beautiful voice. Is he from the region?"

For some reason this question seemed to unsettle him. "Not really. He is a student at the college in Nantes. He is here only for the summer—a distant kin of my wife's—Alan Pommard."

Just like the police chief, Penny was about to say, but bit it back in time. As a tourist she wasn't supposed to know that.

"Did you get into the chateau?" His question was abrupt.

"Oh, yes. Very interesting." She did not elaborate. "Mr. Winton is giving me another interview tomorrow afternoon."

"And did you go to see the famous 'Dragon's Teeth'?" She realized he was watching her closely.

"As a matter of fact I did," she said, with what she hoped was convincing honesty. "Mr. Winton told me about them. I'm afraid I don't know much about such things."

"Oh, really?" Now there was definite mockery in his gaze. "That surprises me. I would have thought you had learned a lot about archaeology from your colleague, Sir Tobias Glendower. You see, Dr. Spring, I know about you and what you are famous for. We are both celebrities in our fields, are we not, *ma chère madame*?"

CHAPTER 11

"I feel in need of a breath of fresh air and a stroll to stretch my legs," Toby said firmly to the trio who had returned to his prison bearing gifts of supplies and information. "It is dark outside now, there are three of you and only one of me, and anyway I haven't the faintest intention of trying to get away. So how about it?"

There was a surly growl of dissent from Shaun, but Nicole quelled him with a glare and asserted her leadership.

"All right, but it can only be for a short while. Alan has to get back to work soon."

They sandwiched him between them and went up the narrow winding stone stair from the Abbey's crypt to the shelter of the ruins. The gibbous moon was still full enough to illuminate his surroundings, and a quick glance to the right confirmed Toby's diagnosis of where he was. The lights of the Auberge du Dragon twinkled at him a kilometer away. "So," he said, strolling briskly around the ruins and puffing away at his pipe. "What do you have for me, and what news of Yves?"

"He's in the chateau and has set up his first contact with Shaun," Nicole replied. "Patty sneaked him in and he's holed up in a deserted part of the chateau. She said there was no other way to do it, but if you ask me she didn't want him tempted by all the other women there. Old Winton has a regular seraglio by the seem of it—ten all told, though I don't know if you'd count an old baggage like Jane Smith."

"No other men?"

"One. Another oldie like Winton and American too. Yves says he looks like a real thug. Goes by the name of Brother Tom; they are *all* sisters and brothers." Her young voice was scornful.

"Any redheads among the women?"

"Again, one—and short-haired." She was thoughtful. "But

107

according to Patty she's a bit simple as well as being gaga about Winton. Comes from off the Tongue, from Le Pouldue to the south."

"Is Patty close to any of these people?"

"No, I don't think so. When she got there and saw what an odd setup it was, she insisted on having her own room. Jane Smith has one to herself, too, but the other nine of them sleep in one of the big rooms like a school dormitory. Brother Tom has a room of his own, as does Winton. She's told Yves a couple of interesting things though—doesn't seem to realize what they mean, so I've a feeling she's none too bright herself. Her room is in a separate part of the house from the rest, and every night the door leading into their wing is locked after dinner."

"So she has no idea what goes on after dinner time?"

"None. But she did say the lights burn late."

"And the other thing?"

"Well, once a month she says she sees lights in the greenhouses. There's a whole bunch of them near the house apparently. Again in the evening."

"Once a month, eh?" Toby murmured, his thoughts still running on witches' sabbaths. "And how about the henge?"

She shrugged. "On that, nothing. Either she doesn't know or isn't telling. Yves asked about the dog. A bit odd really. She claims she found him as a small puppy, shortly after she arrived. He was just wandering about the grounds. Jane Smith—who's a regular old bitch—wanted it killed, but Patty made such a fuss her uncle said she could keep it. Apart from her, he's the only one who likes the dog, but Jane Smith insists it be penned up when she's around. Claims she's allergic to dogs. Patty sneaks him out whenever the old bat is not in evidence, and he often gets away from her and runs off—or so she claims."

It did not quite jibe with what Toby had seen of the dog, but he let that go for the moment. "And has Yves himself noticed any odd goings-on or done any exploring?"

Behind his back the trio exchanged quick glances. "There's hardly been time," Nicole said shortly. "After all, he only got in today and he's just had one meeting with us. He did say Patty told him there had been a hell of a row between her uncle and Jane Smith. She likes listening at doors, does Patty.

About some American writer who turned up there today—a woman.''

Toby felt a little surge of elation; so Penny was on the scene! ''Anything else?''

''Only that Jane Smith was dead against him allowing the woman in again. Alan says she's staying over at the Auberge du Dragon.''

''Hmm.'' He didn't want to appear too interested. ''I couldn't ask much with Yves around yesterday, but I would be interested in knowing more about the setup in the Rouillé family. How many of them are there?''

Nicole and Alan looked at each other before he replied, ''Apart from Yves, there's just the judge and one sister, Marie.''

''The mother?''

''The judge has been a widower since Yves was about ten.''

''And where does Yves get his red hair from?''

''His mother.''

''And the sister?''

''The same.'' This came out reluctantly.

''The judge was the only one who championed me about the henge,'' Toby said carefully. ''And I have heard the Rouillé family have a history connected with it. I have also heard that the judge is a man of high principles but many problems. Do you know the nature of these problems?''

''Money and his kids—in that order.'' Nicole said. ''He never did have a great deal, but Madame Rouillé had a long and expensive illness, which just about wiped him out. He's always been a tightfisted old tyrant with the kids. It was all he could do to scrape together the money to send Yves to college, and then when Yves got involved with the Cause and his marks fell off, his father got so furious he just booted him out. He's an awful old chauvinist, too. Marie's the older and yet there was never any question of her being sent to university, even though she's always been a lot brighter than Yves. So she has to stay home and rot.'' Nicole's tone was bitter.

''And she resents that?''

''I don't know her that well. I certainly would.''

''What does she do?''

''Nothing, except stay home and look after her father.''

A bored and thwarted young girl, Toby reflected, was indeed a likely candidate to turn to witchcraft to liven up her rustic days. "And is there any friendship or relationship between the Rouillés and the Villeforts?"

"The judge doesn't like Villefort. After all, his father was more or less kicked out of the district by Villefort's father, and he's had several run-ins with Villefort over Pommard since he came back here. As to Villefort—who knows? He's not a man to wear his feelings on his sleeve. Marie and Jacqueline see something of each other, because Jacqueline Villefort is distant kin of the judge's wife. She comes from Morgat, and her father owns several fishing boats. A bit of money there, but not a lot. Everyone around here thought Villefort had married beneath him when he took her on after the first Madame V. died, but he's absolutely crazy about her."

"And she?"

"Jacqueline fancies herself a femme fatale," Nicole said, with an angry glare at Alan. "But I think the only one she cares about is herself, and she knows she's onto a good thing with Villefort."

"So you don't see her in the role of practising witch?"

"No, I can't say I do. For one thing, Villefort keeps too close an eye on her."

"Unless he was involved, too," Toby murmured.

She laughed. "I wouldn't put Villefort above making a pact with the devil, but I can't see him capering around the henge muttering mumbo jumbo."

Toby was about to launch into a dissertation on the differences between Wicca witchcraft and devil worship, but thought better of it. He had the feeling they were humoring him as it was, and didn't wish to add to his eccentric image. He changed the subject. "Any idea if Favet is making any progress?"

"According to him, yes. He's doing mounds of paperwork to establish where practically everyone in the area was at the time of the murder. Anyone who claimed to be alone he's been giving one hell of a hard time to, so consequently everyone local is swearing they were with everyone else and he really isn't learning a damn thing. The only people who've admitted to being alone at the time are the Curé, whom even

Favet doesn't have the nerve to suspect; the judge; and Jean Sommelier, for the brief period before he was with you.''

"Which doesn't get us one bit further,'' Toby said gloomily. He still felt uneasy about the pointed way Sommelier had drawn their attention to the time of his appearance. "Does Sommelier have any family or close kin on that farm of his?''

"If you mean children—no. He does it all with the help of one old man who's a bit touched and Madame Sommelier, who, he claims, is the strongest woman in Brittany. People around here say that's why he married her. He certainly works her like a horse.''

"And are any of these people we have been talking about involved in any—er—extramarital affairs?'' Toby said with some embarrassment.

"Sommelier certainly isn't. The only thing he's in love with is money. Villefort isn't. They say the judge goes twice a month to a brothel in Chateaulin, and Pommard has a thing going with a widow who keeps a shop in Crozon. But who cares!'' She was suddenly impatient. "I don't think any of this is getting us anywhere, and it's time we were shoving off. You'll have to go back down. We won't be around much tomorrow. There's something we have to take care of.''

For a moment he was tempted to protest and then thought better of it. He would wait and see what the lad in the chateau came up with before demanding his freedom. He meekly allowed himself to be escorted back and locked in his prison.

As the young people emerged into the moonlight, Shaun raised a hand in farewell. "Got to be off to see Yves,'' he said and hurried off into the night. "Do you have what I gave you?'' Nicole called after him. "Sure!'' he yelled over his shoulder.

Alan looked at his retreating back with a frown. "Do you think this is wise, Nicole?'' he asked. "I must say I don't much care for him and what do we really know about him? I mean, if Yves is onto something, as he says, how do we know Shaun isn't going to cash in on it?''

"It's a case of needs must. You have to be at the Auberge and I'm damned if I am going to go capering around those woods alone at this time of night, Yves or no Yves.''

"You could have gone with him,'' he said stubbornly. "I don't trust him.''

"Nor do I, which is why I didn't. Mighty fast hands has Shaun. Quite the macho man, in fact."

"Oh!" His tone was blank.

She took his hand and gave it a squeeze. "Don't worry, Alan. I had a word with Yves before he left and I'm going to have a rendezvous myself with him tomorrow afternoon. It's a sort of test to see how honest Shaun is. After all, if this thing is as big as we think it is, we'll have to get word to the others in Brest."

He put his arm around her waist and drew her to him with a faint sigh. "You know, Nicole, sometimes I wonder if it's all worth it. Why can't we just get married and finish our studies and get out of here? I mean, what difference do we make to the Cause?"

She kissed him lightly. "One day maybe, but not yet."

"Walk me back to the inn?" It was a plea.

"*Bien sûr!*"

They walked in silence for a while, their arms around each other's waist. "You know, I wonder if we shouldn't have told the old boy about all this," Alan said uneasily. "By reputation he is supposed to be very good at sorting out things, and perhaps holding back this information is a mistake."

"Oh, he's so hepped up about all this witchcraft business, I really wonder about him. In any case, I can't see what this has to do with the murder, but it could be damn useful for *us*," Nicole responded.

"But what if Yves runs into any trouble?"

"Yves can look after himself. The only men there are Winton, who strikes me as a weak old sod, and that other gimpy guy. Anyway, I told you—after tomorrow we'll get the big boys in Brest in on it. That girl is so dim-witted she doesn't seem to realize what she told Yves. Now, it's only a question of him locating the tunnel. He has a pretty shrewd idea of where it must be from what she said, and I got him the photocopied plans of the chateau from the record office today. That's what Shaun is taking to him," she replied.

"Didn't the record office people wonder? And you know how word spreads around here."

"I said I needed it for a history project. You *are* an old worrywart, Alan."

He looked at his watch and let out an exclamation. "*Merde!*

I'd better run or I'll be late! Don't want your uncle to fire me, though the last time I saw him he was too busy to notice me. He was making goo-goo eyes at one of the guests—that funny old dame with the green Triumph Shaun was so upset about. Besides, I'd like another look at Jacqueline Villefort's decolletage—*c'est magnifique*!'' And with this parting shot, he sped off into the dark, leaving her frowning after him.

Penny was not feeling too happy with herself as she sped towards the chateau the following afternoon. She had not received the expected call from Toby and was furious with him, and for someone who was supposed to be undercover, she felt she had blown it in record time. Grandhomme knew who she was and so did Canard. If this goes on, she thought bitterly, I may as well wear a sign around my neck ''Undercover investigator—Please answer all questions.'' At least she could control Grandhomme so long as he stayed at the site, but Canard was a different matter. She had salvaged what she could of the situation by making much of her interest in the cult center at the chateau, and by asking him to help her conceal her other reputation as a detective. He had obviously taken a fancy to her and she had played on that, but exactly how discreet could she trust him to be? ''I must get Grandhomme to teach me some of those fancy French swear words,'' she muttered grumpily. ''I certainly could use them to effect just now.'' She drove up to the main gate with a savage jerk and did her bell-tolling act; nothing happened. She was about to try again when a floridly decorated panel truck came chugging along the road and drew up at the gate, and Jane Smith gazed out of its open window. ''Oh, it's you again! Didn't you get Father Winton's message at the inn?''

''No. What message?''

''It slipped his mind yesterday, but today is his period for Cosmic Communication. He cannot be disturbed.''

Penny controlled her rising temper. ''If he can't see me, I'll talk to the other cult members; Mrs. Winton for instance.''

Jane Smith's eyes slitted. ''That would be difficult. She's been dead nine years.''

''She died here?''

''No, she returned to the States. She fell away from the Path.''

"All right then, how about the others?"

"They are unavailable also, and you would have to get his permission. I cannot give it."

"You're here. How about you?" Penny couldn't keep the sarcastic edge off her voice.

"I have work to do."

"You're not being very cooperative." Penny snapped. "I don't think Winton would like that, and sooner or later I am going to talk to the others, so make up your mind to that. You know your face is very familiar to me. I think it is coming back to me where I've seen you before."

It seemed to take the wind out of the woman. "I can spare a few minutes," she said. "What do you want to know?"

"What impact has the center had locally?"

"We leave them alone and they leave us alone. We don't try to proselytize—people find us. We want no trouble and we make no trouble."

"Has the nuclear power plant made any difference to your local relationships?"

"They don't like the idea any more than we do."

"I should think a power plant in the vicinity would play merry hell with cosmic vibrations," Penny purred. "Are you planning to move the center when it's built?"

"Never! It will not happen, it cannot happen." There was a desperate note in her voice. "However much Villefort would like to get the chateau back, we are here to stay."

Penny pricked up her ears at this. "He wants to buy the chateau back?"

Jane Smith snorted in disgust. "He was glad enough to sell it when we came—but now! It's that wife of his, she's behind it. She has everything else, so now she wants to be lady of the manor. Well, there's no way short of murder he's going to get it."

"I hear there's been one," Penny said idly and was surprised by the vehemence of the reaction. "That has nothing to do with us," Jane Smith shrilled. "Nothing at all! We are people of Peace, there is no blood on our hands. No one can accuse us. They can't get to us that way."

"Has anybody tried?" Penny interjected.

"Well, no." She calmed down with a visible effort. "But

when one is a foreigner there is always the feeling one might be victimized."

"What is the nationality breakdown of your group?" Penny asked. "Are you mostly Americans?" The question did not appear to please Jane Smith, who said grudgingly, "No, counting Patty Winton there are just four of us. We have two Belgians, one English, the rest are French."

"So five French. From around here?" she persisted.

"Two; the others are from the Midi."

"And the sex ratio?"

"Two men, ten women."

"So the Path is more eagerly sought by women," Penny couldn't resist saying and got a hard bright look in return. "Do you let outsiders in for services?"

"No." Jane Smith was becoming monosyllabic with impatience.

There was a faint noise inside the gate and Penny turned to see the tall man limping towards it. "You're wanted," he said tersely. "We've been waiting, sister."

Jane Smith gunned the car. "Wait!" Penny called. "When will Mr. Winton be free to see me?"

"No idea. He'll contact you." Sister Smith zoomed through the gate and up the drive in a cloud of blue exhaust.

"Could I talk with you?" Penny said desperately to the man who was locking the gate behind her.

"Go to hell!" he said with a pronounced New York twang, and limped up the drive.

Penny's eyes narrowed as she watched his painful progress, the fugitive memory gaining substance in her mind. "I wonder. I think a call to John Everett may be in order. I need some information and I need it fast. It seems incredible but it just might be. And, if so, no wonder Winton's running scared!"

She turned the car towards the henge and rattled down the track to find Grandhomme sitting with his back to one of the stones, his head bowed on his arms. She extracted the fresh bread and a flagon of cider she had brought for him and got out. As she went towards him he looked up to reveal one eye almost swollen shut and blackened and his lips puffed and bruised. "What on earth happened to you?" she exclaimed in shock.

"I'm sure the official version would be that I slipped and fell," he returned grimly. "But I've had a visit from Pommard and Favet, and things got a bit rough."

"But that's terrible!" she stuttered. "Why did they beat you up?"

"Pommard seemed to think I'd like to change my story," he said, accepting the flagon from her and taking a hearty swig. "They came out to see the witchcraft things. When I tried to tell him what happened yesterday, neither of them believed me. In fact, now they don't believe any of it. They think we threw in this witchcraft business just to confuse the issue—though God knows why! They were trying to make me say Sir Tobias and I were not together all that morning. I did not oblige them, but I can tell you one thing. Favet is out for his blood. I had to show him the note and he has the Paris police hunting for him. Have you heard from him? He ought to get back here fast, wherever he is."

"I wish to hell I knew where that was," Penny returned grimly. "But I can tell you one thing also. I don't like the way things are shaping up, not one little bit!"

CHAPTER 12

"John, I desperately need some information, and only you can help me." John Everett's plump features took on a faintly resigned expression as he sat at the other end of the phone line in his Boston office. Since in essence he owed Penny his life and liberty, any request from her was impossible to refuse, and yet he had the sinking feeling it was, as usual, going to take up considerable time and money.

"You are—er—involved in another case, I assume?" he said.

"Toby got us into this one." Penny was all aggrieved virtue. "It was none of my doing. I was started on the new book, honestly."

He drew a notepad towards him. "All right, shoot. What do you want to know?"

"First, if you can, track down where, when, and how the wife of Gareth Winton died. That would be about nine years ago. I think her name was Vanessa and she was heiress to one of the big tobacco fortunes. I'd also like to know what happened to her money. Second, do you remember a nasty bombing incident in Chicago in the late '60s? 1968, I think. Several innocent people were killed in an explosion. The Minutemen were involved in it and one of them was injured in the blast. There was a woman leader to that particular group, she had a nickname—something like 'Long Lena.' Could you find out if they were ever caught, or what happened to them, and try to get a good description of her? The FBI should have one on file."

"I'll do my best," he said patiently. "Do I need to know what all this is about?"

"Not really. It's just that, unless my memory is playing tricks on me, I think I may have run into 'Long Lena' or whatever her name was, hiding out in a small Breton village under the alias of Jane Smith. There's been a local murder

117

here and it is possible the group she is in may be involved in some way. Gareth Winton heads it up. Remember him?''

"Indeed I do." He was becoming intrigued. "How would you like me to contact you?"

"You can call me here." She gave him the inn number. "And at a set time; say, six by your time, which would be eleven in the evening our time. If I don't hear from you tonight, I'll assume you don't have anything for me and will wait again tomorrow. OK?"

"Right. Take care now," John said with feeling, knowing all too well her propensity for trouble. "And my regards to Toby."

"I'll give them to him when I can find him," she said irritably.

"He's not with you?"

"No. He sent for me, but when I arrived he apparently had hopped off to Paris without a word. Infuriating!"

"That's not like him." John's voice was concerned.

"No, it isn't, is it?" Her own uneasiness surfaced. "However, I don't quite know what to do about it."

"The French police?"

"They are already looking for him with blood in their eye. I don't want to make things worse," she confessed.

"Heavens, like that, is it? Well, again do take care," he urged. "I'll get on to this right away."

She put the phone down with a worried frown. Another evening and morning had passed by without a message from Toby, and she was becoming increasingly worried and frustrated. The only small comfort she could find was that he had evidently packed and gone somewhere in the expedition Jeep, but she had not the faintest clue where to look. "I simply have to do something to keep busy or I'll get the screaming mimis like Grandhomme," she exhorted herself. She toyed with the idea of making another onslaught on the chateau, but then decided to wait for the added ammunition she hoped John Everett would provide. There had been no message from Winton either and she feared the tough-minded "Jane Smith" had probably persuaded him from further contact. If her own suspicions proved correct, she could well see why. "The only thing I can think of is to go into Cormel and act like a tourist, and see if I can pick up anything on the redhead, though for the life of me I don't see how," she muttered. She drove off in the Triumph, trying to think of some credible excuse for going to see the judge's daughter; no inspiration came.

In his dungeon, Toby was also starting to worry. He simply had to get some kind of message to Penny, but how? There had been no sign of his captors all day. He had finished all the work he could do on his henge notes, and he was feeling increasingly bored and frustrated. In his head he began to compose a "Liberty or Death" speech. The time had come, he decided, to re-emerge and take an active part in affairs.

Above him, in the ruins, a heated argument was going on between two very worried-looking young people. "I don't like it," Alan was saying. "I mean, if Yves didn't show, at least he would have left some kind of message for you."

"You saw yourself there was nothing," Nicole replied, irritable from worry.

"What exactly did Shaun say about the other night? And where the hell is he?"

"I don't know! And I told you what he told me. Yves took the plans and said he would have to be a bit careful because Winton had been on at Patty about seeing someone, and he was afraid that somebody there had spotted them together. He said he had found out about the greenhouses and it was just what we had suspected. Then, just before Shaun left, Yves got all uptight and said he had to see Marie—wouldn't say why. Shaun tried to talk him out of it because of the danger of being picked up, but he did not think Yves took it in."

"But we know he wasn't picked up," Alan broke in. "I checked Cormel again this morning. Nothing. Except that Pommard's been after Sommelier again. I vote we tell the old boy and see if he has any ideas. Honest, Nicole, if Yves is in trouble up at the chateau we ought to get help fast."

"Our people in Brest . . ." she began.

"To hell with them! It'll take all day to get anybody here, and chances are they won't even want to come, knowing the Sûreté snoopers are around. How about your uncle?"

"I wouldn't dare disturb him at this time of day," she said with horror. "Not while he's preparing dinner!"

"Well then, that leaves us only one choice. Let's get Glendower in on it. If need be, he could probably get in to see Winton. Let's face it, he carries a lot more heft than we do."

"Oh, all right!" Her dark eyes suddenly brimmed with tears, and she looked a lot younger than her nineteen years. "But if Yves is OK and we've blown our plans, I'll never forgive you."

Toby's carefully thought-out speech died on his lips as he took in the distraught expressions on the two young faces and the fact that the girl had evidently been crying. Instead, he simply said, "What's up?"

After a swift glance at Nicole, Alan became spokesman. "It may be nothing, but Yves failed to keep a rendezvous with us yesterday. We're a bit worried he may have run into some trouble."

"It could be he just can't sneak out of the chateau too easily in daylight," Toby pointed out.

"But then he'd have sent a message that Patty would have left under a rock we had picked out. That was all arranged."

"When did you see him last?"

"Shaun saw him the night before last." Alan summarized their conversation for Toby. "We were going to meet him the following afternoon, and when he failed to show, we tried it again that night, but still no sign of him."

"So why were you meeting him again so soon?" Toby asked, getting straight to the point.

"We—er—wanted to be sure Shaun was to be trusted to tell us everything."

"Trusted? What about?" Toby looked at him keenly. "You are not telling me all of it, are you? Look, if you really believe Yves is in trouble, this is no time to hold anything back from me. What else is there?"

Alan glanced helplessly at Nicole, who just stared straight ahead, her mouth clamped in a determined line. "Hell, Nicole, I have to," he stuttered and turned back to Toby. "It's like this. We thought the people at the chateau may have been up to something illegal and it looks as if we are right. There's an old tunnel that leads from the chateau grounds to a beach near here—a relic from the old smuggling and wrecking days of this area. There have been unidentified boats seen off the coast by our people recently, and Yves was going to check if the tunnel was still being used for smuggling by the Winton crowd."

"Smuggling what?"

"Pot—marijuana. They are growing it there in some green-houses on the estate. It's still worth a bundle, you know, with all these half-assed laws making it illegal."

This was an angle that had not even occurred to Toby and he was quietly staggered. "How, may I ask, did you get onto all this?"

"Patty never leaves the grounds and yet she always has plenty of joints to hand out. Yves found out that her uncle gives her all she wants—part of his 'mind-liberating' program. Yves began to wonder where it all came from. The other night he snooped around the greenhouses and found out. It makes a heap of sense: why Winton is so hysterical about keeping people out; the activity in the chateau at night; the boats off the coast . . ." Alan stopped.

"It certainly does," Toby snapped. "Why the hell didn't you tell me all this before? I would never have countenanced Yves even going in there. What did you think? That I'd be shocked and blow the whistle on you? Young man, ninety per cent of my students smoke it. I even tried it myself in my youth in the form of hashish." He stared angrily at Nicole. "Or were you thinking of horning in on the racket for 'the Cause,' or perhaps using the tunnel for your own purposes once you had Winton over the barrel?" Nicole's chin jutted a little higher in the air, but she said nothing. "In any case you are all getting involved in something potentially very deep and very dangerous. I have to get out of here and see what's to be done. Let us hope Yves is just delayed by something, but we have to get him out of the chateau. Take me to the rendezvous point and if there is still nothing from him, I'll take a crack at getting in and having a confrontation with Winton." He did not mention that his alarm was not solely for the redheaded boy, but also for Penny, who was in all innocence walking into this nest of vipers. "Where's Shaun?"

"We don't know. That's another odd thing. He never showed up this morning when he was supposed to meet us."

"What do you know of him?"

"He's a student at Liverpool University and part of the undercover wing of the IRA. Supposed to be an expert at organizing underground support cells. He's over here for the summer as a sort of liaison and to give us tips on operations."

"And you don't trust him?" Toby was blunt.

Alan shrugged. "I just don't know. He's not one of us, and he's got some pretty rough ideas that we're not used to. He may be OK, but if there is a lot of money involved. . . ."

"He hasn't been picked up by Favet?"

Alan shook his head. "No. I checked in Cormel before coming here. Favet is flapping around, getting nowhere as usual, and no sign of Pommard. He's probably running Villefort's errands."

"Where's my Jeep?"

"Hidden near here. You're supposed to be in Paris, remember?"

"How do you lot get around?"

"Yves and I have motorcycles. Shaun's been using Yves'."

"Well, I certainly don't intend to start cavorting around on the back of a motorcycle. We'll take the Jeep. I have to come out of hiding now. My story will be that I've been up in Paris for a couple of days. There will be no mention of any of this. Agreed? I'll get my stuff together."

"I don't know . . ." Nicole began.

"But you do know," he cut in firmly. "You do know this whole thing has gone too far, and we've got to do something fast. Drug-smuggling is not usually an amateur operation, and even if Winton is not a professional, the people he is involved with in it probably are—and they play rough. So we have to get Yves out first and then see what is to be done. They may have one murder to their credit already." She blanched at that and then nodded her head in dumb misery.

They helped him pack in silence and set out over the cliffs to where, in a small brush-filled dell, the Jeep was completely camouflaged. "A neat job," Toby observed, hoping the battery wasn't dead. After a little coaxing, the engine spluttered into life and they bumped their way back onto the deserted side road and took off for the chateau. They abandoned the Jeep on a cart-track and walked cautiously in through the heavy-laden apple trees of the orchard to a point near the iron fence where a small granite boulder shone whitely through the underbrush in the gathering dusk.

Nicole felt underneath it. "Still nothing," she whispered.

Alan was peering through the iron railings. "No sign of life in there either."

Toby paid no attention to either of them. He stood listening intently, a chill trickling up his spine at what his acute ears had picked up. Far, far to their left in the direction of Cormel there came from the woods the baying of a hound.

"You know the paths into the woods from the Cormel side?" he said with some difficulty.

"I do," Alan said.

"Then I think we'd better get over there." Toby tried to keep his voice calm. "If I'm not mistaken that's the dog again. We'd better find him and see what's disturbing him."

They set off again, Alan at the wheel, and, after casting along the edge of the wood on the Cormel side, turned down another trail from where the baying of the dog sounded loud and clear.

"This is as far as we can go in the Jeep," Alan announced and jumped out.

Toby was looking at his pocket compass. "That direction, I believe," he pointed, a frown on his face. "Damn it, we are angling back towards the other side of the henge!"

They walked in silence, ears straining for the hound's cries, which had now changed to an ululating wail, adding fuel to Toby's fears. "I see him!" Alan cried and broke into a run. His voice floated back to them strangely altered. "Sir, don't let Nicole come, but hurry yourself."

With a sinking feeling, Toby hurried ahead and almost bumped into Alan's stocky figure, as he stared at a huge oak whose branches swept low to the ground, forming a natural arbor. By the bole of the tree the dog sat on its haunches guarding a figure that seemed to be resting quietly against the trunk, its eyes closed, the face gleaming palely under the dark red hair.

"Oh God! It's Yves!" Alan choked out.

"Stay back and keep Nicole with you," Toby said, taking out his flashlight. "I can handle the dog." He advanced cautiously and the dog stopped its wailing, looked at him with intelligent amber eyes, and then quietly loped off, its message again delivered. Toby trained his light on the still figure and a small shock ran through him. A white-handled knife, the twin of the one he had found in the henge, lay low on Yves' breast, its blade unsullied. He felt for a pulse at the neck, but encountered ice-cold flaccid flesh. He tried to fight down the murderous rage that was growing inside him; to think calmly about the dead boy in front of him. There was no blood on the partly open mouth, none of the hideous mutilation that had been done to Dubois, no sign of violence at all. Cautiously he eased the body away from the tree and looked behind. Sticking out of the middle of Yves' back was a dagger, its handle carved with crude cabalistic designs. Toby knew what it was: an 'athame,' the ritual dagger of a witch. There was one just like it in the Ashmolean Museum at Oxford. Fighting the emotions that swelled up in him, he went on with his methodical search. The blood had soaked darkly from the wound down the back of the boy's T-shirt and jeans, and he could follow a trail of blood spots that showed dark against the dry earth and leaves to a point some four feet away from the trunk. So the murder had taken place right here. On this very spot, someone had crept up on the unsuspecting boy and had planted a knife in his back. By the position of the wound, he surmised it had gone straight to the heart—a skillful thrust of considerable strength, for the dagger was buried to the hilt.

He straightened up and gazed blankly at the tree. What a hell of a situation, what a hell of a mess. There was nothing to be done for the dead, but how could he protect the living? —the two young people who were clasped motionless in each other's arms at the edge of the bushes.

He turned abruptly away and went back to them. "There's nothing to be done here," he said gruffly. "He's dead. Stabbed in the back."

Nicole let out a little moan and, burying her face in Alan's shoulder, burst into quiet sobs.

The boy's face showed sick and white in the gloom. "We'll have to go to the police, we'll have to tell them everything," he whispered.

"Not for the moment. I need time to think," Toby said. "If you tell your story, they'll lock us all up and throw away the key. If possible, I'm going to try and keep you out of it." Again he checked the compass. "I'd like to keep myself out, but I don't think it is possible. They are not going to like this habit I have of finding bodies. The henge can only be a few hundred yards farther on. We'll make for that, and I'll see if I can cook up something with Grandhomme.''

"But . . . but . . . we can't just leave Yves here all alone like that!'' Alan exclaimed.

"Don't be childish. We've no choice for the moment,'' Toby returned roughly. "Pull yourselves together. This is no time for breast-beating. Come on.'' He pushed on through the wood, the young couple following dazedly behind him. He emerged at the back of the dolmen to see a small fire flickering and Grandhomme's tall thin figure outlined against it.

"Who's there?'' Grandhomme demanded.

"It's I, Glendower,'' Toby called out.

"Oh, thank God you're back!'' Grandhomme came towards him and Toby saw his discolored and bruised face.

"What happened to you?'' he exploded.

"The police got a bit rough trying to make me think again about. . . .'' He trailed into silence as he became aware of the two other figures behind Toby.

"Well, I need your help urgently now. There's been another murder. These young people and I have found the body, and for a number of reasons I want to keep them out of it. So you and I will refind it, if you follow me, and then we'll get the police.''

"I don't think that will do,'' Grandhomme said. "Not if you don't want to get arrested. Favet's out for you as it is.'' He rapidly filled Toby in on the events of the past few days; the theft from the henge, Penny's visit, his own beating. "I heard that damn dog tonight,'' he finished, "but I was not about to go into those woods to find out what it was howling about.''

"Have you seen Dr. Spring today?'' Toby asked in increasing alarm.

"No, not today. She was hoping to get into the chateau again, but I don't think she could have or she would have dropped by here.''

All other thoughts were banished from Toby's mind. He had to make sure Penny was not walking into danger—had not already walked into it. He had to find her, immediately. Ignoring all the other pressing problems, he turned to the two young people behind him. "There is something you must do right away," he declared. "I want you to take the two of us back to the abbey, then I want you to go to the Auberge du Dragon and contact a Dr. Penelope Spring, who is staying there."

"And?" Alan said in a mystified voice.

"I want you to kidnap her without anyone knowing and bring her to the abbey," Toby concluded.

CHAPTER 13

In the darkened hallway of the sleeping Auberge, Penny was hugging herself with glee. "Bingo!" she crowed. The phone call from John had taken a solid hour, but every minute had been a nugget of pure gold. "Now let Winton try and keep me out!" she exulted. "I'll have the lot of them spilling the beans to me in no time flat—that is, if they are in the clear, as they claim, on this murder."

A grandfather clock leisurely chimed the midnight hour as she climbed the stairs to mull over her discoveries. She let herself into her room and was reaching for the light switch when a cold ring of steel pressed against her temple and a deep voice said, "This is a gun. Don't move a muscle and don't make a sound. You are a hostage of the Breton Underground Army of Liberation. Do exactly as I say and you will not be hurt."

She was too surprised to resist as her eyes were blindfolded and a gag thrust into her mouth. The muzzle of the gun was removed, and she had the presence of mind to slip her shoulder bag quietly off her shoulder in the dark and let it fall to the floor before her hands were loosely tied. She was taken by both arms and carried down the creaking stairs; there was a rush of damp air as a door opened, and then she was lifted into a car. The minute it started she recognized it as a Jeep, but she was puzzled by the hand around her shoulders, which steadied her against its jolting progress. It was small and soft—a woman's. So there are at least two of them, she thought, no use trying to make a break for it, may as well see what develops.

The jolting got worse before the Jeep stopped and the same half-carrying process was repeated down stone stairs. A door opened and an all-too-familiar voice boomed out, "Good heavens! Don't you two have any sense? When I said kidnap,

127

I didn't mean kidnap like Chicago gangsters! Undo her at once!"

The blindfold was whisked off and she saw Grandhomme and Toby outlined against a paraffin lamp, sitting at their ease at a wooden table and apparently swigging cider.

Penny's eyes narrowed with fury, and when the gag came off she spluttered furiously, "Toby! What the hell is all this? And where the devil have you been? Grandhomme, have you been holding out on me? Because, if so. . . ."

"Calm, calm!" Toby said. "I'm very sorry about all this, but I had to get you out of the inn fast and couldn't think of another way. You were in danger."

"Danger!" She glared at the two white-faced young people and recognized the folk singer from the auberge. "What do you think being kidnapped at gunpoint is? They could have blown my head off. Danger, indeed!"

"It wasn't loaded," Alan said feebly.

Her eyes fell on a suitcase in the girl's hand. "And you have my things—of all the nerve!"

"Penny, will you shut up and listen," Toby appealed. "There's been another murder, and I wasn't about to risk you being added to the list." He led her back to the table, sat her down, filled her a glass, and began to explain.

As she listened, her anger faded, to be replaced by a sick, sinking feeling. "Oh, dear God!" she whispered, "I may have blown the whistle on that poor boy."

Toby stopped in the middle of a sentence. "Oh? How?"

"When I was in the chateau I saw him and Winton's niece together. I thought he was a cult member—I mentioned it to Winton and Long Laura. So that's why . . ."

"Long Laura?" Toby echoed blankly.

"Yes, well, I've been busy. Since I didn't hear from you, I went ahead on my own and, taken together with what you've found out, what I have uncovered makes a whole heap of sense. I had just got off the phone with John Everett when I was seized." She shot a frosty glare at the young couple, who were huddled miserably at the other end of the table. "I had asked him to find out a lot of things for me, and he came through in magnificent fashion. To boil it down—I'll give you the details later when we've sorted everything out— Winton's wife, Vanessa, was his chief source of money.

Apparently, not too long after they came to the chateau, she got fed up with the setup, went back to the States, and got a Reno divorce. She overdosed on sleeping pills and booze not long after that, but not a cent of her money went to Winton. He must have been strapped, so he turned to this profitable little sideline of pot-growing. Now—as to Long Laura. I thought there was something familiar about 'Jane Smith' the first time I saw her, but then yesterday I saw her in conjunction with the lame American, who is also a cult member, and something clicked.

"In 1968 there was a nasty incident in Chicago. A house used by a cell of the Minutemen exploded, the debris killing two innocent passers-by. The dead body of a Minuteman was found in the house by the police, and they also picked up evidence that a wounded member of the group had been removed by the Minutemen. From evidence they found in the house, they zeroed in on a Minuteman leader who was called 'Long Laura'—real name Laura Jane Smitt. Murder warrants were issued against her and several others, including a Brooklyn man who had worked with explosives and who, I strongly suspect, was the wounded man and is this lame man at the chateau. Anyway, the FBI never found them. They completely disappeared and haven't surfaced since, and I am virtually certain that 'Long Laura' is none other than 'Jane Smith.' With those two around, I don't think we have to look much further for our murder suspects."

A frown wrinkled Toby's smooth brow. "On the face of it, yes—but . . ." he murmured, ". . . there are certain things that don't quite fit. Obviously these two—if they are the people you suspect them to be—would not be above murder, but logically I cannot see why they should have committed these murders in the way they did or in those places. Young Rouillé was killed right where his body lies on the Cormel side of the woods and with those witchcraft trappings on him. Why? If they had found him snooping around and had known their secret was uncovered, surely it would have made more sense to do away with him right there and dispose of the body quietly in the sea. Why draw attention to it at all? The object of Dubois' murder I can see—to shut his mouth and presumably to spook the nuclear power plant scheme and warn off others by the method of his death. But the boy's murder? To shut his mouth certainly, but he has no connection with the nuclear plant. If they were following along the same line of intimidation, by rights he, or at least his body, should have been treated in exactly the same way as Dubois'. And why, if the chateau people were involved, would they let him get as far away from the chateau as that before they murdered him? When I saw the white-handled knife I naturally assumed it was a twin of the one found in the henge burial, but having heard of the robbery, I think it probable that it is the very same one; again as if the murderers were bringing our attention to the witchcraft angle."

"Mm, I see what you mean." Penny was perplexed. "But maybe that's just a red herring to throw us off."

"The operative word is red, I feel," Toby said. "Who is the redheaded woman? So far we have three candidates among those connected with this affair: a French girl from Le Poldue living at the chateau who is supposedly simpleminded and devoted to Winton, Jacqueline Villefort, and Yves' sister, Marie. Now, if it is the girl from the chateau, again why, in heaven's name, would they draw attention to it? If it is not she, we are left with the murdered boy's sister and Jacqueline Villefort."

"There is another angle to this, too," Penny mused. "Whoever took those things from the henge, as Grandhomme has pointed out, must have been watching and saw us go off together. Both of our local candidates were having dinner at the inn last night and both of them were evidently curious about me. That doesn't get us much farther, I grant you, save that Canard mentioned the Villeforts were frequent guests, whereas it was the first time the Rouillés had ever been to the auberge."

"Not a very pretty image you are building," Toby said.

"There is the further point, which Grandhomme also spotted," she went on. "Why did they wait so long to recover those things from the henge? It was left unguarded several times after you had made the find and had talked about it, when you and Grandhomme were off the site together. The only answer to that seems to be that they too were occupied elsewhere at the same time. Right?"

"Right," he agreed. "Well, we'd better collate notes before we go any further."

"Good idea. By the way I read all that stuff you had left in your room at the inn, so you can skip that," she said. To the astonished trio watching them, it seemed as if a human computer was at work, as the two different beings became to all intents and purposes one mind.

Finally, Toby leaned back with a satisfied sigh and glanced at his watch. "Good Lord, it must be dawn! I think that about does it. Interesting tidbit you picked up in Cormel yesterday about Villefort's three-day absences every month. Even if he does keep a close eye on her, it would give Jacqueline plenty of opportunity, if she is our witch."

"Yes, I was rather pleased with that myself," Penny said smugly. "I've always found the post office a mine of information in rural places, particularly if it is run by a post mistress of uncertain years. This one was a gushing spring— very proud of the fact their local mayor was important enough to spend three days in Paris every month. I wonder what he does there."

"He used to be a lawyer in Paris at one time. Maybe he still has clients," Toby suggested. "Anyway, I'm too tired to do any more tonight. I suggest we all turn in for a few hours and tackle the problem of what to do about the new murder later in the morning."

"You expect me to stay here?" Penny said incredulously.

"Why not? There are enough sleeping bags to go around." Toby looked around him with a proprietorial air. "It's a very comfortable dungeon," he added defensively.

"But you know how you snore," she said accusingly. "I wouldn't get a wink of sleep, and I'm damned if I'm going to sleep on a cold stone floor when I have a perfectly comfortable bed waiting for me back at the inn."

"I'm not at all sure it's safe," he started to say, when there came a dramatic interruption. The door to the dungeon flew open, and the small figure of Francois Canard appeared, and bristling with rage.

"What insanity have you two young fools been up to now?" he snarled and, rushing over to Penny, he clasped both her hands. "My dear, dear lady, are you all right? The maid alerted me to the fact that your room was empty and the bed had not been slept in. When I found your purse on the floor and saw your car in the parking lot, well, I was afraid something like this had happened; that these two young idiots had found out the connection between you and the archaeologist and had acted in their usual irresponsible fashion.'' He glared ferociously at them. ''This is the end,'' he shouted. ''I am packing you both off to Nantes today!'' He turned back to her. ''I will never forgive myself for this, never! What can I possibly do to make it up to you?''

''Bringing Dr. Spring here was my idea,'' Toby managed to get in. ''You must be Francois Canard. How do you do? I am Toby Glendower, and this is my assistant, Paul Grandhomme. I'm afraid there have been some serious developments, and I thought it unsafe for Dr. Spring to remain where she was.''

''Unsafe! Under my roof?'' Canard looked as if he were about to burst with indignation.

''Uncle Francois—it's Yves,'' Nicole cried. ''He's been murdered. I think the people at the chateau found out about him and . . . and. . . .'' She buried her face in her hands and started to shake.

''Impossible!'' Canard was speechless, and Toby continued.

''Until we know more about the situation at the chateau, and knowing Dr. Spring was already involved there, I really did not want to risk putting her in danger.''

''Yves dead?'' Canard muttered dazedly. ''But why?''

''That is indeed the question,'' Toby's voice deepened into a growl. ''Whether it stemmed from his having discovered the drug-running activities of the people at the chateau, or his connection with your Nationalist movement, or some other source, has still to be determined. But our immediate problem is a rather gruesome practical one. We have not yet reported the finding of the body. Knowing the way Favet's mind works, I was going to try and keep Nicole and Alan uninvolved and have Grandhomme and myself 'find' it. But now Grandhomme tells me that Favet is equally certain we have been lying to him, and so it is highly likely he will arrest us, and that would also be unfortunate. At the moment we have not had time to come up with any good alternative ideas.'' He looked hopefully at Canard.

But the latter was still concentrating on the first part of his statement. ''Drug-running? From the chateau? Unbelievable!

Why did you say nothing of this to me?'' he demanded of his niece.

"We wanted to be sure," Alan said, avoiding his accusing gaze. "Everything has happened so fast . . . we thought. . . .''

"You *thought*—that will be a change certainly!'' the little man scoffed.

"About the body," Toby said firmly, bringing everyone's attention back to him. "I was thinking perhaps *you* could find it, Monsieur Canard.''

"They know I'm a Nationalist," Canard snapped. "And if Favet is as unreasonable as you say, and from my own brief brush with him I am quite prepared to believe it, he would probably arrest me.''

"Perhaps then you and Dr. Spring could find it together," Toby pressed. "As a supposed tourist, he would scarcely have grounds for suspecting her.''

"You may have something there," Canard said, with a sudden roguish twinkle. "We could go for a romantic stroll in the woods, eh, *chère* Madame?''

"Well, I'm game," Penny said absently. "But I think we should deal with something even more pressing than that first.''

"What's that?'' They both looked at her.

"If Yves Rouillé's death is related to the goings-on at the chateau, there is another young person in imminent danger—the one who smuggled him in, Patty Winton. We should try and get her out of there. Winton didn't strike me as the type of man who would liquidate his own niece, but with those other two involved. . . .'' She rubbed a weary hand over her eyes. "God, I'm so tired I can't think straight.''

Toby was equally tired, but a sense of urgency drove him on. "How did the setup at the chateau strike you?'' he persisted. "You're usually good at sensing the atmosphere.''

Penny yawned. "Basically innocuous, which is so strange in view of what we know. Winton strikes me as a loser who can't accept the fact and who has retreated into a crackpot ivory tower, and Jane Smith also struck me as semi-cracked, as if she too believed in all that gibberish he comes out with. Of course everyone else there is an unknown factor, but it is obvious they must be 'in' on the drug angle; whether for the greater good of 'Cosmic Consciousness' or for the money involved is hard to say until we find out more." She looked over at the two young people, who had quietly fallen asleep in each other's arms, and at the red-eyed Toby. Only Grandhomme, who was still quite happily swigging away at the cider, seemed at all alert. "Anyway, how about a few hours rest to revive ourselves? You can stay here if you like, but I'm going back to the inn with Francois."

"She will be quite safe with me," Francois Canard assured him frostily. "And we will return this afternoon."

But dramatic interruptions seemed to be the order of the day. This time the dungeon door was opened stealthily and a dark figure walked in, gun in hand; it was Shaun. They stared at him in amazement, an amazement that matched his own. Canard broke the startled silence. "What the hell do you think you are doing, O'Reilly? Put that gun down!"

"I heard strange voices and I. . . . What are you doing here?" Shaun spluttered.

"Never mind that." The raised voices had awakened the sleepers, who sprang to their feet at the sight of Shaun.

"Where have you been?" Nicole shrilled. "Do you know what has happened to Yves?"

Shaun's eyes shifted uneasily. "I went to Brest," he said. "I thought our people should know. I thought we could use some help."

"You went without consulting me!" Canard roared, flying into a tantrum.

"It seemed like a good idea. Everyone here is so embroiled I thought. . . ."

"And what did they think?" Canard asked furiously.

"They said the situation was too hot here for them to get involved; that you should handle it as best you can, but to keep them out of it." The second part of Nicole's question suddenly seemed to have penetrated, and a look of alarm crossed Shaun's face. "Don't tell me Yves has been arrested! I told him not to see Marie. I just knew she'd turn him in!"

With a quick glance at the others, Alan came to life. "You didn't explain much about that before you left," he said evenly. "What exactly did Yves have in mind to do?"

"I don't know what he was so anxious to see her about. He wouldn't say," Shaun replied. "I just know he was planning a meeting at their usual place."

"Where was that?"

"The spot they've been using since his father kicked him out of the house—the trysting oak, he called it, somewhere near the Dragon's Teeth." He looked at them curiously. "Why? Was he picked up there?"

"No, but someone did meet him there, and stuck a witch's dagger in his back," Toby said. "He's dead."

Shaun's reaction was unexpected. His eyes rolled back in his head, his pale skin turned a sickly green, and he slid to the floor in a dead faint.

CHAPTER 14

"And your story is that you were just walking through the woods and happened to stumble across the body?" Favet's ferretlike eyes flicked suspiciously from Penny to Francois Canard, standing shoulder to shoulder and looking, in these sylvan surroundings dappled by the late afternoon sunlight, rather like two slightly oversized representatives of the elf kingdom.

"That's right." After several hours sleep and a huge gourmet brunch cooked by her companion, Penny's pep was renewed and she was all set to do battle with anyone and everyone. A hasty postbrunch conference had resulted in a fabric of white lies which they fervently hoped would not come apart, but would give maximum protection to everyone in the group. "As I've already explained, we were taking a stroll. We were headed for the Dragon's Teeth, where Monsieur Canard's niece and her boyfriend, an employee of Monsieur Canard's, have been camping out, giving a helping hand to the man who is watching the site during the absence of the archaeologist."

"I wanted to discuss Pommard's program for the coming weekend with him," Francois put in, with a sly glance at the local police chief, who was standing silently by, a surly expression on his heavy face. "He sings folk songs at the inn."

"This Pommard is a relative of yours," Favet snapped at the policeman. "Why haven't you mentioned him?"

"A remote connection only," the police chief said. "I know nothing of him. I did not even know he was still here."

Favet turned his attention back to Penny. "And both of you claim not to know the murder victim?"

"I didn't say that," Francois said quickly. "I told you I recognized him as Judge Rouillé's son."

Favet grunted and muttered something to one of the local

constables, who had been diligently searching the environs of the trysting oak. Much had happened in the two hours since Penny and Francois had reported the grim discovery. The doctor had been summoned and had pronounced a rough estimate, pending autopsy, of time of death at about forty-eight hours previously; cause of death, a stab to the heart. There were no other marks of violence on the body. The two daggers had been tested but no fingerprints had been found, to no one's surprise. Penny had identified herself as an expert on witchcraft and had pointed out they were both ritual witchcraft objects, a statement which had caused Favet to look ready to commit murder himself. The body of the unfortunate Yves had been removed, and the next of kin notified. Thinking ahead to just such an eventuality, they had sent Shaun to lurk around the judge's house in Cormel to pick up on reactions there.

The temporary lull in the proceedings was brought to an end by cracklings in the underbrush and the appearance of the stocky Sergeant Auvergne, shepherding Grandhomme and the young couple before him. Favet immediately flourished the white-handled dagger under Grandhomme's nose. "You recognize this?"

"It looks like the one I reported to you as stolen from the henge burial." Grandhomme, who was still well fortified from his night's drinking, gazed unperturbed at his erstwhile tormentors.

"And this?" Favet held up the carved 'athame.'

"I have never seen that before."

"Account for your movements in the past fifty-six hours," Favet said.

"Movements?" Grandhomme echoed innocently. "I haven't made any. I have been at the henge—only not alone. After the unfortunate incident there three days ago, I thought it wiser." He looked blandly at the policemen. "These two young people kindly agreed to keep me company until Sir Tobias Glendower returns."

"And how long have you been there?" Favet wheeled on Alan.

"The past three nights and two days."

"All the time?"

"One of us has. I have been into Cormel for supplies and

to the inn to perform for Monsieur Canard's patrons. It is my summer job," Alan explained.

"And you have been staying in these woods all summer?" Favet said slyly.

"No, just the past three days. Before that we stayed at the Auberge du Dragon, but there is no longer room there."

"You knew the dead man," Favet said, accusingly.

Nicole was very pale, but she seemed in control of herself. "The sergeant here told us it was Yves Rouillé. Yes, we knew him. We were all students at Nantes University."

"He was a Nationalist," Favet snarled. "Are you two also? Come now, it's no use lying. I'll find out soon enough."

Penny began to perspire; he was getting on dangerous ground. They badly needed a diversion.

"We are proud to be Bretons," Alan said quietly. "All the students at Nantes feel that way."

"Oh, Inspector," Grandhomme chimed in. "You were concerned about the whereabouts of Sir Tobias Glendower. I have heard from him in Paris. . . ."

Favet's attention was diverted and Penny gave a silent sigh of relief. "Why didn't you inform me of this? You knew we were looking for him."

"It only happened last night," Grandhomme continued, a picture of aggrieved innocence. "Naturally I was going to let you know. Pommard here brought the message. Sir Tobias has been staying all along with Professor Latour of the Sorbonne."

Toby's alibi had been cooked up after he had been sneaked into Francois' private sanctum at the inn. He had plotted this particular little diversion over the phone with the convalescing Latour.

"He says he'll be back in the next day or two," Grandhomme went on. "But I have the number to call if you want to talk with him sooner. He's going to be very upset when he hears what's been happening."

Favet was looking increasingly frustrated. "Later," he said and turned back to the young couple. "And during the time you have so conveniently spent together at the henge, did you see or hear anything unusual?"

"No, except last night we heard a dog howling somewhere

in the woods," Nicole volunteered. It was the first truthful word that had been said, and it sounded odd.

"That damn dog again!" Pommard spoke uneasily, and Favet silenced him with a glare. "And?"

"And nothing. That was all."

"Not good enough. You admit Rouillé was a fellow student of yours; you must have seen something of him during the summer," Favet rasped. "Didn't you visit him at all in his home?"

Pommard intervened. "His father had barred him from the house," he whispered in Favet's ear. "Bad blood there. He wasn't living at home."

"Then we must find where he did live." Favet continued to glare at the young couple. "And if I find you two have been lying to me . . . !"

"I believe he was visiting his girl friend," Nicole replied. "He was friendly with Patty Winton, up at the chateau."

Damn, Penny thought, I wish she hadn't volunteered that. God knows what the smitten Yves had confided to the young girl, and if Favet got to her first with his bullying ways, it boded ill for the future of the young Nationalists.

Francois Canard was evidently thinking along the same lines, for he attempted another diversion. "Inspector Favet," he interrupted testily. "I have an inn to run and a dinner to cook. My guest and I have told you all we know and have done everything in our power to help you. I must ask that you let us return to the auberge without further delay."

"One moment!" Favet held up an imperious hand. "I will tell you when you can go." He turned back to Nicole. "And where was this Yves Rouillé staying all this time?"

"We never discussed it," she said honestly. "We just ran across him from time to time and chatted casually."

"Did you search them and their belongings?" Favet suddenly demanded of the sergeant, who nodded and said, "Nothing, nothing at all."

"What if I told you your friend had in his pocket a handful of joints? Would that surprise you? Was he into drugs? Was he a pusher? Was that why he was hanging around here? Come on—out with it!"

"I know nothing of it," Nicole said stiffly. "I know nothing of such things."

"Maybe a day or two in the lockup would refresh your memory," Favet growled.

Canard bristled. "Inspector, I will not stand by and see you browbeat my niece in this fashion. You heard your sergeant. You have no grounds whatsoever to make these stupid accusations against two innocent young people. And I warn you, if you dare arrest either one on this flimsy pretext, I shall have a lawyer on your back inside of an hour and I shall not rest until I have your discharge as well."

"Don't you dare threaten me!" Favet retaliated, but to Penny's amusement he completely backed off; he turned to the police chief. "We have delayed too long already with these foreigners in the chateau. You say you have seen Winton twice and that he cannot help us. I am not satisfied. We shall visit the chateau and interrogate everyone there. If you cannot gain entrance, as you claim, then get a search warrant from the judge. I will be in there before the day is out or know the reason why!"

That should send the balloon up with a vengeance, Penny thought. We've simply got to get that kid out of there before it's too late. "I wish your sergeant would take me to the police station," she stated firmly. "There I intend to contact the American Embassy and lodge a formal complaint with the French government over your treatment of me."

"But I haven't done anything to you," Favet said in amazement.

"You are detaining me here unnecessarily, you are ruining my vacation, and you are upsetting me by your bellicose manner," she complained. "Those are grounds enough."

"Well, all right. You can go. So can Monsieur Canard. But neither of you are to leave the district until I say so."

"Oh, so now you're threatening *me*." Penny was beginning to enjoy herself.

"Not at all, this is standard procedure in a murder case," he spluttered.

She sniffed expressively. "I have given you my statement; there is nothing further I can add to it, and that, so far as I am concerned, is that."

"And I must insist on taking my niece with me," Francois put in. "This has been a shock to her and I must consult with her mother concerning future action."

Favet evidently did not like the sound of that 'future action' so he repeated, "All right, she can go for the moment, but she too may not leave the area."

The three went off in Francois' gleaming Mercedes, leaving Grandhomme and Alan gazing wistfully after them. "So far so good," Francois said cheerfully as he headed back to the inn.

"Not so good. I have to talk to Patty before Favet does," Penny said. "Nicole, did you say there was a gap in the fence around the chateau? I wonder if I could get in there and get Patty out on the quiet. Unless I unleash my big guns, I haven't a hope of getting in at the front gate, and I don't think I dare do that until she's out of there."

Nicole looked dubiously at Penny's plump form. "Well, as I understand it from Yves, Patty used to squeeze through two of the railings that had been bent out of shape. She's very small and thin. Even he couldn't get through. According to Shaun, he had to climb in. I don't really think. . . ." She tactfully did not finish her thought.

"Could you take me there and show me the place? Perhaps among the three of us you can boost me over somehow."

"Dear lady, I simply will have to put together tonight's dinner," Francois said. "My assistant chef is good, but not that good. I cannot leave immediately."

"Then we'll have to sneak Toby out to help us and hope for the best."

Toby was more than a little wary of the project. "Even if you get in, what if they catch you snooping around?" he fussed. "They may harm you or they may call the police, and you'd have a hell of a time trying to explain it to Favet, given the mood he is in."

"Don't be silly, Toby. If there's one thing I'm sure about, it's that those people would never draw attention to themselves by going to the authorities. Besides, I've no intention of getting caught." Seeing the determined gleam in Penny's eye, Toby knew it was useless to argue, but there arose the further problem of transport. They dared not use the Jeep, which was officially in Paris, and Penny's Triumph was too small to accommodate the three of them. Perforce, Canard's Mercedes was once more pressed into service, Nicole at the wheel.

Parking its gleaming white bulk inconspicuously was no easy matter. By the time they had reached the orchard and were approaching the iron railings, shadows were already long and dark in the woods, though the sinking sun was turning the windows of the chateau before them into myriad fiery eyes. They found the bent railings close to a granite boulder, but it was evident that there was not the faintest hope of squeezing Penny's plump form through.

Toby looked up at the soaring spikes. "I don't like this. Even if we get you over with the aid of a rope, this place is in full view of the chateau. We can't see in, but they can damn well see us. I think you should wait until dark."

"And miss my dinner?" Penny said indignantly.

"It would have other advantages. They lock themselves away after dinner, remember? You'd have a clear shot at searching for her room."

"If the outside doors aren't all locked by then," she pointed out. "I can hardly go around throwing gravel up at all those windows waiting for the right head to pop out, can I?"

"She may come out," Toby replied. "Don't forget the dog. She often wanders around with it after the rest of the household are out of the way."

"If they are allowing her that much liberty any more. She may be penned up in there. Still . . ." Penny looked at the sunlit vegetable garden that stretched before them, offering little in the way of cover. "Maybe it would be better to wait a while until at least the fence is in shadow." They sat in silence, lulled by the drowsy summer sounds of the wood. Toby puffed contentedly on his pipe, while Nicole sunk into a state of miserable sef-recrimination. Penny felt for her, but knew better than to give comfort; in the girl's present condition, that would only end in tears and possibly hysteria. The time for tears would have to come later.

They all tensed as subdued cracklings in the wood signaled the cautious approach of someone through the overgrown orchard. A person materialized and Nicole let out a gasp. "Shaun! What on earth are you doing here?"

He leaped back in fright. "I . . . I . . ." he stammered and gulped. "What are you doing here? Has anything else happened?"

"Not yet, but it soon will if you don't explain yourself,"

Toby said. "You were supposed to be watching the Rouillé house."

"I was. I did. I couldn't find any of you, and I thought . . . well, it struck me after what happened to Yves that someone should tell Patty what's been going on. She's probably worried out of her skull by him disappearing like this. I thought she might come looking for him—and this is the way she gets out."

It sounded a bit thin to Toby, but he thought quickly. "All that is being taken care of, but now that you are here we can use you. First though, tell us what happened at the Rouillés'."

"Not a great deal. I was there when the police car came up and the judge rushed out all white and tight-looking and went off with them—to identify the body, I suppose. Word must have spread in the village, because little knots of villagers kept strolling by the house, some of them actually standing around and gaping at it. Marie almost came out at one point, but then, when she saw all the people, she went back into the house. Her face was all swollen from crying. Jacqueline Villefort arrived shortly after that, but she was only in there about fifteen minutes before Villefort came along, his face like thunder. They both came out together a few minutes later, neither of them looking at all happy with one another. Then the judge returned with the priest, and I heard some shouting through the open windows, but that stopped and nothing else happened. So . . ." he shrugged. "I got fed up and left."

"Well," said Toby, "now that you are here you can make yourself useful. Go over to the henge and see if Grandhomme and Alan are there. If they are, bring them back. We may need them. No need to hurry, we'll not be moving before dark."

Shaun looked inclined to argue, but Nicole put in, "Yes, Shaun, please! That'll be a great help."

After hovering uncertainly for a moment, he said, "Okay, Nicole. If you say so."

Penny waited until his footsteps had died away before asking, "Why did you do that?"

Toby grunted. "I'm not too sure of that young man, and if and when Patty does appear on the scene, I don't want him to hear what she has to say. If he gets back before that happens, I'll make sure he has something else to do away from here.''

''Look!'' Nicole exclaimed, a catch in her voice. A white-clad figure had emerged from a window to the far right of the building and was running swiftly away from it, using the tall-growing, staked-out runner beans as cover. It disappeared briefly out of sight as it reached the line of the fence, but within a minute came into view again, bent double and creeping along the inside line of the fence.

They drew back into the shadows as the person squeezed through the iron railings and stood up, revealing the small figure of Patty, her long fair hair in disarray over her face.

''Patty!'' Penny called softly and stepped out, causing the girl to shrink back against the railings with a faint shriek. ''We are friends, friends of Yves! Don't be afraid, my dear, we've come to help you.''

The girl looked frantically at them with wide eyes. ''Who are you?'' she panted. ''The police—they say he's dead—murdered.'' There was a desperate appeal in the thin voice. ''They are lying, aren't they? It's not so, it can't be so!''

''I'm afraid it is,'' Penny said gently. ''But we're here to see justice done and to help and take care of you, as he wished.''

The girl did not appear to hear her. ''I had to get away,'' she whispered. ''They've not let me out of their sight for days. When the police were finished with me, I ran, and they couldn't—didn't dare—follow. I have to get away,'' her voice rose. ''I ve got to get away!''

''Good. We'll help you. We've a car waiting. We'll take you to safety,'' Penny coaxed. ''And you can tell us all about it. Tell me, when you last saw Yves, what did he say to you?''

The girl came over to her and grasped her in painful intensity with her thin-bony hands. ''It's what I don't understand,'' she whimpered. ''The last thing he said to me was 'I'll be back for you, but don't worry, I know they couldn't have done it, so you'll be quite safe.' ''

''Done what?'' Penny prompted.

''Why, the murder,'' the girl said. ''The murder in the wood!''

CHAPTER 15

It took some time before anything like a coherent story could be drawn from Patty, who went in and out of a foggy daze, induced partly by the shock of the news and partly from the drugs she had been encouraged to take over the past several days. It was not just marijuana, which she admitted to smoking constantly, but Quaaludes and other pills as well, which her uncle had recently introduced her to. Since her rescuers did not dare call a doctor, they were obliged to fall back on their own limited knowledge of what to do. "Time, good feeding, and rest should bring her back to normal eventually," Penny opined. "At least I hope so. Luckily she seems like a strong kid and has a pretty good tolerance. Otherwise she'd have been a basket case long since, by the sounds of it. Winton ought to be shot for this."

They had brought her surreptitiously back to the inn and sneaked her up to Penny's room, where she was fed a substantial meal and put to bed. But what had appeared to jolt her back towards normalcy was the appearance of Nicole bearing gifts in the form of a pair of her own blue jeans, a T-shirt, and a sweater, which Patty scrambled into immediately with a thankful cry. They were several sizes too big for her, but she hugged them and preened before the mirror, the haze receding from her blue eyes. The men had departed, leaving Penny and Nicole to cope, and between them they managed to coax out of her what Yves had been up to during the time he was in the chateau. It came by fits and starts, but it began to add up to a coherent picture.

Late at night, when Patty was finally in a deep sleep, Nicole and Penny collected Francois and made for the ruins of the abbey, where the rest were waiting. Shaun was there, so Penny cocked an enquiring eye at Toby. He gave an imperceptible nod, and she sat down at the head of the wooden table and took out a notebook from her shoulderbag,

147

donned her glasses, and looked at them like a chairman of the board bringing a meeting to order. "Well," she said flatly. "If the story Patty has been telling holds up, there seems to be no possibility that any of the people at the chateau were involved in the murder of Armand Dubois.

"According to her, the day of the murder was a very fine, warm day . . ." Toby nodded corroboration, "so all that morning from 8 A.M. onwards the entire population of the chateau, herself and Winton included, were out in the garden, weeding, hoeing, and harvesting. The only exception was Jane Smith, who at about 10:30 A.M.—so far as Patty remembers—took off in the van to go marketing in Cormel and was back by the noontime break. And I think it unlikely, given the time factor and Toby's feeling that it would have taken two people or one enormously strong one to commit Dubois' murder, that she could have done all that. Furthermore, although Patty is not so sure where everyone was for the rest of the day, she says the work went on in the garden all afternoon until the supper break. That evening, she says, was one when the lights were on in the greenhouses until very late. She took the opportunity to slip out with the dog, who ran away from her. It was she you must have seen at the henge, Toby, because she says the dog did not come back until after midnight, and she had gone there because she knew the dog often visited it. Incidentally, she is very upset about her pet. It seems to have disappeared; she hasn't seen it in the last two days."

"Did she say whether she heard the dog that night?" Toby asked.

Penny frowned slightly. "One thing you have to realize is that I got all this in bits and pieces as she wavered in and out of her fog, and some of it does strike me as odd. After Hercules ran off, she tried to find Yves. He wasn't at the orchard, but there was another place they sometimes used to meet, closer to the sea where he camped from time to time."

"I know where that is," Alan said quickly.

"Well, she went there but he wasn't there either, so she thought she'd check a third place, near the road to the Sommelier farm. It was then she heard the dog, but she says something about it frightened her. She was heading for the henge when the crying stopped. She got really scared when she heard you, Toby, crashing after the dog, and ran all the way back to the chateau. It was then she saw six of them, the six including the three Americans, coming back from the tunnel.''

"She knew about the tunnel then?" Shaun said excitedly.

Penny shook her head. "No. This was one of the things she and Yves discovered in the short time he was there. She told him what I have just told you, and he got very excited and had her lead him to where she had seen them emerging. He had some plans with him, she said." Shaun nodded impatiently. "So they hunted around and found the entrance behind an ornamental fountain in the grounds, and they explored it. It came out at that beach you mentioned." She looked at Toby.

"La Haye beach?"

"Yes, that's it."

"And what was in the tunnel?"

"Nothing. Nothing at all. But she says Yves was very interested in all the footmarks he saw in the sand. She says she doesn't know why."

"And what did she say about the marijuana?"

Penny sighed faintly and shook her head. "The child is a nice enough kid but a bit on the blank side. She claims she knew nothing about the greenhouses and what was in them. It seems incredible, I know, but Winton had spun her some tale about how the greenhouses were where they practised advanced power techniques of the cult, and that they were full of dangerous vibrations to the uninitiated, hence she must keep away from them; and she seems to have swallowed it hook, line, and sinker. She didn't question the source of the pot, which her uncle handed out like manna from heaven."

"Did Yves tell her about it?"

"Apparently not."

"Sounds like she's having you on!" said Shaun.

Penny looked over at Nicole. "What do you think?"

Nicole ran a hand through her short-cropped curls. "I'd say she was speaking the truth," she said in exasperation. "She seems so incredibly dim about everything."

"So what happened after they found the tunnel? I am anxious to get some sort of time table on his disappearance," Toby said.

"They went back to her room for a while and smoked some joints. Then Yves said he'd better turn in because there would be a lot to do on the next day, but that must have been when he investigated the greenhouses. She cleared up one point that had been worrying me: how he made contact with his sister, Marie. To tell it in chronological order, the next morning, Patty had an unpleasant session with her uncle and Jane Smith, who accused her of having sneaked somebody into the chateau, based, unfortunately, on my slip of the tongue the day before. She was frightened, but stoutly denied it and thinks her uncle may have believed her. She did not dare go back to Yves until they were all busy at their meditation period, and she found him restless and very anxious about something. He told her the same thing he told Shaun— that he had to see his sister. Apparently there is a public phone on that little side road; a pretty peculiar place, but some farmer who is a noted miser and who was on the local council succeeded in having it installed several years ago at public expense. At that time he was about the only one to use it, but even he has one of his own now."

"Sounds like Sommelier," Toby interrupted.

"Probably, but Patty did not know his name. Anyway, Yves, while he was staying out in the woods, used to phone his home from there. If anyone but Marie answered he'd just hang up, but she usually did pick up, because they only have a daily maid and the judge is not usually there during the day. Then Yves would set a rendezvous with her at the trysting oak. She often used to slip him a little money and sometimes food on the sly."

"And on that particular day?"

"Patty was upset, she said, about her uncle going on at her, so Yves said he'd better take his things with him and push off because they might search the chateau. He said he'd meet her at their usual place that evening; that he hoped to lay his hands on some quick money, and that maybe they could go off together. She was so thrilled that she does not seem to have taken in much else he said, although she recalls something about having to square something with someone and that he had people to see."

"Besides Marie?"

"Yes. Then he asked her for some more pot for his friends,

which she gave him and which was still in his pocket when he was found. At that juncture the noon bell rang for the midday meal and she got panicky and left him. She claims she never saw him again; that when she went back that afternoon, his things were gone and so was he."

"That brings up an interesting point," Toby commented. "His knapsack and bedroll were taken from the chateau, but they weren't found at the trysting oak. Where are they?"

"I know several of the places he used to camp," Alan volunteered. "I could go and look."

"Good—as soon as we are finished here. What time were you supposed to meet Yves?" Toby looked at Nicole.

"Five o'clock. But, as we told you, when we went there, no Yves, no message." Shaun's eyes were suddenly hard as they looked over at her.

"Then I think we are safe in assuming that some time between noon and five of that day Yves met his end," Toby stated. "Obviously, the next order of business is to get hold of Marie Rouillé and see what she has to say. We may be able to narrow it down a lot more, depending when and if his meeting with her took place."

"It may be your next order of business," Penny said firmly, "but mine is to do something about Patty. That child needs medical care and, knowing who is in that chateau, I'm not going to risk keeping her around here. I thought I'd take her up to Paris and tell the American Embassy what's what. It seems she does have another relation she could go to—her mother's sister, who lives in Texas. Gareth Winton may be her legal guardian, but he is obviously an unfit one. Do you realize the child has not had an hour's schooling since she arrived here? I think they could probably break the guardianship on that alone. Winton has been sitting on about sixty thousand dollars of her money, too. In Paris she can stay with an old student of mine, Angela Redditch, whose husband is stationed at the British Embassy. You recall him, Toby? They were nearly blown up in Israel when we were out there."

"Well, if you think it's all necessary," Toby replied. "And if you are going to Paris you may be able to do something else to advance this case. Shaun here came up with a very interesting bit of information while we were waiting for you." He looked intently at Penny. "It appears that when he was in Brest he heard from the Nationalists there a very significant tale that had been passed on from their Paris contacts. An Arab diplomat—we'll leave the country out of it for the moment—got in his cups in a night club one night and was heard boasting that the nuclear power plant in Brittany would never be built; that he had someone big 'in his pocket.' The waiter was a Breton, so he paid attention. No names were mentioned, but the Arab kept repeating that the plant would never get off the ground and what they were paying to stop it was a real bargain. There was something about 'casting very little pearls before very little swine,' but enough to achieve their ends. So, reluctant as I am to admit it, it really does seem to indicate Favet was right up to a point and that Arab oil is somehow involved.''

"But Brittany is a big place," Penny protested. "He might mean someone in the state government."

"No, he specifically mentioned 'on the spot,' and when one of his fellow drinkers asked him if he meant the Dragon's Tongue, he just laughed and repeated 'on the very spot,' which would bring us back to Winton.''

"Who, on the face of Patty's testimony, cannot be involved in the murder," Penny pointed out. "How about Sommelier? He fills the bill, particularly in that rather significant passage about pearls before swine. After all, he is a pig farmer."

"Yes, that's true," Toby agreed uneasily. "But to an outsider, Cormel might also be considered 'on the very spot,' which brings in all the others. It could even be an oblique reference to the henge and whoever is doing the witchcraft there.''

Or someone who had so very conveniently been planted there, like Grandhomme, Penny thought to herself. Had Dubois and Grandhomme been co-conspirators? Favet had thrown out dark hints about Dubois' oil connections in Algeria, and he had access to sources closed to them. Grandhomme was from Algeria and was of unusual caliber for a drunken hobo. Yet, on Toby's knowledge, he could not have killed Dubois, so that seemed to be a dead end. Still. . . . "So what had you in mind for me to do in Paris?" she said out loud.

"Well," Toby looked thoughtfully at Canard, "I was rather hoping Monsieur Canard here would have some helpful suggestions. He knows a great many important people, and what we are after is someone who can get a line on bank accounts. Not a very easy task, I fear, but if we could just find someone who had recently become a lot richer. The starting point would be that Arab's bank account. Any payments from it down here or to another Paris bank to any of our principals."

"But we don't even know who he is!" Penny exclaimed.

"Oh, yes we do." Toby was a little smug. "That Breton waiter was a very smart man. The Arab was a regular customer and so he got his name and address from the credit card."

Canard cleared his throat. "It will be a little difficult for me to make arrangements at the inn and I will be unable to stay long, but I would be delighted to accompany Dr. Spring to Paris. Yes, I do have contacts who will be able to assist us, I think, but it may take time. It would help if we had a specific list of suspects."

"Up to a point we do," Toby returned. "Winton and Sommelier, both money-hungry; Villefort, with an expensive wife; Rouillé, with many money problems and yet who can suddenly afford one of your expensive dinners, M'sieur. Perhaps even Father Laval. . . ."

"The priest?" Penny exclaimed.

Toby shrugged. "Rather remote, I grant you, but he struck me as a thoroughly miserable man living a thoroughly miserable life, and with little hope for the future."

"How about Pommard? Why haven't you included him?" she demanded.

"Again an outside possibility, but he is so under Villefort's thumb and is, by all accounts, so lazy, I can't see him acting independently."

"Your list is a little chauvinistic, isn't it?" she said acidly. "I should think after all the cases we've been involved in, you might stop thinking of us as dear sweet creatures and add a few women to the list."

Toby looked faintly shocked. "But the method!"

"If the witchcraft angle is involved, you would not be dealing with one single woman but a group," she pointed out. "And a group would be perfectly capable of dealing with a small man like Dubois, or an unsuspecting lad like Yves Rouillé. So I would add Jane Smith—whom we know has a violent past. Jacqueline Villefort—who seems to be insatiable in her wants. Marie Rouillé—who, you've said yourself, is probably as frustrated as all hell. And even Madame Sommelier, 'the strongest woman in Brittany,' remember? Or, for that matter, it could be a male-female partnership. It does work, you know. Look at us," she grinned.

"Er—did you get anything from Patty on the witchcraft angle?" Toby asked weakly.

"Only this. Winton's group did do something at the henge on Midsummer's Day. Patty did not go, but says all the rest of them went, and she heard something about 'saluting the sunrise.' "

"Well, that would fit neatly enough. That was the period just before I arrived, when the henge was deserted. And Winton may have tumbled to the solar alignments," Toby said. "It has one axis oriented on the midsummer solstice. What did she have to say about the redheaded girl at the chateau?"

"She couldn't remember whether the girl was always shorthaired or not. Apparently, they have a general shearing session every now and then, though judging by the looks of the inmates I've seen, it isn't that frequent." She looked at her watch. "Good grief! I've lost another night's sleep. I think I'll have to have a few hours if we are going off to Paris. How about you, Francois?" He nodded and got up. "What are your plans?" she asked Toby.

"I am probably going to remain out of sight until you get back," he answered. "The rest have been doing a good job of finding out what has been going on, and I am depending on Nicole to set up a rendezvous with Marie Rouillé. She is more likely to be willing to talk to her, anyway."

They moved a little away from the group and Penny muttered in his ear. "There's one other angle you are probably thinking about but which in present company I did not wish to make an issue. That remark of Yves'—whom do you think he was going to get the money from? And who had to be 'squared'?"

Toby made a shushing motion. "I know, but not now and not here. One thing is for sure—someone in this company is a viper in the nest. But don't worry, I'll take care of it. Just keep a close eye on the girl. She may still be in some danger.

She knows too much and she doesn't realize it." He looked at her meaningfully. "Don't leave her alone with Canard at any time."

Now she was shocked. "You really think. . . ?"

He shrugged. " 'So may the outward shows be least themselves, this world is still deceived by ornament,' " Toby quoted softly. "Just be careful, Penny, be very careful."

CHAPTER 16

Penny had thoroughly enjoyed her battle with the American Embassy, who had been beaten back from "It is none of our affair" to "We will look into it in due course" to "We will certainly take some action" to "What are your suggestions, Dr. Spring."

The FBI man from the Paris field office, who had been summoned by the harassed diplomat she had managed to corner, had been plunged into deep gloom by the news of "Jane Smith's" and "Brother Tom's" presence in his bailiwick. "It was all so long ago," he sighed. "Getting convictions against such people now is all but impossible—look at the Hoffman case!"

"I thought murder cases were never closed," she said with asperity. "And in any case, I should think it would not look too well for the American image when it is disclosed—as it may well be any moment now—that two wanted American criminals have been involved in drug-running activities in France, and that you were aware of this."

"It will certainly have to be looked into now that you have brought it to our attention," he muttered, glancing helplessly at the equally gloomy diplomat.

"Anyway, that is your affair," she said briskly. "All I'm concerned about is the welfare and safety of this young girl. The sooner she is returned to the States, the better. I know the Embassy has ready access to telecommunication services direct to the States. Her aunt in Texas should be contacted and apprised of the situation. If she is willing to take care of her, that would be by far the best solution. The girl does have money of her own. Unfortunately it is all in the hands of the uncle. The Embassy should send her back and get the expense money out of him later."

"It's a very ticklish position, with Winton being her legal

guardian." The diplomat tried to reassert his authority. "And we have no funds at the Embassy to cover such contingencies."

"Well, you'd better find some fast," she snapped. "The girl has been neglected, drugged, and thrown into highly unsuitable company by this man. We feel she may be in some physical danger. At the moment she is staying with friends of mine in the British diplomatic community. I repeat, it is not going to look well for the American image in diplomatic circles here if it gets noised abroad that the British government has provided protection for a threatened American girl, while the American Embassy sat on its hands and did nothing. I expect some action on this."

"I will see what we can do," the diplomat said unhappily. "You do not happen to know if Winton has any funds in a Paris bank? Perhaps we could do something about attaching a portion of them to provide the costs of the trip."

"According to Patty Winton, her uncle did have her sign deposit slips to the Credit Lyonnais here in Paris. Part of her inheritance was in stock. Although she is a minor, they are in her name, so it is her own money."

"We'll look into it," the diplomat repeated.

"Good. Then I'll be back tomorrow to see that the arrangements are going forward," she said. "And while you're at it, you might also try and find out if any unusual sums have been credited to Winton's account recently, and let me know."

"We can't do that!" he said in quiet horror.

"Why not? It may clear him of suspicion of two very nasty murders that have occurred on his doorstep in Brittany and which I am investigating. On the other hand, it might indicate that he is the guilty party—in which case it would simplify your actions regarding the girl. And you would not want to obstruct French justice, would you?" she demanded. "He may also be involved with Arab interests to sabotage the French government's energy program." And with that Parthian shot, Penny took her leave of the two very dazed officials.

"You just have to be firm with these people," she informed Francois, who had taken her to lunch at La Coupole in Montparnasse. "One never gets anywhere by being at all nice to officials."

He was looking worried. "I'm not at all sure what we are getting ourselves into," he informed her, peering dubiously at the plate of langoustines in front of him. "I have made some enquiries, but I talked privately to a cabinet member, who is a friend of mine—he adores my Crème Bavarian aux Oranges— and he became very upset. It seems that for some time there have been suspicions that a very highly placed member of the government may be tied up with this Arab sabotage move- ment in the energy program. If this affair in Brittany is tied in with it and is uncovered, it might even bring the government down. We could be about to become highly unpopular."

"Does that worry you?" she asked in surprise. "I am so used to being on the outs with officialdom that it doesn't even concern me any more. After all, as a Breton Nationalist you must be fairly used to it, too."

"Luckily they tend to think of me as a great chef and not as a Nationalist," he said with engaging frankness. "But when all is said and done I am still a patriotic Frenchman. What is bad for La France is bad for me also."

"Surely it is not bad for France to rid itself of its rotten apples? If top level officials are in Arab pockets, the sooner they are uncovered and got rid of, the less damage will be done. And I think you will find," she added drily, "that if it is all connected and does go to high places, it will all be dealt with very, very quietly. You may not be given a Legion of Honor ribbon for your part, but they certainly will not blame you. It may even help your cause."

"I've already got a Legion of Honor," he said absently. "The prime minister of the time was from Normandy and I think it was for my 'Tripes à la Caen-Canard.' But you are probably right, *chère* Penny, so we will press on regardless. *Hélas*! It may take some time—the red tape involved is simply unbelievable! I can only stay one more day—the August flood is about to begin—but I will leave instructions that the information be given to you. Can you occupy your- self here?"

"Oh, I can occupy myself all right. In fact I'll pay a call on some colleagues in the Musée de l'Homme and see what's cooking in the French anthropological world. Who knows what I might pick up!"

"And no doubt you will be spending much time with Mam'selle Winton. Where is she, by the way?"

Penny fought down the suspicions Toby had planted in her

mind. "With friends of mine." She was equally casual. "But I have every hope of getting her out of France in the next day or so. That child is so muddled she scarcely seems to know her own name at times. It is shocking what drugs do to the human memory. I was so pleased to see your niece does not indulge in such things."

"My niece by marriage." He seemed preoccupied. "Her mother was my wife's sister. Made a poor marriage—no money to speak of. Since we had no children, my wife was always devoted to her. Yes, Nicole is a very dedicated and ambitious girl who knows what she wants of life."

"Is she related to the young man who is obviously so devoted to her? They look rather alike."

"Yes, I believe so." He smiled faintly. "When you have ties to the Dragon's Tongue, everyone sooner or later is related to everybody else. What is the term you Americans use? 'Kissing cousins?' I believe they are that. Yes, Alan is a nice lad, but I am not sure he is strong enough to manage her—and a little lazy too. It seems to run in the Pommards." He grew quiet.

"Well, I hope they manage to stay out of trouble." Penny applied herself to a plate of 'papillon' oysters. "But then," she comforted herself, "Toby will see to that."

Her words were being echoed to the sound of pounding surf. Toby stood in the ruins of the abbey, a brisk southwest gale teasing his silver hair into flying strands. "Try to avoid being seen," he was saying. "And stay out of trouble in Cormel. You understand what I want you to ask Marie? Nothing to be said about the witchcraft until you have found out about the meeting with Yves."

"Yes, yes, I understand all that." Nicole was snappish with impatience. "You don't have to keep on repeating things. I'll be off now."

"Hadn't you better wait for Alan to get back? He's out hunting for Yves' things in the woods."

She raised her eyebrows at him. "No, I don't need Alan holding my hand. He would just be in the way."

"But how are you going to get into Cormel?"

"I'll borrow the assistant chef's motorbike." She gave him a tight smile. "He often lets me use it—thinks it gives him an 'in' with my uncle. See you!"

"I certainly hope so," Toby muttered and returned to the cosiness of the crypt.

A short while later, Alan came breezing in, a triumphant smile on his face. "Found them!" He held up a knapsack and the bedroll. "He had stashed them in a place on the beach where we both camped together about a month ago. There's something here I think you'll find interesting." He extracted a dog-eared student's notebook from the knapsack and brought it over to the table. "Here," he pointed. Under a date which Toby recognized as being that of Dubois' murder, Yves had listed the cult members, all of whom had been methodically crossed off, save Jane Smith. Next to her name was a small query and the note 'not much time.'

"Looks as if Yves was doing his own deducting," Alan said.

Toby grunted and read on. Underneath was another list: Sommelier, Villefort, Jane Smith again, Pommard, and Jacqueline. There was a series of brackets beside the names, linking Villefort and Jane Smith, Jane Smith and Pommard, Pommard and Jacqueline, and Jacqueline and Sommelier, and underneath them a note heavily underscored: "*Ask Marie.*"

"I wonder why he did that," Alan said, leaning over Toby's shoulder and breathing hard. "Bracketing all those together like that."

"Umm. No idea. I wish Nicole had waited though," Toby rumbled.

"She's gone already?" Alan sounded surprised. "She said she was going to wait for me."

"You can come here. My father's in Crozon—he'll be gone all day. I'm alone in the house. Come round to the back." Marie's voice trembled: "I hoped you would call. I must talk to you." She cradled the phone and stood looking at it with unseeing eyes, running her hand nervously over the back of her short-cropped red hair. Her hand went to the phone again, then drew back, and she ran out of her father's study into the old-fashioned kitchen. She gripped the edge of the stone sink with such intensity that her knuckles showed white and gazed out of the window at the formal garden, her lower lip caught in her teeth and her eyes full of tears. These she brushed hastily away as a slim figure slipped past the window, and she went to unlock the back door, relocking it again carefully after Nicole had come in. "Did anyone see you?" she asked anxiously.

"No, I don't think so." Nicole looked her over with a critical eye. "You're looking terrible. We have a lot to talk over."

"I've been half out of my mind. Do you want something to drink, or shall we go into the parlor?"

"No, nothing for me."

Seated on the stiff, old-fashioned fauteuils of the parlor, they looked at one another in silence for a minute, then Marie burst out. "What did Yves want to see me about?"

"I was hoping you'd tell me." Nicole was grim. "You didn't see him?"

"No . . . I . . . no." Marie gulped and shook her head.

"It might help if you tell me exactly what did happen that day."

"Yves called and said he wanted to see me; that it was important; that there were some things he wanted me to find out and that he couldn't do it," Marie said.

"Did he say where he was calling from?"

"No. I assumed it was that call phone he used to use on the chateau road. He sounded upset. Father was home that day, so I did not dare say much, because I was afraid he'd come in at any minute. I told Yves that. I said I would try to get away but that it wouldn't be easy."

"What time did he call?"

"It was just after one. I was clearing the things off the dining room table after lunch and father was in there finishing his wine."

"Did he hear you?"

"No, I don't think so. As soon as I heard Yves' voice, I shut the study door."

"What time were you supposed to meet him?"

"I said I'd try to get there by four, but to go to the oak and wait. He said to make it earlier if possible because he had to meet someone else on the other side of the wood."

"That would have been Alan and me," Nicole interrupted. "We had a rendezvous for five o'clock, which he never kept. What time did you go?"

"I didn't. I couldn't get away. Father suddenly decided he

wanted some typing done—some law article he was writing. I tried to get out of it, but he was in one of his moods, so. . . ." She shrugged helplessly.

"Did you talk about anything else?"

"I asked him if he needed money, that I could let him have a little. He said no, that from now on he hoped the shoe would be on the other foot and that he could give me some. He muttered something about some good coming from all this bad, which I didn't understand. I asked him what he'd been doing, and he laughed and said he was one up on my dear friend, Jackie; that he'd been staying in the chateau, which was more than she would ever do."

"And is she?" Nicole asked. "Is Jacqueline Villefort a friend of yours?"

"Yes, she is." Marie's tone was defiant. "Yves never liked her, he was always poking fun at her, but she's been a good friend to me; the only one who made this damned hole bearable. Yves could never understand that and Patrice is just as bad—he's so jealous. She's as bored as I am by the whole dreary setup."

"You didn't tell her this, did you?"

"No!" The reply was a little too swift, a little too vehement, and Nicole scented evasion, but let it go for the moment. Instead she asked casually. "Did Yves ask you about your hair?"

"My hair?" Marie's face took on a pinched look. "What about my hair?"

"Look, Marie, normally this would be none of my business, and, believe me, I sympathize with your lot here deeply, but we have to get some answers to Yves' death and get them fast, so let me lay a few facts on the line for you. Somebody has been monkeying around up at the Dragon's Teeth, and somebody—maybe the same, maybe not—murdered that government man. During Yves' stay at the chateau, he more or less proved that nobody up there could have been involved in either matter. So that means it is somebody local. The only thing we're positive about is that one of the people involved up at the henge had hair the exact color of yours. We've got to find out who it was. This may have nothing to do with the murders, but we still have to find out who, to clear the ground. So if you have been fiddling around with witchcraft, for heaven's sake tell me!'' The minute she said "fiddling'' she knew she had made a mistake. Marie's face became tight and closed. "As you say, it's none of your business, Nicole.''

"But it is now,'' she cried. "Marie, don't you realize? Yves was killed by a witch's dagger, and that white-handled knife, which was formerly planted at the henge, was right there lying on his breast when he was found. Don't you want his murderer caught? It may have been someone involved in this witchcraft who wanted to silence him.''

Marie had gone very white. "No,'' she whispered. "No, that's just not possible, I know it isn't.''

"Then if you know, you have to tell me,'' Nicole said. "Don't you see that?''

"Some things are sacred and beyond your understanding,'' Marie faltered.

"Life is sacred, and Yves' was taken from him. That's what I understand.'' Nicole flared.

"No—it just can't be that.''

"Then if you know, tell me!''

"I can't. Oh dear God, what am I to do?'' Marie buried her face in her hands and started to sob.

Nicole had an urge to shake her until her teeth rattled, but restrained herself and said gently, "For Yves' sake, you must, otherwise his death will be meaningless.''

"The witchcraft had nothing to do with it,'' Marie's voice came muffled through the sobs. "It's just someone trying to make it look that way.''

"Then you were involved,'' Nicole pressed. "Please, Marie, you have to explain.''

Marie's head came up and she looked at Nicole defiantly. "There are powers you don't understand. It was important that the henge stay where it was; important to us all. It is the Luck of Crozon. Jackie said that where Patrice and my father had failed to save it, we would succeed. In the past our ancestors were *sages-femmes* in these parts. We had the power. I have it on both sides—the Rouillés as well. . . .'' She did not finish that thought. "So we did what had to be done. We aren't responsible for what has happened since.''

"You mean Yves . . .?'' Nicole was appalled.

"No, no! I keep telling you, that has nothing to do with it.''

"Tell me then."

Marie gulped. "That day when Yves rang up and my father was being so difficult, I called Jackie to come over and help me get out of the house, so I could go to him. I had to tell her why."

"Then she could have . . ." Nicole started excitedly, but Marie almost snarled. "Hear me out, damn it! She came right over; that was about half an hour after Yves called, but my father was firm. He said that when I had finished, I could go shopping with her. So she stayed, hoping he would go. He did—about 3:30—but I was nearly finished by that time so, for the sake of peace later, I finished up. I walked with her to her house in case anyone was watching, then she took me in the car and dropped me off on the track near the trysting oak. It was about 4:30 by that time. She said she'd wait and take me back. I walked in and . . . and. . . ." She broke down again and sobbed into her hands. "He was there under the tree—dead. I touched him and he was cold, so cold . . . I did not see how, but I did see the knife just lying on him. I was so shocked I ran back to her screaming. She was as terrified as I was—so we drove away. We drove all the way to the beach and . . . and when we had both stopped crying and shaking, she said someone was trying to frame us; that we should not tell a soul about any of it. And you see someone is. She couldn't be involved, she was with me the whole time."

Nicole was trying to digest all this at a gulp. "And no one else was involved in this witchcraft business with you?" she questioned.

Marie swallowed hard and shook her head. "No one—just us."

"And it was your hair in the henge?"

"It was hair from both of us," Marie said proudly. "We cut each other's and plaited them together."

"Then who took the things away?" Nicole asked.

Marie looked frightened. "I don't know," she whispered. "Until I saw the knife on Yves, I thought it was still in the henge."

"So somebody else had to know."

"I don't know who," Marie whispered. "What am I going to do?"

"For the moment nothing. Do nothing," Nicole said firmly. "And don't tell anyone, not even Jackie, you have talked to me. All right? We'll see everything is sorted out, never fear. And I'll keep in touch. Don't worry, Marie, we'll pin it down now, you'll see." She was in a hurry to be gone. "You mustn't blame yourself, it's not your fault."

As she emerged from the back gate, she was startled by a figure emerging from the lilacs behind the house. "Oh, it's you, Alan," she gasped. "You startled me!"

"You did not wait for me, so I was waiting for you. Did you get anything?" he asked eagerly.

"Yes. Quite a lot." Hastily she filled him in on the high points.

"We'd better get back to the old boy right away with this," he said.

"You go on then, I have to go to the post office and get this letter off to my mother. She's all upset and screaming for me to come home. God knows what Uncle Francois told her, but I'd best calm her down."

"Oh, all right," he said reluctantly. "See you back at the abbey then?"

"Okay." They parted company.

She had finished her errand and was just emerging from the post office when her path was blocked. Inspector Favet, Sergeant Auvergne at his elbow, stood before her, a triumphant grin on his face. "Nicole LeBrun," he said, "You are to accompany us to the police station, and I should warn you that anything you say may be used in evidence against you. Acting on information received, in the name of the Republic of France, I have a warrant for your arrest for complicity in the murder of Yves Rouillé. The jig is up, my Nationalist friend! We'll have the rest of you terrorists by tonight!"

CHAPTER 17

"Nicole will give it to you verbatim when she gets here, but that's the essence of it," Alan said excitedly. "Taken in conjunction with Yves' notebook, what do you think it all means, Sir Tobias?"

"A good question," Toby ruminated. "On the face of it, we have two bored women playing at witchcraft up at the henge. If we assume Marie is telling the truth, she is out of it so far as Yves' murder is concerned, and so is Jacqueline Villefort. But it is also evident that, apart from Marie, only two other people could have known definitely where Yves was going to be that afternoon and when—Jacqueline and the judge, if he had overheard all or part of that telephone conversation. He left the house a good hour before the two women, so he could have made it to the wood very easily."

"But his own son!" Alan exclaimed in quiet horror.

"His estranged son," Toby pointed out grimly. "We'll have to find out where the judge was in that time period. However, I think it far more likely that Jacqueline Villefort, while having an unbreakable alibi herself, passed the information on to someone else. She had half an hour before she came over to the Rouillé house. Plenty of time to make a quick call or . . ." he paused significantly ". . . to tell her husband. There is the third, and to my mind least likely, possibility that someone spotted Yves and followed him to see what he was up to. That stretches probability pretty thin, because it would mean that same person was handily carrying around the witchcraft objects. This brings us back to the other point Marie's testimony clearly shows—somebody else, possibly in cahoots with Jacqueline, knew about the witchcraft activities and moved the ritual objects from that grave. Somebody who, possibly in the first murder but undoubtedly in the second, wanted to make quite sure that these two women were implicated by association with the objects and therefore would (a) be silenced and (b) would potentially be in our Mr. X's power. Now this would seem to rule out Villefort, who is apparently devoted to his wife. On the strength of Yves' list—and we have no idea what he had in mind when he made it—we have the interesting bracketing of Pommard and Jacqueline. Plus, we cannot rule out Sommelier and Jane Smith, who live close enough to the henge perhaps to have seen our witches at their nocturnal capers.''

"What about the stone over the grave?'' Alan objected. "Jane Smith couldn't have moved that by herself, could she?''

"No, but she could have with the assistance of Brother Tom, or even Winton.''

"But how could they have possibly known about it? I mean, they were all locked up in the chateau most of the time.''

"True, but Patty wasn't. In her nightly wanderings with the dog, she may have seen something in one of her drug dazes that she subsequently let drop and alerted them. A remote eventuality, I grant you, but possible.''

Alan sighed. "It doesn't seem to get us a whole lot farther, does it?''

"Oh, I wouldn't say that. I think it has moved us a whole lot nearer to bringing the various threads together. It has given us some definite avenues to explore, and coupled with what I hope Dr. Spring turns up in Paris, it should lead finally to the right path. Anyway, it is high time I got back into the action. My gear is all packed, I think I'll be getting back to Morgat.''

"Nicole is certainly taking a long time,'' Alan said uneasily. "She should have been back by now. I think I'll wait here for her.''

"You'll be over at the auberge working tonight?''

"Yes.''

"Well, if anything comes in from Dr. Spring, would one of you contact me? She doesn't know I'm out in the open again. Where's Shaun?''

"He went into Cormel to see what he could pick up about Favet's raid on the chateau. I imagine Favet's got them all under lock and key by now for the pot-growing, if for nothing else. I wonder if that will mean Villefort will get the chateau back after all." He broke off. "Speak of the devil!"

The door had opened and Shaun came in, perplexity on his raw-boned face. "If that doesn't beat everything!" he burst out. "Do you think Yves could have been having us on?"

They gazed at him blankly. "What do you mean?"

"I saw Jane Smith in Cormel doing the marketing as usual. So I asked around. One of the constables is a chatty sort and tells everything to the whole village. And Favet searched the chateau yesterday—greenhouses and all. He didn't find a bloody thing!"

"What!"

"It's the gospel truth! In fact, Winton has him all het up looking for Patty. Favet has scrubbed them off his list of suspects and thinks Patty may be victim number three."

They looked at one another in consternation. "How the devil. . .?" Toby started and then exploded. "The tunnel! That must be the answer. They must have anticipated a visit from the police and moved the plants to the tunnel. Come on!"

"Where are we going?" Alan asked.

"To La Haye beach. We have to find the other end of that tunnel."

"What about Nicole?"

"Leave her a note," Toby said impatiently. "Come on, we simply have to nail Winton now or he may get off scot-free, and Dr. Spring and Canard might be in serious trouble for having spirited Patty away. We have to get proof!"

They piled into the Jeep and lit out for the beach, which could be reached from the land side only by a difficult scramble down the rocky cliffs. The small, crescent-shaped beach was tucked between deep granite spurs, which stuck out into the ocean like protecting arms. "At least we won't have a large area to search," Toby observed.

"No," Alan panted, sliding on the slippery rocks. "It is almost certainly in one of those caves you see at the base there. This beach is hardly ever used. For one thing it's too damn difficult to get to, and for another the sand is completely covered at high tide, so people can get trapped on it."

"Hmm, by the looks of it we'd better put a move on then. The tide is coming in," Toby grunted, as they arrived, breathless and bemired at the base of the cliffs. "Let's split up, it'll save time. Whoever finds it, give a yell to the others."

They crossed the wet sand, the breakers crashing ominously on their heels. In the second cave Toby hit pay dirt. The entrance of the tunnel was well camouflaged by the cave narrowing down to what appeared to be an impossibly narrow cleft, but just before the cleft a fissure opened out to the left and a big boulder almost masked the low rounded tunnel behind it. Toby stooped and shone his flashlight to reveal a flight of rough steps disappearing into the gloom. He bellowed "I've found it!" which sent reverberations thundering off the rocky walls.

The two young men appeared together at a dead run.

"Back here!" Toby called and began to climb the steep stairs. The stairs ended and a tunnel, which was only an uncomfortable 5½ feet high, stretched away into darkness ahead of him. Bending low, Toby played his flashlight up ahead as Shaun and Alan crowded eagerly in behind him; the impression was that of a miniature jungle. On both sides of the tunnel, with only a narrow footpath left between, stood rank upon rank of healthy looking marijuana plants, neatly potted. "Eureka!" he breathed and fumbled at his camera bag. Shaun tried to push past him, but Toby stayed him with a restraining arm. "Aren't we going to explore it?" Shaun asked indignantly.

"No." Toby pointed the light at the pathway, which showed the imprint of sandaled feet. "We need the evidence intact for Favet, not messed up with our own footprints." He took out the Polaroid that Penny had brought him from one of her American forays and which he normally eschewed as being too gadgety; now it was a godsend as he quickly snapped a whole roll of shots showing the footprints, the plants, and the general setting. "All right, let's get out of here."

"Is that all we're going to do?" Shaun said, in disappointment. "Aren't we going to see where it comes out?"

"Yves told us that. And I've no intention of being stuck in here until the next low tide." He shone the light towards the opening to show the waves pounding almost to the entrance. "As it is we are going to get a dousing." He tucked the prints safely in an upper pocket and waded out. By the time they had scrambled back up the cliff, the three were not only wet, but liberally plastered with mud.

"Now what?" Shaun panted as they reached the crest, while Alan gazed anxiously around.

"Still no sign of Nicole," he said. "I don't like this. Where can she have got to?"

"The first thing I'm going to do is go back to the inn as planned," Toby wheezed. "Clean up and get into some dry clothes. I advise you to do the same."

"I'm going back into Cormel," Alan said. "I have to find Nicole."

"No, don't. Go back to the abbey and wait for me there." Toby, who was a little worried himself, tried to appear calm. "As like as not you'll find her there, but I want you all to keep out of sight as much as possible until I find out back at the inn how the land lies, and I go to Favet with this information. Chances are he has probably checked up on all of you by this time and I don't want him to nab you. To take the heat off, I intend to set him after Winton and then stall until we get some more information from Paris."

"But . . ." Alan started to protest.

"No!" Toby was firm. "We still have a lot to do, and I don't want things complicated by having any of you taken out of action, however temporarily." He detoured back by the abbey and watched them until they had disappeared into the ruins, then turned the Jeep towards Morgat. Slipping unobtrusively into the inn and up to his room, he luxuriated in a hot bath, changed, and, feeling a new man, descended to the crowded bar. The loud buzz of conversation stopped dead on his entrance, and the landlord hurried out from behind the bar where he had been serving. "You're back!" he stuttered. "We were beginning to think you had left us."

"No—just went up to Paris for a few days. Didn't Grandhomme tell you?"

"Well, yes—but we thought with all that's been happening . . . er. . . . What's your pleasure?" The landlord struggled to recover his composure.

"A tankard of cider. And what has been happening?"

He was bombarded on all sides by accounts, in varying degrees of inaccuracy, of Yves' murder, Favet's abortive raid on the chateau, and the lack of progress on the Dubois murder.

"Seems to have done the trick though," said one incautious local. "I don't see any other government men down here about the plant, do you? Scared off they are."

Toby sensed a profusion of undercurrents in the crowded room. There was a certain sense of relief, but there was anger here also—anger bottled up and seething.

"That's one thing, but how about the boy?" another growled. "One of our own. Somebody's got to pay for that and pay quick. If you ask me those weirdos at the chateau are behind it. Just because Favet didn't find anything there doesn't mean to say there's nothing to find. He couldn't spot his hand in front of his face, that one! We ought to do something about it ourselves, that we should. Have 'em out of there and shake it out of them." There was a low rumble of assent from a large portion of the crowd.

"Does Favet still have his headquarters here?" Toby asked, when he could get a word in.

"No. He's moved in on Pommard. Can't think what's come over Pierre. He's all buttering him up now," the landlord grumbled. "He better remember he's going to have to go on living here after that lot clears out—if he knows what's good for him! If you ask me, Villefort's none too pleased about it either."

"There's a lot of things Villefort wouldn't be pleased about, if he had his eyes open," someone added and chuckled significantly. There were a few answering laughs, but more heads shook in warning disapproval, with sidelong glances at Toby. So they knew something—probably about Jackie, he thought, but what? He didn't feel the mood of the group was right for probing questions. Instead he drained his tankard and said, "Well, I'd best be off to Cormel then—I hear Favet has been asking after me." He turned to leave, but as he did so the door to the bar parlor swung open and Jean Sommelier came rushing in. "Favet's made an arrest for the murders," he shouted, then stopped dead as he saw Toby. "You!" he gasped. "You came back. Well, it looks as if your precious henge is safe, at least for a while." His normally red face was an unpleasant mottled bluish-red and he was panting for breath.

"Steady, Jean!" Someone spoke from the crowd. "You look all in. Who has the inspector nabbed?"

"A girl from Nantes." Toby's heart sank into his boots. "With the chateau people out of it, Favet's going hell-bent after the Nationalists. Says that they killed Dubois and then murdered the Rouillé boy because he was backing out—had left the group and was about to blow the whistle on the whole Nationalist setup here. I heard it from that sergeant. Favet has a couple of other warrants out, too. Says he'll have the lot of 'em by nightfall." Jean stamped over to the bar and stood there, grasping at his heart. "Give me a cognac."

Ten thousand hells, Toby thought, this has really torn it! He stood rooted to the spot with indecision. Should he try to warn the others at the abbey? His mind raced, but looking at Jean's distraught face he came to a sudden decision.

"A mistake has been made," Toby barked. "A mistake which I think you realize, by the looks of you. So I want to ask you one question, Sommelier, and please give me an honest answer, for a great deal hinges on it. Where were you between 1:30 and 5 o'clock in the afternoon four days ago?"

Jean said nothing, but gazed at him through narrowed eyes.

Then a voice spoke from the crowd. "He was with us." Three burly men shouldered their way through the throng and took up protective positions around the farmer, frowns on their weatherbeaten faces.

"All that time?"

"All that time."

"And where were you and what were you doing?" Toby asked.

"That's none of your damn business," one growled.

Toby's temper flared. "It is my damn business," he roared. "I happen to know those young people are innocent of the boy's murder. What is more I can damn well prove it but, if I do, it might mean the real murderer gets away scot-free. I may be wrong, but I don't think any of you want to see people railroaded just because they happen to be Breton patriots." There was a rumble of assent from the room. "But in order to see my way clear I need an answer to that question." He looked hopefully at the quartet of men, but they remained silent. A flash of inspiration came to him. "Was it to do with the Lammasghal?" One of the group gave an involuntary exclamation. "Was that it?" Toby demanded. "Because if so, for God's sake tell me! Don't you see what it means?"

"No, we don't," one snarled. "And if you want to stay around here, you'd better learn not to talk about things like that that are no concern of yours."

Jean's breathing had been easing and he looked at Toby shrewdly. "I see what it means and I know what you are after. You want to be quite sure I had no hand in the Rouillé boy's murder, isn't that it?"

Toby said nothing, but gazed steadily at him.

"All right—you win. I was at the farm all that afternoon—with them." He jerked his head towards his circle of protectors. "We were locked in the barn—for the first pressing. It has to be done in stages, you know."

"And the final pressing is on Lammas Eve—tonight?" Toby was guessing.

Jean nodded, an ironic smile playing about his mouth. "So you still had me on your list of suspects, even though I was with you when Dubois was murdered. That doesn't speak very highly of your opinion of me."

"When the stakes involved are as high as the ones being played for here, no one is above suspicion," Toby said. "Do you swear to this?" he looked enquiringly at the silent men.

"He was with us all right," one growled, "but if you dare tell Favet any of this. . . ."

"I have no intention of doing any such thing. I fully recognize the sanctity of the brewing rites," Toby said stiffly. He turned his attention back to Jean. "And you did rather force yourself on my attention as to the time you were at the henge that morning."

The same tight smile stayed on Jean's face, which had regained most of its natural color. "You know a lot about us, but you don't know everything. I don't suppose this would mean anything to you, being a man of science." There was a slight edge of sarcasm to his voice. "But one does not get to be a maker of the Lammasghal merely by being a good cider-maker. I am what you might call a psychic. Ask the people here. They will tell you. I knew there was danger around that morning—danger to me. I did not know how or why, but I knew it was there and that I had to be with someone; that someone, for better or ill, was you.'' He appraised Toby. "Let me tell you something else. You haven't been to Paris at all, have you? You have been hereabouts all the time."

Toby nodded. "Yes. I have been investigating undercover, aided by the very same young people Favet is after."

"So now, if you are convinced I am out of it," Jean continued dryly, "where does it leave you? What are your plans?"

"I have in my pocket evidence that should make Favet at least look in another direction," Toby said carefully. "However, I am virtually certain that it is not the direction in which the murderer lies. Before this is over, I will need a lot of local support from you all, because some of the things that will be revealed may well rock the fabric of life on the Dragon's Tongue to its very foundations. I think, in spite of that, you will help me because, as you have said . . .'' he looked around the silent circle of faces ". . . one of your own—a boy who was guilty of nothing but having a too-enquiring mind—has been killed. And for that, justice must be done. Are you with me?" There was an uneasy murmur of assent. "Then," he sighed, "I must be on my way."

"To do what?" Jean was blunt.

"To put this evidence before Favet—and then to visit Judge Herve Rouillé," Toby said heavily. "The field narrows—it narrows fast."

CHAPTER 18

Toby's paternal instincts got the better of him. Regardless of the rashness of his course, he rushed back to the abbey to warn the two young conspirators still at large. The crypt was empty and dark, and on lighting the lamp, he found evidences of a hasty exit. Knapsacks and bedrolls had disappeared and Yves' notebook had been left lying open on the table. He took the notebook and made a cautious approach to the Auberge du Dragon, fearing the worst. The demoralized staff there informed him that it hadn't happened yet, but probably would at any moment. An incautious constable had returned the assistant chef's bike to him, with the unwelcome news of Nicole's incarceration and the report that Favet was after Canard. Alan had been at the inn at the time and had taken off, in the words of the desk clerk, "like a meteor bent on destruction." This did nothing to lift Toby's spirits, although the young desk clerk's common sense earned his approval.

"I tried to contact the boss in Paris—to head him off from coming back to this mess," the latter confided. "But he had already left. If only we could somehow contact him en route!"

"To whom did you talk?"

"That lady guest he went up there with."

"Good—then get me her number. It's urgent I talk with her, and if Favet and his men turn up while I'm on the phone, stall them until I can get out of here." He retreated to Canard's private study and with considerable relief contacted the peripatetic Penny, to whom he quickly related the latest disaster.

"If you have anything that could help," he begged. "I have no idea where those two young idiots have gone off to now, but I'm about to throw Winton to the wolves in the hopes of gaining some time. Canard will just have to take his chances, since there appears to be no way of heading him off. Among other things, they'll probably arrest him for kidnap-

177

ping Patty Winton, and you won't be in any too rosy a position either.''

"Not to worry," Penny sounded cheerful at the prospect of battle. "I put Patty on a plane to the States this morning, so she's safely out of it all. She left behind a sworn statement at the Embassy that should let us off the hook. I had to lean on the Embassy a bit, but—bless their hearts!—when you get the old wheels moving they do come through in style. The FBI man is sending someone down about *our* two terrorists, and in general they are stirring things up in a highly satisfactory manner. Also, I might be able to head off Francois, who got a late start. He finds it hard to leave my fascinating side," she added impishly, eliciting an outraged grunt from Toby. "Anyway, we stopped at a very nice inn run by a friend of his to have lunch on the way up, and he was planning to contact the same man on the way back, so I'll send a message to him there. His contacts haven't come through with a thing up here yet, but the Embassy has found some interesting stuff on Winton. I'm not sure it is what you want to hear though. Tell me, when was the power plant scheme for the Dragon's Tongue first discussed?''

There was a brief pause while Toby flipped through his notebook. "Two years ago. Villefort managed to hold things up for a year on one pretext or another, and then it has taken that much longer to clear up all the legalities about the land and contracts.''

"Hmm. That's what I was afraid of. Well, the Embassy did find that Winton has had considerable annual deposits going into his accounts here, but that's been for six years, long before the power scheme was an issue. The amounts are not as large as you would expect from a successful drug-running operation, but I strongly suspect that if Jane Smith's or Brother Tom's bank accounts could be found and dug into, they would show similar deposits. I think this may have been a cooperative adventure in all senses of the word.''

"And there have been no additional payments from any other sources over the past two years?" Toby queried anxiously.

"For the past three years the amounts have increased by a few thousand dollars, but that may reflect the rising profits in the drug trade rather than an Arab payoff. For one thing it's too small and for another Winton's role up to now has essentially been a passive one. He really hasn't been in the active fight to stop the plant at all, even Sommelier has made more of a nuisance of himself than Winton.''

"Sommelier seems to be out of it." Toby filled her in on the revelations of the bar parlor.

"Fascinating! A psychic cider-maker—what next?"

"What next indeed!" Toby growled. "Well, stay where you are until you get something definite. No sense in you coming back to this maelstrom. If I'm not in the jug, I'll call you back tonight. Keep leaning on whomever you can—we need ammunition quickly."

"I'll stop Francois on the road and get him onto it again. Now that Nicole is in a spot, that should rev him up a bit," she said with undiminished cheerfulness, and rang off.

Toby had another quiet word with the able desk clerk. "I think we may have headed off your boss," he said, "but in case young Alan shows up again, will you tell him from me to lie low and do nothing. I have things in hand and he is not to worry about Nicole." He sounded a great deal more confident than he felt, but the clerk, who was deluged with a crowd of new arrivals, gave him a quick nod and returned to his work. Bracing himself, Toby turned towards Cormel.

He located the Pommard house, a relatively humble and rundown, two-story building just down the street from the imposing Villefort residence. Its view was equally gloomy, for it overlooked the graveyard adjacent to the church. There was a police car parked outside and, he noted with interest, a brand new Citröen in the barn beside the house. He was surprised and not a little relieved when, in answer to his knocking, the door was opened by the placid Sergeant Auvergne, in his shirtsleeves and with a steaming cup of coffee in his hand. The sergeant looked equally surprised to see him.

"I have some vital new evidence to put before Inspector Favet," Toby said formally. "Evidence which I hope will prevent a gross miscarriage of justice."

Looking even more surprised, Auvergne stepped back and waved the coffee cup in the direction of a fusty-looking formal parlor. "Inspector Favet was recalled to Paris this morning. Commissaire Pommard is temporarily in charge, but isn't here at the moment. Do you want to wait or is there something I could do?"

"I would be immensely relieved if you could," Toby said with a slight emphasis. "I have a lot to say to the Sûreté which I would not at the moment like divulged to local ears." He perched on a hard green plush-seated chair and looked severely at the sergeant. "You have struck me from the first as a reasonable man in an unreasonable situation—a situation which becomes more complex by the minute. Inspector Favet has been approaching this case from a single—and I fear mistaken—angle, as I hope to show you. You are familiar with the appearance of the marijuana plant?" He held out the color photos and the sergeant, who had progressed from surprise to astonishment, nodded dumbly, as he hastily leafed through the series of instant photos.

"These plants were originally housed in the greenhouses of the chateau—this testimony comes from the late Yves Rouillé," Toby said quietly. "They were removed prior to your police search of the chateau to a secret tunnel, which runs from an ornamental fountain in the grounds to La Haye beach—again information from the dead boy. These photos were taken at the La Haye beach end of the tunnel by myself this morning in the presence of two witnesses. In short, Winton and his followers have been running a drug business out of the chateau. The reefers found in young Rouillé's pocket were supplied by Winton to his niece Patty—now on her way to safe haven in the United States—but who has left behind a sworn affidavit at the American Embassy in Paris to all of this. You fingerprinted the people at the chateau?"

Auvergne, who was gaping at him in disbelief, nodded again. "Then you may save some time by extracting the fingerprints of Jane Smith and the man who goes by the name of Brother Tom and sending them on to Paris, where they will be matched against prints on hand with the American FBI office there. We have strong reasons to believe they are wanted criminals—wanted terrorists—in America." He paused to let that sink in. "La Haye beach is inaccessible until the next low tide, but if you send your men there, you will find the evidence, along with the footprints of the chateau inhabitants. An FBI man is reportedly on his way to take care of the other matter."

Auvergne gulped and recovered his voice. "How do you know all this if you've been in Paris?" he squeaked.

"I have not been in Paris all the time," Toby said loftily. "I have been doing some undercover investigating, and since we are presently alone I must confide in you that the activities of the group at the chateau are only part of what I have uncovered. That, as your inspector suspected, there has been Arab oil interests involved in plans here to sabotage the power plant scheme, and that these may involve some of the higher authorities in the area, including the man you tell me is now in charge of the case." He looked blandly at the dumbfounded sergeant. "So you can see we shall have to proceed very, very carefully, and I suggest you get in some reinforcements from Paris as soon as you can. I still have some questions to answer, but it seems inevitable, the way things are pointing, that one or more of the highest local officials are involved in the murders. Information that will shortly be on its way from Paris will clarify who—but at the moment there are not enough concrete facts to make an arrest. I am on my way now to see Judge Rouillé. I hope after that to see my way even more clearly, but I hope you appreciate the potential dangers in the situation?" He left the questions hanging.

"I'd better get on to Paris," Auvergne mumbled. "But I find it very hard to believe Pommard is involved in any way. He has bent over backward to head off Favet from any precipitate arrests. It was only with the greatest reluctance he gave up the information on the Nationalists."

"So it was he who was behind Nicole's arrest?" Toby said quickly.

"You know about that? Well, yes, in a way," the sergeant admitted. "But he kept telling Favet there was no real evidence. I think in view of what you have brought in, it is far more likely the chateau people are behind it."

"In any case that is what you must tell him," Toby said significantly. "Though, as I've said, I'm afraid it is not that simple." He got up. "Well, I'll leave you to proceed with it. How do I get to the Rouillés?"

Auvergne told him, adding, "The funeral should be over by now. That's where everyone is. I'm not sure the judge will see you, but you can try."

Toby exited to the doleful sound of the death knell tolling from the little gray church. At the gate he almost collided with two black-clad figures, who recoiled at the sight of him.

It was Villefort's changed appearance that struck Toby. The big man was looking every one of his fifty-plus years and there was an air of uncertainty about him that sat ill on his proud, beak-nosed face.

Pommard, on the other hand, seemed to have grown in stature, and he loomed over Toby, his burly figure radiating authority. "What the hell are you doing back here?" he growled.

"I was laying some new information about the case before the Sûreté," Toby said suavely. "Information I think you will find extremely interesting. If you will excuse me, gentlemen?" And he walked off, aware of their eyes boring into his back.

The door of the Rouillé house was opened by a stranger, and Toby stated his business, conscious of the low murmur of many voices from the parlor.

"This is not a very opportune moment," the man was saying, when the judge appeared, his dark eyes cold and hard. "What is it?"

"I would not intrude at such a time if it were not an urgent matter," Toby said. "But it is about the murder of your son, and the mistaken arrest of his friend and comrade, Nicole. I wish to avoid further tragedy."

"Come into my study then. I can spare you a few minutes." It was difficult to read any emotion in the deepset eyes.

Toby stood his ground. "I would also like your daughter to be present. I think she would prefer to be. Would you tell her that I know everything Nicole knows? She will understand even if you do not." They eyed one another for a few more seconds and then the judge turned away.

"Very well—in there." He waved his hand towards a closed door to the rear of the hallway.

Toby went into the somber, book-lined room, where he was joined a few moments later by the white-faced Marie, whose black attire enhanced her air of fragility, and by her father.

Their inner misery was so evident that only the knowledge of Nicole's plight and Alan's imminent danger kept the embarrassed Toby from leaving them to their mourning. Instead he said stiffly, "Before going into things which will be painful to you, may I say how deeply I feel for you in the present circumstances? I knew Yves only briefly, but enough to know he was a very sensitive and intelligent young man. It is only the desire to see his murderer brought to justice that brings me here at such a time. But there are some things that I must know and that only you can tell me." He paused. "First, let me say that the police are on completely the wrong track in trying to pin the murder on his Nationalist friends, nor were any of them involved in the murder of Armand Dubois. I have discovered that that morning they were all at a Nationalist cell-meeting at Crozon." He could have sworn a flicker of relief passed over the judge's frozen features. "However misguided and rash their actions may have been, those young people are harmless. I think one of them may have been guilty of passing on information as to Yves' whereabouts and activities which may have aided the murderer, but he himself at the time of the murder was not even on the Dragon's Tongue. He was in Brest. I am referring to Shaun O'Reilly." There was no reaction from either of his listeners. "And apropos of the time of Yves' murder, I gather that the police have not been able to narrow it down further than between midday and 6 in the evening. We are in a position to narrow it a lot further than that, thanks to your daughter's testimony." Marie drew in her breath sharply and looked at him with wide, frightened eyes. "We know he was alive when he talked to her on the phone after 1 o'clock and we know he was dead by 4:30 when she found him." The judge let out a startled exclamation and looked in horror at Marie. "By the state of the body when she did so," Toby went on, "I would say that the murder had occurred at least two hours previously—that is around 2:30 P.M., or shortly after he arrived at the rendezvous. But, just to clear the record, where did you go at 3:30 that afternoon, Judge Rouillé?"

The judge exploded with dark anger. "You think that I—my own son!"

"Please!" Toby held up a placating hand. "As I said, just to clear the record—it has to be done before I can proceed."

The judge's lips set in a firm line. "I went to see a friend about a private matter."

"Who?"

"Jean Sommelier."

"Judge Rouillé," Toby said quietly. "Only the truth can serve us now. I happen to know where Jean Sommelier was all that afternoon, whom he was with, and what he was doing. If you were with him, tell me what it was."

The judge shot a furtive look at his daughter and then muttered, "At his farm, in the barn. It was the first pressing of the Lammasghal." Marie looked startled and Toby let out a relieved sigh. "At last! So that is out of the way. Now we can go on to more cogent matters. Were you aware of your daughter's involvement in witchcraft up at the henge?"

Rouillé's face again darkened with anger. "Only after the death of my son. Then the priest told me."

"Father Laval? How did he know?"

"He could not tell me—the seal of the confessional, I suppose—but when I faced her with it. . . ." The judge glared at Marie, who glared back. "Such arrant nonsense! And now look what it has led to!"

"In an area where mystical rites and beliefs are still very much part of life, one can hardly blame a young girl who is, after all, just following a natural climate of opinion," Toby pointed out mildly. "And anyway all that is rather beside the point at the moment." He turned his attention to Marie. "There is one matter that I need clarified; the murder weapon— the athamé, where was it?"

Marie looked at him blankly. "Why—in the henge!"

"Oh, but it wasn't—at least, not with the other things in the burial pit," Toby said firmly. "The hair, the strigils, the white-handled knife, the flowers—those were there, but not the athame."

"But it must have been!" she cried.

"You put it there yourself?"

"Well, no. But Jackie. . . ." She stopped suddenly and bit her lip.

"It belonged to Jacqueline Villefort?" She gave a reluctant nod. "And you saw her put it in the pit?"

"No, not exactly. You see I was dousing the candles. We thought we heard something and it was all in such a rush at the end."

"You heard someone?" he pressed.

"We heard some rustling in the bushes and got frightened,

but it could have been the dog. Afterwards we heard nothing," she faltered.

"So you did not actually see her place it with the rest of the things."

"No," she said reluctantly. "But I could have sworn. . . . Maybe you just didn't see it."

He shook his head. "Out of the question. Where did you usually keep those things?"

"In the churchyard," she said simply, eliciting another outraged gasp from her father.

"Where in the churchyard?"

"In the Villefort mausoleum," she whispered. "Jackie had a key to it."

"That pernicious woman! So she . . ." the judge started to say angrily, but Toby frowned him into silence.

"Now if you would just go over again for me the exact sequence of events the afternoon of the murder . . ." he started to say, when there was suddenly an urgent pounding on the door and an agitated face appeared. "Judge, sorry to disturb you, but you're wanted immediately! The sergeant from the Sûreté says can you come quick. Somebody's been stirring up trouble. There's a mob on its way to the chateau— some of them armed. There's talk of a tree-hanging—he wants you to calm 'em down!"

CHAPTER 19

If Toby had not witnessed what followed, he never would have believed it. By the time he, the judge, and all the male mourners at the Rouillé funeral, the priest included, had piled into cars and rushed to the chateau, the main gate to the mansion was encompassed by a seething mob. It was as if time had rolled back two hundred years as the irate crowd, some armed with pitchforks and scythes, others with shotguns, jostled and shouted like latter-day French Revolutionaries after the aristos' heads. The only twentieth-century note was struck by the police car, which Sergeant Auvergne had thoughtfully slewed across the gates to prevent the mob from getting at the padlock, and in which he and one of the local constables were sitting, locked in and looking a little desperate as the crowd rocked the car up and down in frustrated anger. The funeral party formed a wedge around the judge and Toby and shoved their way through.

The judge climbed on top of the car and waved his arms wildly to get their attention. "Stop this at once! Have you all gone mad?" he thundered. "What is the meaning of all this?"

There was a chorus of shouts about justice being done to "them foreigners."

At the sight of Toby, Auvergne had rolled his window down a cautious crack. "Where the hell is Pommard?" Toby demanded, having scanned the crowd in vain for a glimpse of the big policeman.

"He got all excited about the tunnel and he took one of the constables and was going to try and get into La Haye beach by boat," Auvergne spluttered. "I've called Paris and another Sûreté squad is on its way, but it won't be here for several hours. Favet was already on his way back, so I haven't talked with him. God, I hope the judge can cool them down, or we could have a lynch mob. I don't want to shoot anyone. The worst of it is I don't think this is all of them. The constable here says another group went around by the orchard and were talking of scaling the fence. I hope the gang at the chateau has enough sense to lock up and stay put.''

The authoritarian tones of the judge had been joined by those of the priest, who had climbed up precariously beside him on the hood of the car. Half of the crowd was now yelling at the other half to be quiet and let them speak.

When the noise level had diminished somewhat, the judge raised his voice again. ''You say you are here to see justice done for the murder of my son. I too want to see justice done, but not like this; not with guns and pitchforks. I represent the law of France, the curé here represents the law of God. We both urge you in the name of this same law to disperse quietly before more harm is done, more injustice committed. You are hampering, not aiding, the police in their efforts to bring this about.''

The crowd had quietened as he spoke, but then the sound swelled again as its attention fixed on something behind the judge, and Toby saw a small band of men headed by Jean Sommelier hurrying down the drive of the chateau. Jean came panting up to the gate. ''Well, you might as well go home, my friends. The birds have flown. We've been through the house and there isn't a soul there. Isn't that right?'' he appealed to the men behind him, whom Toby recognized as his fellow Lammasghal-makers.

''Flown in one hell of a hurry, by the looks of it,'' one of them growled.

The crowd started to get excited all over again. ''See! What did we tell you, Judge?'' came the cry. ''They are as guilty as sin. We'll track them down!'' There was a new surge at the gates. ''Open up, Jean, and we'll search the grounds.''

Toby thought quickly. ''Judge Rouillé, tell them that in the absence of Pommard you personally will take charge, and will go with the sergeant here and the men already inside to institute the search. Tell them to disperse peacefully to their homes and that tonight there will be an open-air meeting in the village center in Cormel and they'll be informed of developments then. I think I know where the fugitives might be—but hurry!''

With an understanding nod, the judge began to speak, the priest took up the ball, and Jean, after a quick look at Toby, joined his voice to theirs. There were a few minutes of milling around and indecision, and then the crowd began to split up and to move off along the road.

"How the devil are we going to get the gates opened?" Sergeant Auvergne asked peevishly.

"No problem." A man inside, with the shoulders of a blacksmith, produced a crowbar and with a slight strain of his bulging muscles, snapped the hasp of the padlock off. The chain fell to the ground with a definitive clank.

"I'd better leave the constable here to guard the gate in case any of them gets any ideas about coming back," Auvergne said, starting up the car.

"No," Toby said quietly. "We may need him. Two of Jean's men can stay." He smiled grimly. "They seem to have more influence with their fellows anyway." They followed the car in through the gates and shut them again.

"I see the point in dispersing the mob, but what is the point of this?" the judge complained. "Technically we are now all trespassing, and to what end? The people are gone."

"I don't think they've gone very far." Toby turned to the priest. "Father Laval, do you know where there is an ornamental fountain on the grounds? If so, please take us directly there. The house can wait."

The priest nodded and set off at a brisk trot, the rest of them close on his heels. They reached the dry fountain in an overgrown area of the grounds and Toby hurried around it. There was absolutely no sign of an entrance. "Something in or on the fountain must trigger it," he said desperately, fiddling with the bronze scallop shells with which the outside of the fountain was decorated. But it was Sommelier who found that the main spigot, fashioned in the shape of a leaping fish, turned on its axis. As he twisted it, they heard the creak of opening hinges and the entire back of the fountain swung out to reveal a flight of steps running down into darkness.

Toby took a deep breath. "Here we go then," and plunged down them.

"You expect to find them here?" Auvergne asked.

"I most certainly do. In time, I hope." Toby returned cryptically. "Get your gun out—just in case."

The tunnel took a sudden bend and they rounded the corner to a dramatic confrontation. The tunnel swelled out to form a low-vaulted chamber lit by the light of hurricane lamps. It was crowded to suffocation by people and plants. At the other side of the chamber stood Pommard, his crouched bulk filling the small opening, a drawn revolver in his hand. The cult members looked terror-stricken.

For a moment there was startled silence as the two groups faced each other, then Pommard recovered his voice as Auvergne emerged from behind Tony's tall figure, his own gun in hand. "Collared the lot!" he cried. "And with the evidence."

Toby took a quick inventory of the group. "Not quite all, I fear. I do not see Brother Tom," he said quietly. "And what happened to your constable?"

Pommard looked at him, his brows drawing down into a frown. "I sent him back in the boat for some help. Why? What is it to you?"

"All the available help is now here," Toby said, edging aside to let the other constable and the judge through. "And in view of what has been happening outside, I think you had best take your prisoners back the way we came in and confine them in the chateau. Judge Rouillé will explain." The judge did just that as Pommard's face grew dark with anger. "I am in charge here," Pommard growled. "It is for me to say what is to be done with this gang of murderers."

Winton, who had appeared to be paralyzed with terror, suddenly came to life. "We are not murderers," he squeaked. "There is no blood on our hands. We have done no wrong. These plants, they were for our own use—that is not against the law! You are trying to victimize us because we are foreigners."

"You shut your trap!" Pommard roared, with a menacing gesture.

Winton shrank back but continued to shrill, "You can't threaten us like this. If there's an angry mob out there, it is your duty to protect us."

"There are only three cells in the Cormel jail," Auvergne put in practically. "One of them is already occupied. You are either going to have to take this lot into Nantes and turn them over to the police there, or do as Sir Tobias says, keep them under guard in the chateau. Favet is on his way back; he'll want to question them too.''

"There are cellars at the chateau," the priest said. "The windows are barred. They could not escape.''

Pommard looked from one to another in angry frustration. "All right. Auvergne, you and the constable cross to this side and we'll herd them back up. For the moment we'll take them back to the chateau. Then we'll see what a little individual questioning will shake loose." He leered menacingly at the huddled women. "Favet had better hurry if he wants any of this case to himself. These little birds are going to sing fast and loud, if they know what's good for them!''

Toby emerged into the late afternoon sunlight with a sense of relief tinged with an equal amount of guilt. He was not happy about leaving the cult members in Pommard's ungentle hands, but was still in no position to take them off the hook. His uneasiness increased when Pommard incarcerated Winton and Jane Smith in one cellar and the rest in another, and then sealed off a room for himself and the constable. He obstinately barred the participation of anyone else, including Auvergne, who was no happier about this than Toby was.

They went into a quiet conference with the judge and it was decided that he should return to Cormel to await Favet and direct him to the chateau.

"I think I had better stay here," Auvergne said. "Just to make sure things don't get out of hand. I certainly do not care for Pommard's methods.''

"All right if I wander through the chateau?" Toby said diffidently. "I'd like to get a general feel for the place." He wandered off through the melancholy desolation of the great house; only two things of interest emerged from his tour. He located what had been Patty's room, to find it in a state of complete disarray. It had evidently been torn apart and searched. A torn-up photo lay in confetti shreds in one corner and patiently he pieced it together until it showed two heads close together, one blond, one dark red. So the hapless Patty had been ill-advised enough to keep a picture of her young lover and that, with Penny's unwitting revelation, had been enough to tip them off, he reflected gloomily. And yet he still could not believe they were responsible for the boy's death.

The other find was in a small room on the ground floor, which smelled strongly of dog and which reminded him of the unaccountably missing Hercules. What had become of the dog who had been so omnipresent at the decisive happenings and yet now had vanished? Was its carcass lying somewhere out there in the woods, in the grounds? But why dispose of it? He prowled on, half-expecting to find it. His prowling took him close to the interrogation room, where the sound of a woman's shrill scream and sobs chilled his blood. Feeling helpless and very upset, he fled the house. He had to take action soon, he could not let this sort of thing go on; he must get through to Penny again, he must see Grandhomme.

He detoured by the henge which, in the twilight and in his state of nerves, appeared to him full of silent menace, as if the ancient stones had been catalyzed and charged by the surrounding violence. There was no sign of Grandhomme, but when he checked the dolmen-shelter, he found him in sodden sleep, an empty bottle of cognac by his side. Toby was aware that tonight was Lammas. Although he thought it unlikely, he had been prepared to tell Grandhomme to keep his eyes open for activity at the henge. Now there was no question of that. He looked at the snoring man with a mixture of pity and anger; somebody had been supplying either money or liquor to Grandhomme. Who? he wondered drearily. Who, after everything else that had happened, could still be interested in keeping Grandhomme out of the picture?

Thoroughly depressed, he returned to the Auberge du Dragon. Here he found little to cheer him; there had been no word from the young fugitives, and Canard had phoned to say he was returning to Paris, which faintly puzzled Toby. A call to Penny enlightened him. Madame Spring had already checked out of the hotel, he was informed. Yes, she had left with a gentleman, a gentleman in a white Mercedes. No, the hotel did not know their intended destination.

Please God, it's here, he thought, and that they have something. He fell to wondering gloomily what story could be told to the mass meeting in Cormel to soothe local tempers. He vacillated between going back to the chateau and making straight for the village. He badly wanted to talk with the Villeforts—both of them—but did not want to face them with his present meager stock of ammunition. "Did Canard give you any indication of when he might be returning?" he asked the weary desk clerk.

"He said he hoped to get in about ten tonight. He has already been in touch with his lawyer in Brest, who is on his way here—for Nicole and for himself, if need be." Toby nodded; three more hours to wait. He felt in no mood for mob scenes, so he turned back to the chateau.

His arrival at the main gate coincided with the arrival of the squad car from Paris, which was packed with stony-faced men, and he caught a glimpse of Favet's profile in the back seat beside a well-dressed man with the look of authority stamped all over him. Toby followed them up the drive, eliciting friendly grins as he passed by the Lammasghal-makers still on duty. Before he had parked his Jeep, the official party had debarked and hurried inside, and by the time he had got into the main hall there was no sign of them. "What's been happening?" he enquired of the harassed-looking constable at the door. The man rolled his eyes skyward. "Fireworks! The priest and Auvergne have been after the chief. I don't know what's been going on, but I think all hell is about to break loose with this new lot."

Toby wandered again through the ill-kept, deserted rooms, until he heard a voice calling his name; it was Auvergne. "Glad you're back," he said with relief. "Favet wants to see you in about twenty minutes."

"Who is the big wheel with him?" Toby asked curiously.

"Someone from the Ministry of the Interior. I don't know what's up, but something big must have broken. Favet is like a cat on hot bricks. I'm glad he is here, though. Pommard has been acting off his rocker. We had to stop him beating up on some poor wretched dim-witted girl."

"The redhead?" Toby asked.

"Yes, he had her confessing to everything under the sun and implicating the others, but I don't think it means a thing. He had her scared out of her wits."

"Well, before I see Favet, I think I'd better fill you in on a few more things," Toby said. "It suited my purpose for the moment to direct attention to the cult, but I'm damned if I'm going to stand by and see them railroaded by Pommard and the mob. Lawbreakers they undoubtedly are, but murderers I am virtually certain they are not.'' He got out Yves' notebook and briefly explained its cryptic references. ''There's a statement from Winton's niece which is on its way from Paris and which will back up all this,'' he continued. ''Also we have evidence that Winton has been receiving his cut from the drug trade, but there is no evidence he has been getting payments from Arab oil sources. Information about all this is also on its way.'' He hoped fervently this was true. ''It begins to look as if the murderer or murderers sat with us around the table at that very first meeting with Dubois. Now, I didn't do it. I have eliminated Sommelier and Rouillé as suspects, Winton seems to be in the clear, if the young people's testimony holds up—so you see who that leaves.'' He looked significantly at Auvergne. ''The curé, Villefort, and Pommard.''

Auvergne pursed his lips in a silent whistle. ''But then what about all this witchcraft stuff you've been going on about?''

''Well, this is where it gets really interesting,'' Toby answered. ''I know now the identity of the witches—and one of them is Jacqueline Villefort.''

Auvergne looked at him with a worried frown. ''But that doesn't make any sense!''

''On the face of it, no, but I am beginning to see how it could add up,'' Toby was saying, when there came another dramatic interruption, as shouts were heard in the main hall. They ran out to find a very elderly man in a wrinkled gendarme's uniform, obviously greatly agitated, waving his arms at the other constable. A door opened and Favet and Pommard emerged.

The old man turned to Pommard. ''I'm sorry, sir. It wasn't my fault. I was standing guard in the outer room, letting nobody in, just like you said. Forty years' faithful service I put in here before I retired, as you well know, and I always followed orders. I heard the motorbike but I didn't pay it no mind, they're always roaring around the village these here days. And then there was all this cracking and breaking. By the time I got out me keys and got the doors unlocked it was too late—busted clean out and gone.''

''What the hell are you babbling about?'' Pommard roared.

''The prisoner, sir—escaped. Some young fella on a thundering great motorbike—chains on the bars—pulled 'em clean out and went roaring off with her.''

Favet turned, a triumphant grin on his face, to the man who loomed at his elbow. "See!" he cried. "What did I tell you? The Nationalists again. All the rest of this we've been listening to is a side issue and so much crap. They're the guilty ones!"

"Oh, bloody hell!" groaned Sir Tobias Glendower.

CHAPTER 20

The turn of events was threatening to become very ugly indeed, when the heavens intervened with split-second timing. It had become increasingly oppressive and sultry as darkness fell. Then, with a roll of thunder like the crack of doom the skies opened and torrential rain pounded across the Dragon's Tongue, as the sea lashed itself up to equal fury. There was no open-air meeting, no mob, no scouring of the countryside for the missing fugitives. Action of all kinds was suspended while the peninsula cowered under the lash of the summer tempest, giving Toby what he had so fervently hoped for—a breathing space.

Within the chateau, the acrimonious wrangling had continued. It had been decided, in view of the elements and the sad state of the Cormel jail, that the chateau prisoners should be kept where they were for the moment, until arrangements could be made for their transport off the isthmus. A police all-points bulletin had been sent out for the interception of 'Brother Tom,' Alan Pommard, Nicole LeBrun, and Shaun O'Reilly. There was a brief lull while the two official groups drew apart and tried to think of what else they should do. This respite was shattered when the FBI man arrived, bedraggled and looking extremely irritated, with extradition papers for Jane Smith and Brother Tom, whose fingerprints had indeed matched up with 'Long Laura's' and one Thomas Quinn, late of the Minutemen and Brooklyn. The news that two known terrorists—one now missing—had been among the chateau party set Favet to muttering and Pommard to triumphant demands that the extradition be denied on the grounds that they were suspects in the local murders. As they negotiated heatedly with the FBI man, Auvergne slid up to Toby. "Shouldn't I tell Favet now about what you have found?" he murmured anxiously.

"Not until my colleague arrives from Paris with Patty

Winton's statement and the other evidence,'' Toby replied.
"Without that we do not have enough either to clear the cult
group of the murder charge or to direct Favet away from his
false ideas about the Nationalists. Besides, in present company I do not want to show my hand.''

"But I don't see how you are ever going to be able to bring
it all out in the open without doing just that,'' Auvergne
complained.

"I'm none too clear myself, at the moment,'' Toby confessed. "But I'm beginning to get an idea that I think might
work. For now, however, it is still a question of keeping quiet
until the cavalry arrives.''

"The cavalry?'' Auvergne echoed blankly.

"Just a joke,'' Toby said hastily. "A private joke.''

The cavalry, in the shape of Penny, arrived at midnight,
after everyone had argued themselves into exhaustion and was
preparing to call it quits for the night. She arrived in tandem
with Canard and a bewildered-looking man who turned out to
be the lawyer summoned to help Nicole and who had arrived
in Cormel only to find the bird had quite literally flown.

Favet pounced on Canard like a cat after a particularly
plump rat. "So,'' he purred, "You found it wiser to surrender, Canard! A sound decision in these circumstances.''

"Surrender nothing!'' Francois snapped. He was tired and
testy. "You try and lay one finger on me for this murder
business and you'll have a case for false arrest slapped on you
so fast your sheep's head will swim. I have in my briefcase
sworn statements from six unimpeachable witnesses who can
vouch for my movements during the time of both the murders.''

"Which is not to say you are not involved in the plot,''
Favet snarled softly.

"Produce your evidence of that!'' Francois snapped.

Toby drew Penny aside. "Did you get anything?'' he asked
anxiously.

She grinned at him with delight. "Did you ever doubt it?
Yes. Let's get away from this official mob and gloat in
private.'' They slipped quietly into one of the empty salons
and she subsided with a grateful sigh on to a pile of cushions,
as he drew up another pile and settled beside her. She opened
her shoulder bag. "Item 1. Patty's sworn statement which,

together with what you have, should get the chateau group out of trouble—at least for the murders.''

He leafed through it quickly with a satisfied grunt. ''Yes, that should do it.''

''Item 2. The statement of Winton's finances, which should put him back in trouble for his drug activities,'' she continued cheerfully, and then, with triumph, ''and Item 3, courtesy of Francois' spy network, something that should help pin the murderer. It was Villefort after all, no doubt about it; payments direct from the Arab's account right into his. Here are copies— probably illegal, but to heck with that—of the respective statements. He can be pinned in another way, too. The high-ranking minister who is involved also was a client of Villefort's back in his Paris days as a lawyer. Chances are that is how he was recruited for this particular little caper. As you can see, the payments started two years ago and have continued in increasing amounts until just about a month ago, when there was a real whopper. There is one strange thing though.'' She looked at the paper in her hand with a slight frown. ''Nearly all of that payment was suddenly withdrawn just a few days ago. Of course, he may be getting ready for a getaway and has stashed it in a Swiss bank. They are trying to trace it now.''

Toby grunted noncommittally and began to stuff his pipe, gazing abstractedly into the dark shadows of the room. ''You don't seem either surprised or particularly delighted,'' Penny said with a slight edge to her voice. ''Wasn't this precisely what you had anticipated and hoped for? Isn't it enough?''

''Oh, yes, it's very good, excellent.'' His tone was absent. ''Unfortunately, it is not that simple—and if you think back over the evidence you will see why.''

She screwed up her face in an agony of concentration. ''Oh,'' she said at length. ''Yes. I see what you mean. So what do we do now?''

''Well, I am going to get a good night's sleep for a change. Then first thing tomorrow I'm going to try and bring in those two young idiots to clear up that little mess and get Favet off that particular track.''

''You know where they are?'' she exclaimed.

''Not exactly, but I know quite a few places to look. Young Alan was very chatty about their favorite camping-spots. I imagine they are still very much around. They wouldn't have risked trying to get off the isthmus, knowing the alarm was out, and I don't suppose either of them has any money. They are probably waiting for a chance to get to Canard for a getaway stake."

"And if you succeed in doing that?"

"I need their testimony for what I have to say to Favet and that very diplomatic-looking man, who is so obviously hanging around to see the cats do not escape very far from the bag and no devastating revelations become public. After that, I hope they will agree to set up a meeting I have in mind. It's a bit melodramatic, but a confrontation might be the only means of getting at the truth. If the murderer keeps his head, I think he still has a chance of getting away with it, but he has one vulnerable chink in his armor and it is that I am banking on to bring him down. There is just one more thing I would like to find out and then I'd be sure of my hypothetical reconstruction, but how I'm going to get that . . ." he trailed off with a tired sigh.

"We'll worry about that tomorrow," Penny said comfortingly. "Let's call it a night. I'm all in, and by the sounds of it you are, too."

"There is one little thing you could do for me tomorrow while I'm hunting the fugitives," he suggested diffidently.

"Oh, what's that?"

"See Jacqueline Villefort—this is what I'd like you to say." He went on at some length.

"Little thing!" she snorted. "You certainly saddle me with some lulus, but—all right, I'll take on Guinevere. I shudder to think what would happen if you tried it."

Toby was up early the next morning, stepping out into a rain-washed world where the sun once more shone brilliantly in the clear sky. He checked the abbey ruins first, without much hope, and was not surprised to find them void of life. His second stop was likewise uneventful, but on his third he hit pay dirt. In the dell where the Jeep had previously been concealed, sat, under its own camouflage, the large black motorcycle. "So it's the beach," he thought, and made for another little cove adjacent, just as sheltered as La Haye beach, but with a convenient path that wound sinuously down to its sandy surface. Here too the cliffs were pockmarked by caves. He waited until he reached the beach before shouting loudly: "Alan, Nicole! It is I, Sir Tobias. Come on out! I don't want to have to search every cave for you."

There was a moment of silence as he listened for an answering call above the pounding surf and the screaming gulls. None came, but Alan's dark curly head poked cautiously out of one of the openings. "Are you alone?" he queried anxiously.

"Quite alone." Toby went over to the cave and ducked through the low entrance. Nicole was sitting in a disconsolate heap on one of the bedrolls, her firm chin propped up on her small fists. "We're in one hell of a mess," she declared.

"Yes, indeed." Toby glared at Alan. "That was an extremely foolhardy thing to do and has served no useful purpose whatsoever—in fact, quite the opposite. Favet is all steamed up again and is roaring after you down the wrong track."

"I wasn't about to let Nicole stay in any jail," Alan bristled.

"A noble but senseless thought—she was much better off there than she is here," Toby said. "Dragons, dungeons, damsels in distress, and now a knight in shining armor roaring off with his lady fair on a motorbike—taking a hunk of Cormel jail with him, incidentally! I am seriously beginning to doubt the wisdom of summer holidays for students. The sooner you two are back in college the better it will be for everyone."

"So why are you here consorting with us desperate criminals?" Nicole said, ever practical.

"To take you in—or rather, to have you turn yourselves in."

"What good would that do? They'd just lock both of us up and throw away the key."

"I guarantee that will not happen," he said firmly. "Things are coming to a head, and with your testimony I think I can persuade the Sûreté to set up things for a final showdown."

"But what if you can't?"

"I can and I will." Toby was definite. "Do you know what happened to Shaun?"

"He split on Yves' bike," Alan growled. "He was headed for Brest, and I imagine our people there will pack him off to

England. He turned into a right royal pain all around. I wanted him to help get Nicole out, but he was in such a panic he couldn't get out fast enough.''

"Hmm, I'm not surprised. I fear Shaun had something on his conscience he did not like to think about," Toby gloomed.

"He did not mention to you being picked up or questioned by the local police, did he?"

"Was he?" they chorused.

"I don't know, but I was hoping you would," he sighed. "Come on then. Get packed up. It's time we got things rolling.''

"Well, I hope you know what you're doing, because we don't," Nicole grumbled, but reluctantly did his bidding.

Finding the official Sûreté party proved difficult. Toby stashed the Jeep and its fugitive occupants out of sight behind the church and made cautious enquiries at the Pommard house, only to be told by the sullen-faced Madame Pommard that there had been no room for them there and they had all gone to stay at the inn at Morgat. Another cautious enquiry at the jail revealed one lone constable—the guardian of the chateau door of the night before—on duty.

"What's going on?" he asked Toby eagerly, and admitted complete ignorance as to the whereabouts of his chief or any of the Paris brigade.

Toby was just about to leave when he turned back. "You don't happen to know anything about the fugitive Irishman, do you? Lanky and sandy-haired? Ever see him around here? Any trace of him?"

The constable was eager to share what little information he had. "No, he hasn't been picked up. That other one has, though. What's his name at the chateau—Tom? They caught him on a train trying to get into Belgium. They're bringing him back. I know who you mean though—saw him around the village, several times, I did. Wait a minute though! I believe I did see the chief questioning him one time. Just outside the village, it was. He had a motorbike with him that looked like the Rouillé boy's.''

"Ah!" Toby said with a satisfied sigh. "Well, thank you, thank you very much."

He had hoped to approach Favet through the sympathetic Sergeant Auvergne, but preliminary scouting of the Morgat inn revealed that Auvergne, another Sûreté man, and one of the local constables had been detailed to escort the chateau group tŏ Nantes and would be unavailable until evening. He hustled the two young people up to his room adjuring them sternly to stay put until he came back, and braced himself for Favet, who had taken over the private parlor of the inn for his new headquarters.

"What do you want?" Favet growled, as Toby appeared at the door. "We're very busy." He was sitting at a small table across from the official who had appeared the night before.

"Not too busy, I hope, to finalize this case," Toby said mildly. "I am now in a position to put before you evidence that should lead to a final solution. But first I think I should meet this gentleman," he bowed politely in the direction of the blandfaced man. "Because what I have to say raises some delicate questions involving the government."

"Auguste Velin," the man announced, eyeing him warily, but stood up and proferred his hand. "You are Sir Tobias Glendower, I presume?"

The amenities over, Toby drew up a chair to the table and unloaded sheaves of papers from various pockets. "I would be grateful if you would just listen to what I have to say, for the moment," he said carefully. "When I have finished, I can produce two witnesses to bear out the events of the past two days. After that, it will depend heavily on your own cooperation whether the guilty parties are apprehended or not. That is your affair, but I am perfectly willing to participate in the event I have in mind." He began to expound in his euphonious lecturer's voice. ". . . So you see you were right all along about the involvement of Arab oil interest," he concluded magnanimously to the stupefied Favet, "if incorrect in linking it to the Nationalists. The young people you have been seeking were not even in the neighborhood at the time of the Dubois murder. They were in Crozon. And at the time of the second murder, they were in a completely different part of the Cormel woods, awaiting the dead boy. They are presently upstairs . . ." Favet let out a strangled exclamation ". . . awaiting my summons and will substantiate the story I have just told you." Toby looked at Auguste Velin. "They are unaware of these other vital facts from Paris, and I suggest should remain so."

Velin nodded and looked over at Favet, who was beginning to bristle. "I think we should go along with Sir Tobias' suggestions. Face it, Favet, the terrorist angle is out. And as to the rest . . ." he let out a faint sigh, "it will have to be handled with the greatest delicacy, a lot is involved."

"Then you will get them all together tonight?" Toby asked. "You will arrange it as I have indicated?"

"We'll do everything possible to bring it about, but just in the interests of sheer space, I think the meeting should be here and not in the Villefort house. If things are as you state, all the Sûreté men will have to be present."

"Then we'll have to have a large table around which the original party should sit," Toby insisted. "The psychological buildup to this is crucial."

"You need Winton as well?"

"Yes, it's not vital, since he, in effect, broke up the original meeting, but it would be useful."

"Arrange it," Velin ordered Favet curtly. "And now if we may see the young people?"

Nicole and Alan came down, told their stories, and signed statements. "Now may they go?" Toby queried.

"There's the question of the jail break. They have a lot to answer for," Favet began hotly.

"Sir Tobias, would you wait outside with Mademoiselle LeBrun and Monsieur Pommard for a moment?" Velin cut in.

They waited outside tensely, as the murmur of voices continued behind the door; it eventually opened and Velin, a tight smile on his face, emerged.

"In view of these extraordinary circumstances, I have prevailed on Favet not to pursue this other matter," Velin announced. "However, you two must go back to the Auberge du Dragon until affairs have been completed. After that, I'm afraid I must insist on you leaving the peninsula to return to your homes in Nantes. I'm sure you will understand."

Toby handed the keys of the Jeep to Alan. "Bring it back tonight," he said. "And say nothing of this at the auberge."

Much relieved, they hurried off, hand in hand.

Velin rolled his eyes heavenwards. "The things I do for France," he murmured. "Will you hold yourself available here, Sir Tobias? There is much to arrange and much to discuss, and I am having to hold a tight rein on Favet. Where will you be?"

"If not in my room, then in the bar," Toby said and, suiting the action to the word, made for the latter. The first person he saw was Grandhomme, propped up at the counter and looking shaky and excited. "Sir Tobias, I was looking for you!" he cried. "You must come out to the henge at once. There is something you ought to see. I think it may be what you were looking for. The rain last night . . . one of the dolmens shifted. I think it may be very important."

Toby eyed him levelly. "I can't come now, Grandhomme. Not today. Maybe tomorrow, when everything is over."

"What do you mean? Everything over?"

"After a murderer is caught," Toby replied. "I am not a vindictive man, but this is one murderer I shall be happy to see get his just desserts. And, now that you are here, Grandhomme, this is just where you are going to stay."

CHAPTER 21

As the hours of the day ticked away towards the eight o'clock meeting, Toby could feel his nerves stretching and tensing. He was gambling, he knew, and if that gamble failed . . . but he would not allow himself to think like that.

He had received a cautiously optimistic phone call from Penny. "She is a lot tougher than I anticipated," Penny confessed, "but I think she is thoroughly scared and a little push tonight might do it. Velin came himself, while I was here, to request her presence at the inn tonight. He's a clever one. She was going to refuse when he casually dropped the fact that Marie Rouillé would be there too with her father, and Jacqueline graciously changed her mind. May I sit in on this thing?"

"At the outset, no," he apologized. "It's important to alter the original ambience as little as possible while I do my thing. I'm sorry to foist this role on you, but if you could stay with the Rouillé girl and Jacqueline and somewhat unnerve them with dark hints, that would be very useful. Favet or Auvergne will slip out at the right moment and give you your entrance cue."

He picked without any appetite at an early dinner, then went for a brief walk along the cliffs towards Morgat, just as he had done that first evening. There was anger in him as there had been then, but now it was a cold fury as he recalled the faces of the dead. He slipped into the meeting room to see how far Velin had succeeded and was pleased with the result; a large polished mahogany table had been obtained from God knows where and dining chairs to the exact number of the original meeting stood around it. Other chairs were placed against the wall around the room, two of them flanking the only door. Satisfied, he went up to his room and waited tensely, sitting on the edge of his bed and watching the minute hand of his watch. There were sounds of cars in the parking lot, doors slamming, and the murmur of voices. At two minutes to eight he rose, drew a deep breath, and went downstairs. Bracing himself, he opened the door and walked in.

Auguste Velin sat at the head of the table, and Armand Dubois' briefcase was on the polished surface in front of him. There were empty chairs to his left and right. The rest of the group sat silently in their original places. Villefort, at the head of the table, the dim electric light overhead accentuating the golden glints in his fair curls, looked preoccupied and uneasy. The priest, sunk in deep gloom, looked down at his clasped hands. Sommelier, his vivid blue eyes dancing with curiosity, was beside him. The judge, at Villefort's right, stared straight ahead, his aloof face forbidding in its sternness. Only the uniformed Pommard seemed unchanged, his great fists resting on the table and a slight smirk on his swarthy face, but there was no amusement in the pale blue eyes as they flicked briefly towards Toby and then resumed their contemplation of his hands.

On Toby's arrival, Velin rose and, in a carefully rehearsed voice, echoed the dead man's words. "Ah, good—there you are!" He indicated the chair to his right "*Messieurs*. I think you are all well acquainted with my colleague, Sir Tobias Glendower, a distinguished British archaeologist who has been excavating at the Dragon's Teeth on behalf of the French government."

Outside, the grandfather's clock began to chime the hour on a deeper note than the one in the Villefort house. Velin paused and glanced significantly at the empty chair to his left. The effect was not lost on the men around the table, who stirred uneasily in their seats, their concentration focused on him and Toby. The Sûreté men, sitting silently in the shadows around the walls, seemed like mere props, as the room held its breath.

They had come to the end of the original script, but Velin went smoothly into his next cue. He released the catches on the briefcase with a click that sounded startlingly loud in the silent room and opened it up to display sheaves of folders inside. He cleared his throat. "I, as representative of the government of France, have requested your presence here tonight, since you are all interested parties in the two recent

tragedies that have occurred here on the Dragon's Tongue—
the savage murder of my colleague, Armand Dubois, and the
equally sad murder of Yves Rouillé.'' A spasm of pain
contorted the judge's face for a brief instant. ''I would ask
you now to give your attention to Sir Tobias, who has been
assisting us in the investigation, and who will reconstruct the
sequence of events.''

Toby stood up, his tall figure dominating the table, and
removed two of the folders, which he tapped thoughtfully
with a long forefinger, ·before beginning to speak. All eyes
were riveted on the folders. ''Armand Dubois was a determined
and dedicated man,'' he declared. ''A man with a difficult
job to carry out. He sat down with us that night knowing that
he was in the presence of enemies, that all of us for our
various reasons were against him and what he stood for. But
he had this job to do and he was not a stupid man, so he came
prepared. He wanted no trouble, he wanted to be allowed to
get on with the task at hand. To facilitate this, he had acquired
significant information on certain people, which he could use
as a lever to ensure the job was done but which, being of a
highly sensitive nature, he was not about to reveal to the
world at large. He was, understandably, under considerable
strain, and a certain incident at the end of the meeting at the
mayor's house upset him, showing as it did the depth of local
animosity against him. It made him angry. Some time between
then and eleven o'clock the next morning, when he met his
death, he was prompted to reveal this information to one of
the parties involved. It was a fatal move, for the murderer
panicked and, in his panic, killed. He did not stop to consider
that in obtaining the information Dubois had with him, he
was merely chopping off the branch and not the root; that the
source of such information still remained, if one looked in the
right direction.'' He paused for a significant moment. ''The
method of murder was a clever one, since it was an established mode of vengeance killing used in this region since
World War II and therefore was known to everyone equally.
However, here fate stepped in, because Armand Dubois was
on a decoagulant medicine for a blood condition and bled to
death with such rapidity that the murderer had no time to set
up an alibi. He therefore altered his original plan and determined to point the finger of suspicion at a specific person,

known to be hostile to Dubois, and whom he knew was meeting Dubois that morning. That person was Jean Sommelier.

"He moved the body to a clearing in the woods close to the Sommelier farm," Toby continued. "And, knowing Jean was involved in certain local practices, he removed and sharpened a scythe from his barn, leaving it on the body to mislead us into thinking that someone was practicing black magic. It was here his luck began to run out, for, thanks to the black dog from the chateau, the body was quickly discovered so that the time of death could be accurately pinpointed. Worse, from his point of view, Jean Sommelier had an alibi for that time, having been with me and my assistant. However, in other respects his luck was holding and no finger of suspicion was directed at him because: (a) no one knew what had been in Dubois' briefcase, so the papers removed from it were not missed, (b) a rainstorm effectively wiped out all traces of the murder locale; and (c) those interested in the murder investigation, myself included, went haring off in wrong directions. Inspector Favet, a terrorist expert, arrived, convinced it was the work of the Underground Nationalist movement, and I was mesmerized by the witchcraft angle, due to the fact I had found evidence that the henge had been recently used for witchcraft rites. I had passed this information on, with the opinion that these might well be linked to the cult center established at the chateau."

Again, as if on cue, there came a rap at the door and it opened to reveal the form of Gareth Winton, a very frightened Gareth Winton, flanked by two gendarmes. This time there was no talk of Cosmic Powers. Instead he jabbered, "Why have I been brought here? What is this about? I demand a lawyer. I demand to be allowed to see someone from the American Embassy."

"Ah, Mr. Winton! Come in," Auguste Velin said smoothly. "Kindly sit down. We were just talking about you and your involvement in this affair."

"I was not involved. I had no part in it," Winton shouted desperately, as the gendarmes hustled him in and deposited him, none too gently, in the last vacant seat. "I appeal to you, I appeal to you all!"

Velin ignored him. "Please continue, Sir Tobias. I apologize for the interruption."

Toby had been thankful for the breather, well aware that he was now skating on very thin ice indeed. "Yes, well," he cleared his throat. "Had the murderer been content to sit back and let things take their course, he might easily have got away with it, but this he did not do. And that brings me to another important aspect—the question of motive. A threefold motive for both murders—fear, greed, and blackmail." He paused to let that sink in. "He had killed Dubois in a panic of fear brought about by the latter's knowledge that certain parties on the Dragon's Tongue had been receiving money to sabotage the establishment of the nuclear power plant. But he himself had profited little up to this point from it and saw a golden opportunity to better his position when the time was ripe. With this end in view, he removed the witchcraft objects from the henge, thereby gaining a hold over the women involved, and hoping, no doubt, to plant the evidence on the chateau group when he got the chance, to further strengthen his position. He was thrown off balance, however, when he learned that a group of young Breton Nationalists, angered at having the murder placed at their door, were actively investigating and that one of their number, Yves Rouillé, had gained entrance to the chateau." Again he paused and looked at Velin. "I think it is time to bring in our other informants."

Velin nodded. "Bring in Madame Villefort," he ordered one of the men at the door. Villefort was on his feet in an instant. "No!" he roared, his large frame shaking with anger. "I will not have my wife dragged into this; she is not involved. I forbid it!"

"You are in no position to do that. Sit down!" Velin said with quiet venom, as the door opened to admit Jacqueline Villefort and Marie, followed by Penny. There was a small delay as the women sat down next to Winton. Villefort slumped back in his chair with a groan and covered his face with his hands.

Toby continued to speak in the same even tone. "There was nothing the murderer could do about that—overtly. He could only keep a covert eye on things and hope to get to the boy before anyone else did to find out what he had discovered. Here events played into his hands, because Yves was forced to leave the chateau and, in so doing, contacted his sister. The murderer was alerted, confronted the boy—and killed again. But this time he left behind evidence that definitely implicated the witchcraft practitioners. However, once more he had overreached himself and had lopped the branch but not the root." He quietly got out Yves' dog-eared notebook and placed it on top of the folders. "Yves left behind a record of what he had been doing, a record borne out by the testimony of another young inhabitant of the chateau, Patty Winton. The boy had proved to his own satisfaction that no one in the chateau could have been involved in the murder of Armand Dubois, and he was therefore considering other possibilities. In his written musings the name of Jacqueline Villefort crops up several times." He turned suddenly. "Madame, you are in a very bad position, only the truth can save you now. Tell me!"

But Villefort was on his feet again. "No, no, leave her out of it. Jacqueline, say nothing! If you want a confession, all right, you shall have it. I confess . . . only let her go! Yes, it was I." Favet, in the shadows, came to his feet with an exclamation, but Toby held up his hands in a dramatic gesture and thundered, "No! Monsieur Villefort, we want the truth and only the truth. We want no phony dramatics that will be forsworn the minute you enter a courtroom. If you will not be quiet, you will be arrested and forcibly removed until we have done here!"

Jacqueline, wide-eyed, glanced from her husband to Toby, who reiterated, "Madame, tell me, the day Marie Rouillé phoned you that she wished to meet her brother and wanted your help, did you pass that information on to someone?"

There was a pregnant pause as she looked pleadingly at the men around the table, then a calculating gleam came into her dark eyes. "He made me . . ." she faltered. "He threatened me. I had to tell him, but I did not know what he had in mind to do, I swear it. After, I was terrified. . . ."

"Who?" Toby boomed.

"Pierre Pommard."

"Why, you lying trollop!" The police chief surged up, his face black with anger. "It was all your idea, you bloody witch. You killed him with your dagger."

With a strangled cry, Villefort flung himself at the man, grabbing at his throat. They went down in a crashing heap as the Sûreté men sprang at them from all corners of the room.

They were wrestled apart and forced back into their chairs. "It's lies, all lies!" Villefort screamed, his restraint gone. "He will say anything to blacken her. Listen to me, I will tell you how it was."

"If there is any telling to be done, I'll do it," Pommard snarled. "You and your precious cabinet friend and those bloody Arabs! And I was to do your dirty work and pick up the few measly crumbs you saw fit to throw to me—wasn't that it? I'll tell them how it was! Ever since we were boys I've been expected to lick your ass, Mr. High-and-Mighty. Well, yours isn't the only Villefort ass I've licked—ask your wife. Ask her about our little rendezvous at the trysting oak." His face was a twisted mask of naked hatred.

Jacqueline let out a shrill scream of protest as the two men roared obscenities at each other.

Toby let it go on for a few moments, then lifted his voice sternly. "Enough! I'm afraid it won't do, Pommard. Madame Villefort may have been your accomplice, but she did not commit those murders. You, and you only, are responsible for the murders of Armand Dubois and Yves Rouillé."

"Yes," Villefort cried. "He killed Dubois—I'll testify to that."

"Why, you . . ." Pommard roared, and reached for the gun in his holster. His face registered disbelief as his hand came up empty.

Judge Rouillé quietly rose to his feet, the gun in his hand, and leveled it at Pommard's head. "Is this what you were looking for? Is it this kind of justice you seek?"

"No, Papa, no!" Marie screamed, as a frozen silence fell upon the room.

The judge held the gun steady for a few seconds and then handed it with a slight grimace to the Sûreté man who stood behind him. "No," he said quietly. "That is not my way. I have always lived by the law, and it is the law of France that must be obeyed. Inspector Favet, they are your prisoners, I think."

Favet intoned the formal arrest as his men snapped handcuffs on the two men. He had turned to Jacqueline Villefort when Toby interposed. "I may point out in the absence of certain factual evidence that much will hinge on Madame Villefort's testimony at the trial. If she is a willing witness for the Republic, and if Monsieur Villefort makes a full confession, as he has indicated his willingness to do, perhaps in her case . . .?" He left the sentence hanging.

"Yes, oh, please, yes," Jacqueline cried. "I will do anything, anything. My poor children, oh!" She began to sob effectively into a small lace handkerchief, as Villefort watched her, an enigmatic expression on his proud face.

"D'accord," he said softly, "So be it."

"Whore, witch!" Pommard shouted, and continued his string of insults as he was dragged from the room.

"Thank you," Villefort said simply to Toby and followed, his head bowed.

Favet and his men went after them, escorting Jacqueline out.

Velin, looking more than a little shaken, cleared his throat and looked around at the room's remaining occupants. "Well, Sir Tobias, that was dramatically effective, but for the benefit of the rest of us, would you care to finish your reconstruction?"

Toby heaved a gusty sigh. "Most of it is sheer conjecture," he admitted. "A lot will depend on what Villefort and his wife come up with in the way of corroborative evidence. To backtrack a bit, I think Pommard killed Dubois—or rather laid him out first and then was forced to kill him—in an unthinking panic. He is evidently not a quick-thinking man. He then pressured Villefort, who de facto had little choice, into giving him his alibi, thereby making him his accomplice. He had become aware of the witchcraft activities of the two women, either because Jacqueline had actually become his mistress and had told him, or just from sheer observation. His house, I may point out, looks onto the graveyard and the Villefort vault, where, by Madamoiselle Rouillé's admission, the witchcraft objects were kept. Anyway, he knew what they were up to and where the objects were. His hold on Villefort after Dubois' death was still a tenuous one, but he began to see further possibilities of blackmail and of profiting himself from the Arab money. When he was alerted by Jacqueline that Yves was on his way to the trysting oak, he evidently went prepared. We will never know what transpired there— whether he threatened Yves with arrest and the lad disclosed what he had found out, or whether he had already made up his mind to kill again, using the witchcraft objects to implicate Jacqueline and thereby gain a stranglehold on Villefort. In any case, the result was the same. I think Villefort will admit that the last large Arab payment was transferred to Pommard as the first installment of this continuing blackmail. Having found his golden goose, Pommard obviously did not want to kill it, and here we are fortunate in not having had a whole series of other murders." He looked over at Gareth Winton, who had sat immobile. "You and your company are indeed lucky, Mr. Winton, that we arrived in the tunnel when we did. Pommard had sent the constable back to the boat, and I think it may have been his intention to arrange a very tragic accident for you all. Dead men tell no tales, and if none of you was left alive to testify, the murders could very easily have been pinned on you—at least to the satisfaction of the local population. Then he would have had his helpless milch cow to blackmail, and the Sûreté would have cleared out, leaving the field clear again."

"He was trying to get us to go with him to the beach," Winton said suddenly. "He was very threatening, but I knew it was high tide out there so I was resisting. Then you came along. Can I go now?"

"Mr. Winton, you are under arrest for drug-smuggling," Judge Rouillé said firmly. "You are not going anywhere except back to jail." The cult leader lapsed into a disconsolate silence.

"His later performance at the chateau was a continuing desperate effort along this same line, but again thwarted by the intervention of Father Laval, here, and the sergeant. At this point he really had nowhere to go. All he could hope for was that Favet's original preoccupation with the Nationalists would take hold. He had no means of knowing about the enquiries that were going forward in Paris, so that when he walked in here today he really did not think anything very substantive was afoot. Villefort, being wiser to the ways of the world, was a lot more apprehensive than he. But our psychological gamble worked and so . . ." Toby shrugged, "it is done."

"Very satisfactory," Velin purred. "Of course, in view of certain sensitive aspects of this case, very little will actually come out in court, but we may safely assume that all will be taken care of and that things may now proceed as planned."

"No!" the judge's voice rang out like a clarion call, startling them all. "No," he repeated on a quieter note. "My son was a fighter, and even if I disapproved of his methods, I should not like to think that he died in vain. That shall not happen. In order for things to be 'smoothed out' as you say, Monsieur Velin, you will require our cooperation, and that cooperation has a price. The price is that the government gives up its plans for the Dragon's Tongue."

"But . . ." Velin spluttered, "but that's blackmail!"

"Call it what you like," the judge said, "but to me it too is justice. The government could be seriously embarrassed, may even fall, if we talk; *or* the power plant goes elsewhere and our lips will remain sealed." There were assenting noises from Sommelier and the priest. Rouillé cast an ironic eye at Toby. "If the government should wish to save face, you could always give as a reason the priceless significance of France's only henge monument."

The flabbergasted Velin looked at the determined faces around the table. "Well, I'll see what I can do," he said weakly, and got up. "I think I had better call Paris right now." The others followed him out, leaving Penny and Toby alone.

"Bravo, a masterly performance, Lancelot," she said. "How well you didn't say certain things. Don't you have any twinges about letting Guinevere off the hook like that?"

"After all, she does have two very young children," Toby answered defensively. "And at least Villefort will cooperate."

"Women like that are an absolute menace, and you know it," she scolded good-naturedly. "Turning men of iron into jelly with a twitch of those exquisite shoulders. And I noticed you skated equally easy over those meaningful remarks that Yves made to Patty and his sister about coming into money."

"Why add pain to pain? The Rouillés have suffered enough. Yes, I do have the feeling he may have tried something on Pommard. Judging by the remarks I heard in the bar the other night, I would guess that his and Jacqueline Villefort's liaison, whatever it was, does not seem to have been much of a secret. But if Yves did contact Pommard after he talked with Marie—well, the poor lad certainly paid very dearly for it."

She sighed. "Yes, you're right about that, and chances are Pommard will never talk. So, in a sense, all's well that ends well." Toby was making for the door. "Where are you off to?"

"I've just remembered. I left Grandhomme stewing about something at the henge. I better see what that's all about. See you tomorrow."

Left in glorious isolation, Penny shook her head. "Men!" she muttered. "Can't take your eye off them for a minute! Sometimes I wonder, I really do."

CHAPTER 22

The Dragon's Tongue was in full fête, and Toby, much against his will, the hero of the hour. It had taken several days for the shock waves to settle and this new state of euphoria to set in, but much had happened to bring the inhabitants of the peninsula to this present frenzy of happiness. In Cormel the houses had blossomed with the black and white banners of Brittany, and people had flocked from all over the Tongue to add their voices to the rejoicing. There was music, dancing in the streets, and the wine and cider flowed freely.

What was paramount in everyone's mind was that the power plant scheme was no more. In a carefully worded statement, the urbane Velin had announced that the government of France, in light of the important archaeological discoveries in the area, had decided to shelve the plan: the Teeth were safe, the Tongue was safe, the Luck of Crozon was holding, the Dragon of Brittany was intact—all was well with their world.

Toby had inadvertently contributed to the heroic image the locals had thrust upon him. On returning to the henge with Grandhomme, he had found that one of the monoliths had undergone some slippage due to the torrential rain. Revealed beneath it was a very ancient peg of wood, which he correctly assumed to be one of the original markers laid out by the first prehistoric builders of the site. It had been sent off to the archaeological laboratory at St. Germaine-en-Laye. Word had come back in record time that the henge's date was an early one, 1850 B.C. This brought joy to his heart, for not only did it date the Teeth but the Stannon henge on Bodmin Moor as well. His happiness was quickly tempered when the bearer of the news, the now-recovered Charles Latour, had announced that he was back on the scene to stay and that Toby could retire, covered with his laurels.

"But," stammered the latter, visions of his peaceful puttering vanishing in smoke, "it really would be no trouble for me to finish this up. I mean, I was planning on it."

"I would not dream of imposing on you further," Charles Latour returned, the determined gleam in his eye indicating that he too was going to get his share of acclaim for the henge. "Besides, with all the local activities they have planned for you, you would scarcely have the time."

Disconsolate and defeated, Toby retired to the inn, where the drinks pressed on him by well-wishers kept him in an alcoholic haze. At one of these marathon drinking-sessions, Jean Sommelier, more than a little inebriated himself, said to him with a hiccup, "You know there was one thing I was very wrong about. I don't mind admitting it to you now, but I wouldn't to the others."

"Oh, what's that?" Toby said blearily.

"About the dog. Wouldn't have got very far without him, would we? Led us, you might say, all the way."

"So what about it?"

Jean leered at him. "You seen hide nor hair of him since the murders?"

"No," Toby agreed.

"Nor will you, ever again. Job's done, you see—it won't be around again until danger threatens us."

"What are you talking about?"

Jean's voice sank to a confidential whisper. "It was the Black Dog, the harbinger, all along—just like the others thought. Appeared out of nowhere, didn't he?—and then disappeared into nowhere."

"Nonsense!" Toby spluttered. "Poor wretched creature is probably lying out in the woods somewhere, dead—or the people of the chateau did it in. Black Dog indeed!"

"Well, you have it your way," Jean said amiably. "But I know what I know. Talking of the chateau people, I hear those two Americans got shipped back to the States."

"Yes, they would rather take their chances in an American court than a French one, apparently. A couple of the French cult members sang loud and clear, so Winton's in for it all right," Toby said with gloomy relish. "They have him and the English member, who was the contact for the British market, and one of the French members. They shipped the Belgian back home."

"You've heard about Jacqueline Villefort, I suppose?"

"Only that she is gone."

"She's skipped all right. Took the kids and high-tailed it to her sister's down in the Midi somewhere. Good riddance, I say. Don't think she'll ever dare show her face around here again—a thoroughly bad lot. They say poor old Pierre will get the knife." Jean sighed. "Always was a silly bugger. Feel sorry for Villefort though. Won't seem the same, the Tongue won't, without a Villefort here."

"Well, I wouldn't waste any crocodile tears on him. If he hadn't been on the take, none of this would have happened," Toby said.

"But he was a politician," Jean said. "Only to be expected, isn't it? Anyway, I haven't done too badly out of it. I'm getting all my old orchards back and I've put in a bid for the chateau orchard as well. I'll have that back on a paying basis in no time with a bit of extra help. Offered Grandhomme a job, I have. Can't give him much in the way of wages, of course, but he's very partial to my cider."

"You better not let him drink himself to death." Toby was suddenly belligerent. "A good man that, when he's sober. After all, without him around, both of us would have had a much harder time of it than we did."

"Don't I know it," Jean agreed. "No, I'll see it doesn't get out of hand. Talking of drink, how about another on me?"

Penny was having her own share of problems. With Nicole and Alan packed off to their homes, Francois had returned to his wooing with a singleminded determination. Not only did the variety and magnificence of the dishes lavished upon her palate increase, but also his personal attentions. "I am alone, you are alone," was his theme. "Why not remedy the situation?"

"I could never go along with your political views," said she, hoping to nip further developments in the bud, for she truly liked this gnomelike genius of his trade.

"Then I will give them up!" he announced dramatically. "What are politics when compared to personal happiness? Leave the fight to the young. I have done my share. All I ask in the twilight of my life is peace and a loving companion to share it."

Oh, dear, I had better get out of here fast, she thought in dismay. "That's very sweet of you, Francois," she temporized. "But I'm afraid I have a lot of commitments, a lot of responsibilities."

"Then settle them, by all means," he said magnanimously. "And then, when all is arranged, I shall await your return."

"Well, we'll just have to see," she said, and zipped over to Morgat for a council of war with Toby, whom she found surrounded by his drinking buddies.

"Come outside," she hissed in his ear. "I have to talk to you."

He followed her into the tangy air.

"Are you ready to get out of here? Because I am. In fact, I have to get out of here fast," she urged. "Francois is making his intentions increasingly clear—all of them honorable and permanent."

"Are you considering it?" he mumbled. "He is a famous man, he could offer you a lot—all that good food, for one thing."

"Oh, don't be such an idiot!" she fumed. "On all that good food I've already gained eight pounds—it'll take months to get rid of it. If I went on at that rate, they'd have to roll me down the aisle like a barrel."

He looked down into his glass, which he was still absentmindedly clutching. "I don't expect to last long. I think I'm developing cirrhosis," he announced dismally. "I feel terrible!"

"Of course you feel terrible. You haven't stopped drinking for the past three days," she snapped. "You'll feel a whole lot better once we're away from here and back in Oxford."

"I can't leave until after the ceremony tomorrow," he groaned. "They're going to make me a Son of Brittany or something equally dreadful. I keep trying to tell them all this was none of my doing. It's the judge they ought to be honoring, but no one will listen."

"Then we'll leave right after it." She was emphatic. "No sense in hanging around. We've made our statements and Favet and his merry men have all left."

"In that infernal machine of yours?" he asked with horror.

"I shall be like a pretzel by the time we get across the Channel."

"A few hours of it won't kill you. Really, you're like a spoiled child—worse, in fact. Anyway, get packed, and we'll make it tomorrow right after the ceremony," she said, and returned to the auberge.

Since the mayor and the chief of police were both in jail, the arrangements for the ceremony on the morrow caused a lot of local flutter and bickering as to who should do what. Perforce, the judge was dragged from his house of mourning to officiate. He did so from a hastily erected podium in front of the church, an ironic twinkle in his dark eyes, knowing full well how uncomfortable Toby was about the whole situation.

There was a lot of black-and-white flag waving; many speeches extolling Toby's virtues; much kissing on both cheeks, which embarrassed him beyond belief; and an incredible amount of noise and toasting of the hero. The merrier the crowd became, the gloomier the hero got. The only thing that momentarily lifted his spirits was the appearance of Nicole and Alan, who had sneaked back for the festivities.

"We thought you might like to know we've decided to get married," Nicole announced with attempted nonchalance, but obviously delighted.

"Hmm," he grunted. "High time, too! First sensible thing I've known you two to do. I hope it sets a precedent and you keep out of trouble from now on. No more asinine kidnappings."

"No, sir!" they chorused.

It took some time and much determination for Penny to disentangle him from the mob and herself from the persistent Francois. "You've been just wonderful," she told the latter as she pushed Toby into the Triumph. "I shall never forget my stay at the Auberge du Dragon."

"I sincerely hope not," Francois said anxiously. "But when will you be back, my dear? I shall await your coming with impatience."

"Oh, I'll be sure and let you know about that, Francois. Take good care of yourself in the meantime." And she edged the car out into the crowd, leaving him gazing forlornly after her.

Toby grumbled all the way to the coast, all the way over the Channel, and all the way back to Oxford. Penny bore it with exemplary patience until the spires of Oxford hove into sight. "One more complaint out of you now that we're here, and I'll take the first boat back," she snapped.

He was silenced, at least for the moment.

"I know he has been very clever, as usual," Ada Phipps said in an aggrieved tone a couple of days later. "But that temper of his! I don't think I've heard a pleasant word out of him since he's been back."

"That's because he has to get on with his excavation report, and you know how he loves digging but hates writing it up. And it's the letdown, too. He's missing all that excitement. It does pep him up so," Penny said sagely. "Don't worry, he'll soon be over it. I'm taking him off to Brighton for a couple of days."

"But he hates Brighton!"

"Exactly! An excellent counter-irritant, just what he needs. Besides, they are having a prehistoric conference at the Royal Pavilion, and he'll give a verbal report on how clever he has been about the henge and Stannon and the dates. You'll see, he'll come back as mild as milk."

Ada Phipps sniffed. "Well, I don't know how you put up with it," she repeated. "Him and his moods."

"Don't you?" Penny grinned. "I would have thought that was quite evident to everyone. Some things never change."